What people are saying about the A Fair to Remember series

"Carol Cox is one of my very favorite authors. *Ticket to Tomorrow* is a wonderful blend of historical suspense and romance with a delicious hero, a plucky heroine, and a setting so vivid I could breathe in the scent of Lake Michigan. Ms. Cox owns the genre!"
—Colleen Coble, author of *Alaska Twilight*

"With romance and mystery in the offing, *Ticket to Tomorrow* is a book you don't want to miss. Carol Cox has penned a story with vibrant, memorable characters and a poignant message of forgiveness. Well done!"
—Judith Miller, author of the Freedom's Path series

"*Ticket to Tomorrow* captures the thrill of the Chicago World's Fair with a powerful romance and a thrilling suspense. Cox's mastery of the language and knowledge of the era combined with the riveting setting will keep the reader turning page after page."
—DiAnn Mills, author of the Texas Legacy series

"In *Fair Game*, Carol Cox has created a marvelous story threaded with romance, mystery, humor, and spiritual struggles. Prepare to be transported to the exciting panorama of the World's Columbian Exposition where you will be introduced to characters you'll not soon forget. You won't want to miss this one!"
—Judith Miller, author of the Freedom's Path series

"*Fair Game* is much more than a trip back in time to the greatest fair on earth in 1893. Carol Cox has concocted a delicious mystery and spiced it up with a signature blend of intrigue, danger, and inspiration—and a heaping tablespoon of romance. Kick off your shoes, curl up in your favorite spot, and savor it!"
—Kathy Herman, author of the Seaport Suspense series

FAIR GAME

a romance mystery by

CAROL COX

BARBOUR
PUBLISHING

ISBN 978-1-59789-491-3

For more information about Carol Cox, please access the author's Web site at the following Internet address: www.CarolCoxBooks.com

Cover & Interior Design by Müllerhaus Publishing Arts, Inc., mhpubarts.com

Published by Barbour Publishing, Inc., P.O. Box 719, Uhrichsville, Ohio 44683, www.barbourbooks.com

Our mission is to publish and distribute inspirational products offering exceptional value and biblical encouragement to the masses.

ecpa Member of the
Evangelical Christian
Publishers Association

Printed in the United States of America.
5 4 3 2 1

Dear Reader,

    Some time ago I came across a history of the United States printed in the 1940s. Intrigued, I thumbed through its pages and found my attention caught by a passage about the World's Columbian Exposition, held in Chicago in 1893. Those brief paragraphs sparked my interest and set me off on a trail of research where I discovered a fascinating moment in America's history.

    After winning the honor of hosting the great fair, Chicago opened its doors to the world and invited people from every nation to come to the White City. And come they did! Over 27 million visitors passed through the gates during the fair's six-month duration. Along with sightseers, the fair also drew those who would prey on the unsuspecting, which gave me the basis for this story.

    By the time it was all over, America had established its position as a forward-thinking, cultured nation, and innovations such as the Ferris wheel and the Midway, hamburgers and carbonated soda, Cracker Jacks and ragtime music had become American institutions.

    Thank you for joining me in reliving the moment that ushered in the twentieth century in America. I hope you will enjoy this excursion into the past as much as I have. Please visit my Web site at www.CarolCoxBooks.com. I'd love to hear from you!

Blessings,
Carol Cox

Dedication

To Dave and Katie,
whose patience and support made this book possible.

Acknowledgments

My heartfelt thanks go to:
LeRoy and Lometa Cox,
for providing an insider's look at Chicago,

and Kristin Standaert, assistant dean of
Bibliographic Systems at the Paul V. Galvin Library,
Illinois Institute of Technology,
whose assistance in providing floor plans of
the exposition buildings helped me bring the fair to life.

CHAPTER I

*N*ebraska was never like this.

Dinah Mayhew leaned her elbows on the windowsill at the end of the second-floor hallway and stared down the length of Blackstone Avenue. Brick houses lined the east side of the street, faced by frame dwellings on the west. From her perch, Dinah could see carriages and cabs plying their trade up and down the avenue on this brilliant blue Chicago afternoon. And people, always people in abundance.

She cupped her chin in her hands and felt a broad grin spread across her face. Everything within her view was a far cry from Uncle Everett's farm—a perfect setting for starting a new chapter in her life.

Footsteps clattered on the lower stairs, and a voice floated up to her. "Are you getting settled in, dear? Is everything to your liking?"

"It's perfect, Mrs. Purvis. Thank you."

"I've put the kettle on," the disembodied voice continued. "Come down when you're finished, and we can get acquainted over a nice cup of tea."

"That will be lovely. I'll be down in a few minutes." Dinah turned back to the window and returned to her musings, following the line of the street until trees and rooftops blended as one in the distance. And beyond those rooftops. . . A sigh of sheer bliss escaped her lips.

Only a month ago, she'd been reading newspaper reports that detailed the way Chicago had thrown its doors open to the world, making Dinah green with envy at the knowledge she would never be among the fortunate ones who got to visit the grand exposition with all its wonders. But as of today, she was here in Chicago not simply to see the great fair, but to be a part of it! Her feet tapped out a quick jig on the hardwood floor.

Everything had fallen into place more smoothly than she could have imagined. Take this boardinghouse, for example. She had fallen in love with it the moment she laid eyes on the red brick exterior. It fulfilled the criteria she sought in her new place to live: clean and neat and within walking distance of the fairgrounds. Her room might be small, but it was hers and hers alone, with a motherly landlady who made her feel at home as soon as she stepped into the entry hall. She couldn't have asked for more.

"The tea is ready," Mrs. Purvis called.

"Coming." Dinah gave one final glance out the window and hurried down the hallway to the head of the stairs. She ran her fingers along the panel of the door to her room when she passed it and smiled at the thought of the letter tucked securely away among the camisoles in her top dresser drawer. The letter that had opened up a whole new window on her future.

Mrs. Purvis hovered at the bottom of the stairs. "I started to set the tea things up in the parlor." She gave a little bounce that set her springy, iron gray curls to bobbing around her cheery face. "Then I said to myself, why not just sit in the kitchen like a couple of old friends? I hope you don't mind. I have a feeling we're going to get on very well."

The homey thought made Dinah smile. "That sounds fine."

"This way, then. Straight through the parlor and past the dining room." Mrs. Purvis motioned for Dinah to precede her. "I'm looking forward to getting acquainted. I haven't traveled much in recent years, but I enjoy getting to know about other places from my boarders. You can tell me all about—"

A peremptory knock rattled the front door. Mrs. Purvis tilted her head to one side. "Now who could that be?"

She bustled over to the door and peered out the front window. The pleasant expression slid from her face like ice melting on a summer day. "Henrietta Boggs. Whatever is she doing here?"

"Is everything all right?"

"Shh!" The landlady pressed her finger to her lips and dropped her voice to a barely audible whisper. "Maybe she'll think no one is home." The next instant, her shoulders slumped. "But that wouldn't be right, would it? I guess there's nothing else for it." With a look that reminded Dinah of a chicken cornered by a fox, she reached for the doorknob.

"Henrietta. What a surprise."

A tall, broad-shouldered woman clad in battleship gray swept into the small entry hall with nary a glance at Dinah. "Good day, Ethelinda. I've just gotten back from tending to my sister and knew you would want to hear all about my trip." She lifted her

9

chin and stared down the length of her prominent nose at Mrs. Purvis. "And I, of course, am eager to find out what has been going on in the neighborhood in my absence. Let's go have a nice, long chat. I have all afternoon." She moved toward the parlor with the relentless momentum of a barge.

Mrs. Purvis gave a little yip and trotted off in her wake.

Another knock sounded at the door. Mrs. Purvis started as though she'd been stung. She turned a beseeching look on Dinah. "Be a dear and answer that, will you?" Darting a quick glance over her shoulder, she sidled closer and whispered, "The last time I left that woman alone for more than five seconds, I caught her going through my ledger."

Dinah chewed on the inside of her lip and tried not to laugh aloud in the face of her landlady's obvious distress. "You go right ahead. I'll take care of everything."

Mrs. Purvis gave Dinah a quick squeeze and hurried after her uninvited guest. Dinah bit back a grin. It appeared she wouldn't lack for entertainment here.

The knock came again, louder this time. Dinah swung the door open wide and felt her jaw sag.

Time hung suspended as she gazed into light brown eyes that seemed to look into her very soul. She blinked and drew back, pressing one hand to her throat. "Excuse me, did you say something?"

A slow smile played across her visitor's lips. Dinah decided she liked the way his eyes crinkled at the corners, splaying lines of good humor across his upper cheeks.

"I said I wanted to extend a special invitation to everyone who lives here." He held out a flyer.

Dinah reached to take the sheet of paper, then pulled her

hand back. "Oh, I don't live here. I mean, I do in a way, but. . ." Her voice trailed off. *Idiot! He'll think you're simpleminded, the way you've stared and stammered.* With an effort, she pulled her attention away from his captivating gaze and drew herself erect. "I mean to say, I've just arrived in Chicago today. I'll be staying at this boardinghouse, so yes, I guess I do live here." She clamped her lips together before she made any more of an idiot of herself.

The crinkles around his eyes deepened, and he held out the flyer again. "In that case, I'd like to invite you and everyone else who lives here to attend a meeting tonight on Michigan Avenue. It's part of Mr. Moody's World's Fair campaign."

This time Dinah accepted the paper and held it tight between her fingers. The man's smile broadened, and Dinah basked in the approval that shone in his eyes. She stared into them again, noting the golden flecks barely visible against the light brown irises. The color of caramel, she thought. Like the kind her mother used to stir on the stove.

Right now, the directness of his gaze made her feel as gooey as one of those melted candies. If he kept looking at her like that, she might dissolve into a puddle right there at his feet. The notion brought a flush to her cheeks, warming her more than the heat of the July afternoon warranted.

"Amos B. Hall will be preaching tonight." Dinah could hear the laughter in his voice. "I hope you'll be able to come."

"It sounds like fun." Dinah winced, wondering if the response sounded as inane to him as it did to her.

"More along the lines of inspiring or soul-stirring, I'd say." He trotted down the porch steps, seeming to take some of the afternoon sunshine with him. He looked back long enough to give her a cheerful nod, then started toward the house next door.

Dinah slumped against the door frame and stared after him, weak-kneed after the encounter.

"What was that man doing here?"

Dinah jerked upright so quickly she thumped the back of her head against the doorjamb. She clapped her hand to the tender spot and tried to blink away the stars that blurred her vision.

Mrs. Boggs stepped up beside her and pointed toward the sidewalk. "That man! What did he want?"

Dinah gaped at the demand and held out the flyer. "He came to invite us to a tent meeting."

Mrs. Purvis edged out from behind her neighbor's imposing bulk and peered outside. "Now, Henrietta, he looks like a nice young man."

Very nice, Dinah amended silently.

"Pah!" Mrs. Boggs's jowls quivered. "That just shows how much you know about human nature, Ethelinda Purvis. Why, more than once, I've seen him out on the streets talking to saloon keepers and..." A wave of red suffused her ample cheeks. "To women of ill repute. There's no decent word for it. I find it appalling that he would come up here bold as you please and try to make the acquaintance of your new boarder, using the guise of a religious gathering."

"His coming here had nothing to do with me," Dinah protested. "The invitation was for everyone who lives here." On impulse she added, "I'm sure he'll stop at your door before long."

She found the neighbor's horrified gasp almost satisfying

enough to outweigh the twinge in her conscience. "If he does, I'll soon send him packing. The very idea of a man who consorts with people of the lowest classes coming to a respectable neighborhood like this!"

"Seems to me the Bible has a good bit to say about Jesus consorting with sinners," Mrs. Purvis muttered.

Mrs. Boggs drew herself up. "That trusting nature of yours is going to get you into trouble some day. Mark my words, Ethelinda; one day you'll rue your willingness to take in total strangers."

She fixed Dinah with a steely look. "And you, young lady, you'll do well to heed what I say and stay away from that man. Consider yourself warned." She exited with a huff and stalked down the steps toward a house across the street.

Dinah watched the retreating figure with a sense of awe. "Goodness!"

Mrs. Purvis sagged back against the wall beside the walnut hall tree and fanned herself with her hand. "That woman is the nosiest person I have ever met. She was in the middle of telling me how I ought to rearrange my furniture when she finally stopped long enough to draw breath and heard that young man's voice. Then she charged back out here like a warhorse."

She glanced into the hall-tree mirror and reached up to pat her drooping curls back into place. "At least it got her sidetracked, and she didn't stay all afternoon. That just goes to prove every cloud has its silver lining." The corners of her mouth turned down. "But we missed our lovely tea."

"Why don't you sit down in the parlor and let me get it?" Dinah offered. "You look like you need to catch your breath."

In the time it took to reheat the water for a fresh pot of tea and carry the laden tray to the parlor, Mrs. Purvis had made a remarkable recovery. Her curls had regained their spring, and her eyes sparkled.

"This is good of you," she said, taking one of the floral-patterned cups and saucers from the tray Dinah held out to her. "It seems off-kilter for me to be served something from my own kitchen, especially when you've barely arrived."

"It was no bother." Dinah set the tray on the low table between them and popped a macaroon into her mouth. "You've been very kind to me. I can't tell you how glad I am to have found such a pleasant place to live."

Mrs. Purvis beamed and wiped a crumb from her lips. "And I'm pleased to have someone as thoughtful as you as a boarder. We'll get along; I can tell. I'm just glad you didn't let Henrietta's visit put you off."

"Does she really go through your things?"

"Like a detective looking for clues." The landlady shook her head. "She's been in Ohio the past few weeks taking care of her sister, who was gravely ill. Apparently the sister made a remarkable recovery, and Henrietta returned last evening. It was nice while it lasted, though I suppose it's horrid of me to say such a thing."

A quick grin tilted her lips. "But as long as I'm saying it, I can't help but wonder if the prospect of sending Henrietta packing didn't give her poor sister a good reason to get better as quickly as she did."

The unexpected comment caught Dinah off guard, and laughter made her choke on her second macaroon. "I'm sorry," she said when she regained her breath. "It really isn't funny, but after meeting her once, the thought of having her around for weeks on end. . ." Laughter convulsed her again.

14

Mrs. Purvis nodded sagely. "And being confined like that, with no chance to get away. It would be enough to raise me from my sickbed, that's for certain."

"She does seem to be a woman of strong opinions." Dinah blotted her mouth with her napkin.

"That's been the case as long as I've known her. She didn't waste a moment passing judgment on that poor young man, did she? I'm only glad he didn't hear all the things she said."

At the memory of those caramel-colored eyes, Dinah felt a smile tug at the corners of her lips. "So am I."

Mrs. Purvis clicked her tongue and began collecting the tea things, waving away Dinah's efforts to help. "And all because he was nice enough to invite us to that meeting." She carried the tray back toward the kitchen, mumbling.

The meeting! Caught up in the drama of Mrs. Boggs spouting portents of doom like a Greek prophetess, Dinah had forgotten the purpose of his visit. Her earlier exuberance reasserted itself. Little as she wanted to admit it, she found the prospect of spending her first evening in Chicago alone in her room somewhat daunting. Why not go? At the very least, it would fill in some of the empty time.

And there was always the possibility she might catch a glimpse of their handsome visitor again.

Retracing her steps to the front porch, she peered down the avenue and drew in a deep breath. The very air seemed to exude a sense of excitement.

Oh, yes! If she was looking for adventure, it appeared she had come to the right place.

Or maybe adventure had come to the right place to find her.

CHAPTER 2

A h, the prodigal returns at last." The pleasant-faced woman shoved an arm-load of slim booklets at Seth Howell and pointed to a section of benches. "I've nearly finished putting the songbooks out on the seats. That area still needs them."

"Sorry to be so late, Mrs. Hammond."

"I was afraid I'd wind up having to do the whole job myself. I thought maybe you'd gotten lost." The concern in her expression belied her sharp words.

"Ted Murphy is sick today, so I had to distribute all his flyers in addition to my own. It took a lot longer than I expected."

"Ah, that explains it. Make sure you straighten the rows as you go. The seats get knocked out of line every night." Mrs. Hammond tugged the end of a bench into place as she spoke. "How did things go today?"

"Not bad." Seth reached the end of a row and looked back to make sure he had lined up the seats according to Mrs. Hammond's standards. "Better than usual, actually." *With the exception of that saloon keeper I woke up,* he added to himself. But he didn't see any need to mention that little episode to his coworker.

Mrs. Hammond stepped back and gave the section of seats a final survey. "Do you expect to see a lot of the people you talked to here tonight?"

"I hope to. In fact, I wouldn't be at all surprised if a good many of them came." He shook his head. "Amazing, isn't it? Even when we're up against the biggest exposition the world has ever seen, the crowds just keep getting bigger."

Mrs. Hammond's plump features creased into a radiant smile. "Mr. Moody knew what he was doing when he planned this evangelistic campaign in conjunction with the fair. Truly, the harvest is plentiful. I pray the Lord will reap a good many souls tonight."

Seth nodded. He had prayed for the same thing as he tramped the streets, handing out flyers during the long afternoon. He continued to set out booklets and align the benches by rote while his thoughts played back over the places he had visited. They came to a stop when he remembered a certain diminutive, dark-haired young lady at the red-brick house on South Blackstone Avenue.

He chuckled at the memory of her indecision as to whether she lived there or not and the way her flustered efforts to amend her statement only made things worse.

"It's nearly time, Seth. How are you doing?"

"Almost finished." His thoughts returned to the dark-haired girl. It hadn't taken long for her to regain her pert demeanor. He remembered the way her eyes lit up when she spoke.

As if on cue, a group of crusade workers filtered into the

cavernous tent. The group clustered near the platform at the front.

Seth bent to lay out song booklets along the last row of benches, his thoughts leaving the tabernacle and drifting back to the house on Blackstone Avenue and its engaging occupant. Would she be among those who showed up for the service? Given her comment about it being fun, he wouldn't be surprised.

His mood grew somber as he walked the length of the center aisle to join his fellow workers. Some of the country's greatest expositors of scripture would be speaking during the course of Moody's six-month campaign, yet she only looked upon it as an opportunity for entertainment.

He wondered what her reaction would be when she found herself confronted with the need to tend to the condition of her immortal soul. Would those hazel eyes flash with disdain at the thought of being reconciled with God? Or worse, would they glaze over with a show of boredom?

Seth joined the rest of the group, now gathered into a circle and talking in low tones. He took his place in the circle, his thoughts still focused on the girl. She said she had just arrived in Chicago. Where did she come from? And why? More than most people, Seth was very aware of the numbers of young women who flocked to the city in droves, some seeking employment and a chance to make their own way, others only looking for thrills. His heart grew heavy at the thought that she might well belong to the latter group.

They came by the hundreds in search of excitement, thinking they would find it in the hubbub of the city and not realizing their quest for meaning could be satisfied only by an encounter with the living God.

But some would find Him here. A surge of gratitude welled up within him. Some would.

Seth shifted his weight from one foot to the other. Would this girl be one of those who found true peace and purpose for living? Or would she let the bright lights and frantic pace of city living blind her eyes to the truth? An empty feeling settled in the pit of Seth's stomach.

"Seth? Reverend Howell?"

Mrs. Hammond's voice caught his attention, and he jerked his head upright, suddenly aware of the puzzled looks sent his way from the rest of the group.

"I'm sorry. What did you say?"

Mrs. Hammond gazed heavenward. "I asked—for the third time, mind you—if you would be willing to lead us in prayer."

"Oh. Of course." Seth ducked his head and tried to ignore the snickers that rippled around the circle.

He took a moment to gather his thoughts, to pull his focus away from the memory of soft, hazel eyes and a delicate, heart-shaped face and put it back where it belonged, on the business at hand.

The Lord's business.

Dinah ran her palm across the brightly colored comforter and stared out the window of the room that would be her home for the next few months. In the west, the sun stretched out pale golden fingers as it continued its descent toward the horizon. Dinah twisted a loose strand of thread around her finger and let her gaze return to the flyer she held in her lap.

Only an hour until the meeting began.

It doesn't matter. There are plenty of other things you can be doing. That was true enough. She had more than enough to occupy her mind on this, the eve of her grand adventure. But as many times as she reminded herself of that fact, the attempt at reassurance fell flat.

She knew why. The scene outside the window faded away, replaced by a vision of light brown eyes that crinkled at the corners. A tingle ran along her arms at the memory of his voice. Had he felt a similar sensation when they talked?

The flyer crinkled beneath her fingertips.

Dinah curled her fingers into a ball. She shouldn't go. Her time would be much better spent getting ready for the morrow.

Yes, that would be the responsible thing to do. She could make a final check to be sure the forest green skirt and pin-tucked blouse she had selected with such care for her first day at her new job were in perfect condition.

The rest of the evening could be filled with writing a letter to her aunt, letting her know she had arrived and was safely ensconced in her boardinghouse. *A most respectable boardinghouse.* She must be sure to emphasize that point. Aunt Dora needed all the reassurance she could offer. It had practically taken divine intervention to get her and Uncle Everett to agree to this "mad venture," as Aunt Dora called it.

Dinah remembered the lengthy discussions and the pleading that finally wore down their defenses until they capitulated and agreed to let her come. She felt a fleeting twinge of guilt at the memory. Aunt Dora and Uncle Everett had done so much for her, far more than the demands of kinship required. Their selflessness deserved her undying gratitude and respect.

They know I appreciate them and everything they've done. The confident assertion couldn't quite still the nagging of her conscience. But she had to leave. Uncle Everett, at least, understood that.

"You can't protect her forever, Dora." The echo of his words brought a wistful smile to Dinah's lips.

"How can you expect me to let her up and leave without a moment's pause? I love her like my own daughter, and I'd hardly let Gladys go off on her own like that. We have worries enough with your health the way it is."

"You'll never find the perfect time for her to leave the nest." Uncle Everett broke off into the rasping cough that had plagued him of late. "Besides, we still have our Gladdie."

Yes, they still had Gladys. And good riddance. A shudder rippled across Dinah's shoulders. If the perfect opportunity hadn't arisen to draw her to Chicago and its great fair, the chance to leave behind her cousin with her domineering ways would have been sufficient motivation to pull up stakes and leave.

Reminded anew of her reason for coming to the great city, Dinah felt her spirits rise like the morning sun over Lake Michigan. Tomorrow would mark the beginning of a new chapter in her life.

The flyer slipped to the floor, and Dinah bent to scoop it up. Anticipation of what lay in store for her notwithstanding, she hadn't been able to get the image of that handsome, smiling face out of her mind all afternoon.

She ran the flyer between her fingers, remembering how Aunt Dora fretted about her drifting from her spiritual roots.

"I worry about your reason for leaving," she told Dinah only moments before her departure. "I fear you're more interested in pursuing the things of the world than the Lord."

Dinah tapped her fingernail against the flyer, and a smile curved her lips. Wouldn't her aunt be pleased to hear she had gone to a tent meeting—one sponsored by Moody, no less—the very night of her arrival? Surely, if anything could reassure her of Dinah's sincerity, that news should do it.

And she just might catch another glimpse of her afternoon visitor. Excitement bubbled through her at the thought.

But how was she going to get there? Dinah crossed to the window and peered out at the lengthening shadows. It was one thing to find employment in the Columbian Exposition's fabled White City and secure a safe place to live, quite another to venture out into the unfamiliar streets of Chicago, especially when she would be returning after dark.

A brisk knock broke into her musings. Dinah crossed the room and opened the door to find Mrs. Purvis pinning her flowered hat in place.

"Are you ready?"

Dinah stared blankly. "Ready for what?"

"To go to that meeting, of course. We have just enough time to get there if we leave right now."

It was all Dinah could do to keep a straight face. "The preaching should be wonderful," she said in a neutral tone.

"It should indeed." The landlady slanted a mischievous glance at Dinah, and her eyes twinkled. "And I wouldn't be surprised if we ran into that good-looking young man again, would you?"

Dinah opened her mouth to protest, but what would be the use? She grinned, snatched up her hat and reticule, and hurried to the staircase behind Mrs. Purvis.

Can all these people possibly expect to fit under one roof?

Even the crowds Dinah had encountered at the train platform earlier in the day couldn't compare to the mass of people streaming toward the tent entrance.

For once, even Dinah's adventurous spirit faltered. Her steps slowed, and she looked around at the crush of people that surrounded her. She pressed closer to Mrs. Purvis, who beamed and patted Dinah's arm. "This is a marvelous turnout. Isn't it wonderful?"

"Wonderful," Dinah parroted. The heat generated by the hundreds of people milling about them made the evening air seem stuffy. She fanned her hand in front of her face.

The unflappable landlady didn't seem put off in the least. She forged ahead through the crowd, no more flustered than if she had been out for a Sunday stroll.

What if this thing catches fire? There would be no hope of escape. Dinah held her reticule tight against her body and plunged into the crowd along with Mrs. Purvis.

Her nose crinkled at the odors swirling about them, some of them emanating, she was sure, from an approaching group of workingmen. From their grubby appearance, Dinah felt sure they had come to the meeting directly from their day's labor. She would have found that strange, if not for the look of pure longing on each face.

The line inched closer to the entrance, and Dinah caught the oily, canvas odor of the tent. The heavy scent brought back memories of the time her father had taken her to see a circus when she was a little girl.

Dinah remembered the glow that enveloped her at the thought of having him all to herself on that rare occasion, her joy somewhat offset by the flutter of panic at being in the midst of so many people. But her father's reassuring presence had been enough to settle her nerves and give her the courage to settle back and enjoy the performance.

How ironic that anyone who felt so uncomfortable in a crowd would ever decide to come to Chicago. Once again, it was all because of her father.

A stocky man edged his way in front of Dinah, blocking her view of Mrs. Purvis. Panic reasserted itself. Gathering up her courage, she elbowed her way past him, ignoring his startled "*oomph*" when she pushed by.

Once past that obstacle, she regained sight of Mrs. Purvis and felt her nerves settle down again. Mrs. Purvis slowed for a moment as if getting her bearings, then darted into a space between two benches. Dinah picked up speed and trotted after her.

"Isn't this exciting?" Mrs. Purvis's eyes shone. "I never dreamed there would be so many people. Should we take these seats or see if we can find some closer to the platform?"

"I'm not sure there are any left up there." Dinah stood on tiptoe and peered through the eddying throng. She spotted two empty seats several rows ahead, just beyond a knot of men who stood in earnest conversation.

One of them was. . .

Dinah blinked, then felt her eyes go wide. She grabbed Mrs. Purvis by the elbow and tugged at her arm. "I found a spot up there. Let's hurry before someone else gets to it." Without waiting for a reply, she started forward.

With her gaze fastened on her quarry, Dinah made her way through the crowd, belatedly wondering what she would say once she reached him. Up ahead, the men finished talking and made as if to go their separate ways. *No, let me catch up to him first!*

She shouldered her way around a cluster of chattering matrons. At that instant, he swung around. Their gazes locked.

Dinah's heart stood still, then took off like a racehorse when she saw the flicker of recognition in his eyes. As she watched, a younger man came up from behind and tapped him on the shoulder, motioning toward the front of the tent. He darted one more glance in Dinah's direction, then spun on his heel and followed the youth.

Dinah's sense of victory plummeted to her toes. All around the huge tabernacle, the air buzzed with anticipation, but for her, the excitement had gone out of the evening. She watched his retreating back until he was swallowed up by the crowd. *There went my chance.* She might as well go on back to the boardinghouse. She could always write that letter to Aunt Dora.

"Are those the seats you meant?" Mrs. Purvis pointed to the row beyond. "We'd better hurry if we're going to get them."

Dinah looked about for the nearest exit but saw only people continuing to pour in, with no end to the flow in sight. She would never be able to fight her way through that.

She took in Mrs. Purvis's air of expectation, like a child about to receive a treasured gift. That sweet woman had volunteered to come with her, a virtual stranger, without even being asked. Seeing her evident pleasure, Dinah knew she couldn't be so unfeeling as to suggest they leave before the service even began.

She lifted her chin. "Right. Let's go."

Sliding sideways between seat backs and knees, they finally

reached the vacant seats in the middle of the row. Dinah settled into her place, taking in the packed benches on either side. No chance of leaving now.

Mrs. Purvis prodded her with her elbow. "I've been meaning to come to one of these, but I just kept putting it off, telling myself I was too busy, you know." Her face glowed. "I'm so glad that nice young man stopped by this afternoon, aren't you?"

Dinah mustered up a nod and the semblance of a smile. The meeting wouldn't last forever. Mrs. Purvis seemed satisfied with her response and continued studying the scene as if determined to commit every detail to memory.

Dinah thumbed idly through the songbook, glad to note she was familiar with most of the hymns. At least she could join in the singing. *Nobody forced you to come,* she reminded herself. *Being trapped here is no one's fault but yours.*

Resigned to waiting it out, she settled back for a long evening. Already she wished the benches were more comfortable.

CHAPTER 3

Dusk wouldn't be long in coming. Already shadows gathered in dark pools in front of the buildings that lined the west side of the street.

The evening breeze carried the sounds of voices lifted in song from the crusade tent several blocks away. The man's mouth twisted. The services attracted great numbers by all counts; they certainly seemed to be keeping people off the streets tonight.

I'll give it another thirty minutes. He peered southward, squinting his eyes against the sun's slanting rays.

The *click* of heels along the walk behind him caught his attention, and he swiveled his head. A lone woman—young, from the quick pace her feet tapped out—approached less than a block away.

His lips curved in a satisfied smile. He shouldn't have doubted. Didn't they always come along just when he needed them?

He faded back into the sheltered spot between two buildings and smoothed his mustache with his fingertips. Closing his eyes, he concentrated on the nearing footsteps, trying to gauge the moment when she would reach his place of concealment.

He took a deep breath to compose his nerves. This was one of his favorite moments in the process, that heady rush, knowing that at any instant his target would move within his grasp and the game would begin.

A few seconds more. . .*now*!

He stepped forward out of the shadows, then took a couple of quick side steps to avoid their imminent collision.

The woman—young, he noted with satisfaction—stumbled to a halt.

"I beg your pardon! My mind must have been elsewhere. I didn't see you coming at all."

He doffed his hat and favored her with his most charming smile. "It was my fault entirely." He bent toward her solicitously. "Are you all right? You appear to be somewhat shaken."

His quarry fanned herself with her handkerchief. "I'm fine, really. Just a little startled."

Moving to her side, he gave a small bow. "Allow me to accompany you a little way at least. I feel a bit responsible for you, seeing that I nearly knocked you down. Besides, dusk may fall before you reach your destination if you have very far to go. It isn't safe for a young woman to be out on the streets alone after dark."

The girl glanced at the lengthening shadows. "Yes, I'm afraid I lost all track of the time and walked farther than I intended." She smiled up at him. "Thank you. I should be glad of your company."

She set off, and he fell into step beside her. "Are you on your way home, or to a friend's house, perhaps?"

"Just out for an evening stroll. I needed some fresh air." She reached up to adjust her hat atop her dark brown curls. "And I must confess, a bit of time to myself. The rooming house where I live is unbearably stuffy these summer evenings, and the girls I share a room with aren't the most congenial companions."

He raised his eyebrows. "A rooming house? You aren't from this area, then?"

Her curls danced about her face when she shook her head and slanted a dimpled smile up at him. "My family lives in Missouri. I moved out here to work at the Boston Store."

"But not alone, I hope." His voice held exactly the right note of concern. "Surely you must have come with a friend?"

Mischief danced in the pretty brunette's eyes. "No, I came alone. I couldn't bear small-town life any longer. Why, back home there's nothing more exciting to do than watch the cows graze. I want to see something of real life and experience a taste of freedom before I'm tied down with the demands of a husband and children."

He looked away long enough to mask his elation. "I applaud your sense of adventure. And has your experiment turned out as you thought it would? Have you made a great many friends in the time you've been here?"

For the first time, the girl's confident air dimmed. "Not really. The people I've met at work aren't as friendly as I'd hoped. And the girls at the rooming house don't share my interests."

He shook his head in a show of sympathy. "What a shame. Life can be lonely without companionship. What are your interests, if I may be so bold as to ask?"

Her lashes fanned down over her eyes; then she looked up at him. "My father thinks it unwomanly, but I have a passion for photography."

"Really? Then you must meet my sister. She's a photography enthusiast, as well."

The girl's eyes widened. "Is she? I'd love to meet her. It would be wonderful to be able to discuss it with someone."

"And I'm sure she would be most pleased to make your acquaintance. In fact. . ." His demeanor became solemn. "It might be just the thing to lift her spirits. She has been so unhappy since our mother passed away."

"Oh, I'm sorry! How hard that must be for her. Were she and your mother close?"

"Very. She has taken little interest in anything since our mother's death." He bowed his head and let his steps drag.

The girl laid her hand on his arm with a feather touch. "Then I would be very happy to meet her. Perhaps it would help us both."

"Exactly what I was thinking! It's as if this meeting of ours was directed by fate." He looked around, as if struck by a sudden idea. "Helen—my sister, that is—lives only two blocks from here. Why don't you come meet her now?"

"Right now?" She caught her lower lip between her teeth, then shook her head. "It's getting rather late. I really ought to be getting back to the rooming house."

Careful! Don't lose her now. "It will only take a few minutes to introduce you, and it would mean so much to her. Perhaps the two of you could make plans to meet again later on. It would give her something to look forward to. And," he added when she looked as though she still might refuse, "you don't need to worry about walking home in the dark. I'll be happy to escort you. Better yet, I'll take you there in a cab."

"I don't know. . . ."

"Think of it as doing me a favor. Helping you to make a friend would let me feel I've made up in part for startling you so back there."

The dimple reappeared in her cheek. "When you put it that way. . .all right."

Ten minutes later, he led her up the steps of a compact, white house and opened the front door with his key. "Helen! I've brought a visitor." He stepped inside and turned to the girl. "Please, come in. I'll let her know you're here."

His companion entered the room with slow steps. She gave a quick gasp and drew back in dismay at the sight of a spider web stretching from a lamp shade to the arm of the serpentine-back sofa.

He whipped out a snowy white handkerchief and hurried to wipe the web away. "Please excuse Helen's poor housekeeping. She simply hasn't been herself since Mother died."

The girl murmured in sympathy but drew her skirts closer against her. "Perhaps I should come back another time."

He felt a vein throb in his left temple. If he didn't hurry, she might slip out of his hands. "Helen!" He looked into the back room, then pushed open the swinging door and peered into the kitchen.

"She must have stepped out for a moment, but she won't have gone far. She'll be back any moment. Why don't you sit down while we wait for her?" His throat tightened when she hesitated. "You must be weary after your long walk. Would you care for a drink of water?"

She cast a longing glance at the front door, then sank down into a cushioned armchair. "I hate for you to go to any trouble, but I am tired. Some water would be lovely, thank you."

"No trouble at all. I'll only be a moment." He hurried through the swinging door to the kitchen, where he filled two glasses. Reaching for a small amber bottle that stood beside the sink, he tipped a small measure of a white powder into one of them, stirred it, then carried both of the glasses back to the front room.

"Here, I'm sure you'll find that refreshing after your long walk." He handed a glass to the girl and took a hearty swig from the other.

She murmured her thanks and took a long, grateful drink. "Your sister must enjoy reading." She gestured toward the bookcase on the opposite wall.

"Yes, Helen is very fond of her books. Would you care to look at them while we wait?"

The girl started to rise, then swayed and drew her hand across her forehead.

He moistened his lips and leaned forward. "Is something wrong?"

"I must be more tired than I thought. I feel woozy all of a sudden." Her hands shook as she fumbled to set the half-full glass on the marble-top table beside her. Water sloshed, and a few drops spilled over the rim. She moaned and pressed her fingertips against her eyelids.

"Probably due to the exertion of your walk. I'm sure it will pass quickly." He took another sip of water and watched until she slumped over against the arm of the chair.

Setting his own glass next to hers, he bent to scoop her up

in his arms. He crossed the room quickly and used his elbow to nudge a concealed lever on the bookcase that let the set of shelves swing away from the wall to reveal the door that led to the basement stairs.

Reverend Amos B. Hall looked out over his audience and stroked his graying beard. "I'm happy to see so many have come out this evening."

Dinah fidgeted on the hard wooden bench and stared around the tent, hoping to find some way to occupy her mind for the duration of the evening. What had she been thinking of, coming down here on a whim? Even an evening spent writing to Aunt Dora would have been more entertaining than this.

Snippets of the speaker's message filtered into her brain. Dinah didn't bother to pay close attention, certain there would be little difference between his words tonight and those she had heard during the countless times she sat with her aunt and uncle in their little country church.

She took note of the people seated in the rows nearby, letting her gaze drift to one unfamiliar face after another. So many different types represented here under this one roof! The observation gave her an idea: She could study those around her and try to guess what they did for a living.

That gaunt man in the white shirt and bowtie two rows ahead, for instance. The sharp planes of his face reminded her of Mr. Drew, the storekeeper back home. Dinah could imagine this man standing behind the counter of his shop, ready to show his wares to the next customer who entered.

Encouraged by the success of her flight of whimsy, Dinah turned her attention to a woman off to her right. Her well-made clothing might be of the current style, but her face looked worn and tired. A seamstress, Dinah decided. She could dress herself as well as her clients in the latest fashions, but the hard work of keeping her customers satisfied had taken its toll.

The speaker brought his hand down on the pulpit with a *thud* that made Dinah jump. "I know many of you have been saved and baptized. Those of you who have, raise your hand."

Mrs. Purvis held her hand aloft and slanted a curious look at Dinah when she didn't immediately follow suit. Dinah recovered her wits enough to raise her hand in acknowledgment of the speaker's request.

Reverend Hall nodded as if satisfied. "There are a good many here who have received Christ as your Savior. I am pleased to see that, because my message tonight, in large part, is for you."

Dinah stared around the tent, surprised by the number of people who had responded.

"Blessings untold are yours!" Reverend Hall smiled, yet his voice held a serious note. "But what have you done to share your treasure with others so they, too, may receive these blessings?"

Many in the audience stirred as if beset by the same uneasiness that took hold of Dinah.

"What have you done to be sure that everyone within your scope of influence knows the good news of eternal life?"

The rustling stilled, and the tent grew deathly quiet. Dozens leaned forward with rapt expressions, as if intent on catching every word. To Dinah's great surprise, she found her own attention being drawn back to the man on the platform.

"Many of you raised your hands a moment ago. . .but many

could not. My friends, think of the hundreds, nay, thousands who pass by this spot every day who cannot say they claim the precious name of Jesus as their Savior. And many more than those have never even heard of His saving grace. What a tragedy!"

Reverend Hall scanned the crowd, and Dinah felt as if he were looking straight at her. She shrank into her seat.

"Yet if everyone who raised their hands tonight would take the time to tell a friend, a neighbor, a loved one how much God loves them and has already done for them, how different their situation might be!"

Dinah's throat constricted, and her eyes welled with tears. Beside her, she heard Mrs. Purvis sniffling into her handkerchief. Accompanying sobs sounded throughout the congregation.

"How many have gone into an eternity of darkness because nobody told them about this great hope? Because the people around them were too caught up in their own pursuits—not due to outright selfishness perhaps, but simply because they became too busy with their day-to-day activities to follow one of the greatest command-ments: to love their neighbor as themselves."

Dinah clamped her teeth on her bottom lip to keep it from trembling. The reverend had her full attention at last. That statement described her perfectly. She clenched her hands in her lap and looked again at the people she had been observing, seeing them not as mere strangers or fodder for her game, but as people Christ loved and died for.

Mr. Drew's twin, for instance. Had he raised his hand? Had the woman she labeled a seamstress?

Lord, forgive me! I've been sitting here studying them as though they were exhibits set out for my entertainment instead of seeing them as people who are precious in Your sight.

35

As if reading her thoughts, Reverend Hall went on. "My friends, if this describes you, know that you have transgressed. God is in the sin-forgiving business, but He calls you to repent and turn away from that sin. Don't wait a moment longer to make it right with Him. When you leave this tent tonight, leave with a new purpose in your heart—to put Him first and follow His call on your life."

His tone softened as he looked around the assembly once more. "And to those of you who did not raise your hands, I would address my next remarks to you. . . ."

His voice went on, but Dinah turned her thoughts inward. The speaker's charge touched her in a deep place, bringing back feelings she had ignored for a long time.

The dank basement smells assailed his nostrils as he descended the stairs. Thank goodness he didn't have to spend much time down here. He would never be able to abide that odor for long. Swinging open the door to a small cubicle with his foot, he entered and laid the unconscious girl on the narrow cot set against the rough plaster wall.

Light from the small lamp he had left burning earlier filtered into the tiny room, and he stared down at the still form. Pretty enough, with features more refined than most. McGinty should be pleased.

He closed the door on the darkness and locked it, then stood and listened a moment at each of three similar doors. No one stirred within.

Good. They must still be sleeping off the effects of their laudanum-laced evening meal. It was a perfect time to let McGinty know he had a full shipment ready to be picked up. With any luck, they would all be on their way before midnight, and he wouldn't have to go to the trouble of drugging them again.

Back upstairs, he latched the bookcase back in place and set the room to rights, removing the glasses and blotting up the spilled water with a towel. Over in the corner by the gilt-framed mirror, he spotted another spider web. He twisted the towel in his fists, thinking how he had almost lost his latest conquest over something so insignificant. If he hadn't been able to blame the poor housekeeping on the grief of his nonexistent sister. . . He raised his hand to obliterate it, then paused.

The spider sat at the edge of the web, patiently awaiting its next hapless victim. He caught a strand of silk on the tip of his finger and raised it, lifting the spider into the air. It dangled there, legs flailing. They were much alike, he and the spider. Let others resort to violence; for the two of them, it was a matter of weaving their webs and waiting for their prey to step within. It was all so easy.

Gently, he lowered the spider back to its place, then crushed it with the towel.

He checked his appearance in the oval mirror, then cast one last look around the room to make sure all was in order. Wiping the lampshade clean of any remnants of the web, he blew out the lamp and stepped outside into the calm evening air, taking care to lock the door behind him.

CHAPTER 4

The Lord Jesus opened the way to the kingdom with His own blood." Reverend Hall's voice resounded throughout the meeting tent. "He died to give you life eternal in the world to come. Are you not willing to do His work today, in this present world?"

Dinah twisted her hands in her lap and hung on the speaker's every word. She was no stranger to work—she'd had plenty of that in her years on Uncle Everett's farm. But the preacher's words opened her mind to a new question: To what end had her efforts been? What was the value of it all?

Even her quest, the reason for her being in Chicago in the first place—wasn't that solely for her own benefit?

"You don't have to go to the wilds of the Dark Continent to be a laborer in His vineyard. Just look around you." Reverend Hall spread his arms wide, taking in the multitude assembled before him. "Right now, in this very city, we have people from every corner of the globe come to visit the greatest exposition the world has ever seen. Do you hear me, friends? A veritable mission field is at our doorstep! The fields are white unto harvest. Are your ready to be one of His workers?

"If you have gotten caught up in the things of this world, it isn't too late to change. Right now, you can tell Him you're ready to start afresh, to commit your life totally to Him and to His work."

A chance to turn around, to make a difference! A thread of hope twined its way around Dinah's heart.

"Let us pray, my friends. Take your burdens to the Lord."

Dinah bowed her head with the others, sending up a prayer of her own. *That's what I want, Lord—to serve You. I never meant to drift away and get so caught up in myself. Show me what You want me to do.*

A chorus of "amens" signaled that Reverend Hall had finished. Dinah raised her head and realized for the first time that her cheeks were awash with tears. Pulling her handkerchief from her reticule, she dabbed at the wetness.

"Perhaps God is speaking to some of you right now about serving Him. Again I say, look no further than your own backyard. Opportunities for service abound! Before we close, I have been asked to share with you an urgent need.

"I am privileged to be acquainted with Pastor Seth Howell, who oversees a group of workers dedicated to ministering to the young people of Chicago. The classes they hold have borne much fruit already, as we have seen many boys and girls open their hearts to the Lord."

The tent grew utterly silent, as if each person held his or her breath.

"But there are many yet to reach! The greatest need of the moment is for women willing to take on classes for some of the young girls. These girls come from the poorest of families. Some of them have no mothers, no womanly influence to guide them."

Dinah clasped her hands and leaned forward, feeling the sting of tears that threatened to spill over again.

"These Bible classes may be the only hope for the light of Christ to enter their lives."

Beside her, Mrs. Purvis mopped at her cheeks. "Poor little dears."

"Let's ask God to send the laborers needed to bring these tender souls, and those of their families, into the kingdom. Would you all please stand with your heads bowed?"

Benches scraped against the dirt floor as the crowd complied.

"The Word of God says that no man comes to the Father unless the Father draws him. Is He speaking to you tonight? If so, I would invite you to come forward at this time. Kneel here at the foot of the platform and make it an altar of prayer."

All over the tent, the sounds of muffled sobs and shuffling steps could be heard. With her head bowed and her eyes shut tight, Dinah gripped the back of the bench in front of her and willed her knees to stop shaking.

"I'm speaking to everyone who wants to answer the call of Christ tonight. Perhaps you've realized your need of Him for the first time. Or maybe you already belong to Him, but you've strayed from the fold and now hear the gentle voice of your Shepherd calling you to return."

Someone jostled Dinah's arm while pushing past to make a way toward the center aisle.

"Or maybe there is someone here tonight who wishes to respond to the need I shared a moment ago. If God is laying this on your heart, won't you come now?"

Dinah's feet seemed to want to move of their own accord. She locked her knees and stood fast. *You're not a Bible teacher. You're one of the ones who has gone her own way. What could you possibly have to share?*

"Many are coming. If God is calling you, don't harden your heart. Don't leave here tonight without settling things with Him."

Dinah felt drawn toward the front of the tent like a piece of iron being pulled by a powerful magnet. Her fingers squeezed the seat back so tightly she thought they would freeze in place.

"Is this what You want me to do?" she whispered. From a place deep within her, she felt a resounding *"Yes!"* Sliding past Mrs. Purvis, she stumbled forward to join the throng making their way to the front.

Halfway down the aisle, she remembered her tear-washed face and dried her cheeks as well as she could with her sodden handkerchief. Tears didn't bring sympathy, they only turned people away. She ought to know that better than anyone. With a skill born of long practice, she composed her features as best she could and put a smile on her face to cover her inner turmoil.

Finally she reached the front, only to discover she hadn't the slightest idea what to do next. *Now what?* She looked around, seeking some clue. All around her, people knelt and wept. The sight almost set her own tears to flowing once more, but she made a valiant effort to control them.

A round-cheeked woman stepped forward and led Dinah to

a pair of chairs a little distance from the crush. Taking Dinah's hands in hers, she gave her a reassuring smile. "God bless you, my dear. What brings you forward tonight? Have you come to accept God's gift of salvation?"

Dinah shook her head. "I'm already a believer. My mother told me about Jesus when I was a little girl. But I haven't been following the Lord as I should, and I want to change that."

The woman's face lit up. "We can pray about that right now."

"I've already done that, back in my seat. I know He's forgiven me."

The woman smiled. "Well, then. . ."

Dinah struggled to find the right words. "I also asked Him to show me what He wants me to be doing for Him, and. . ." She glanced down at their joined hands and gathered up her courage. "Well, I'd like to help with that group of girls Reverend Hall mentioned."

The woman's face lit up. "Praise the Lord! Pastor Howell will be so pleased. Let me introduce you to him right now."

Giddy with relief, Dinah allowed herself to be towed along through the crowd. She had done the right thing. For the first time in a long while, she felt the sweetness of God's approval.

The woman stopped and raised her voice to be heard over the noise of the crowd. "Pastor Howell, look who I've brought. Your prayers have been answered!"

Dinah's eyes threatened to film over again, and she blinked rapidly to hold the tears at bay. She had never thought of herself as an answer to prayer before. Forcing the smile back to her lips, she prepared to introduce herself and looked up into the caramel-colored eyes of her afternoon visitor.

42

Turning from his conversation with another crusade worker to answer Mrs. Hammond's call, Seth found himself staring into the face that had haunted his thoughts all afternoon.

The answer to his prayers? He could think of one way that could be taken, but he had a feeling that wasn't what Mrs. Hammond meant. He looked in question at his coworker.

She displayed a triumphant smile. "Ask and you shall receive!"

He focused on Mrs. Hammond's face to keep from losing himself in the depths of the girl's hazel gaze. "And just what am I receiving?"

"This young lady. . ."

"Dinah Mayhew," her companion supplied.

"Miss Mayhew has volunteered to take charge of one of your groups of girls. Isn't that wonderful?"

Seth barely restrained himself from throwing his head back and letting out a shout of "Hallelujah!" He'd put on a brave face in front of the other workers, but truth be told, he had all but despaired of finding anyone to take on that task. The area these girls lived in could make the staunchest heart quail. To have God send him a worker only moments after the need was made public seemed nothing short of a miracle.

He studied Dinah Mayhew again, taking in the broad smile that curved her full lips and her general air of someone about to embark on a thrilling adventure. The thought brought him back down to earth with a thud.

He recalled their earlier meeting. Nothing in their conversation then gave him any indication she had an interest in spiritual things. Indeed, hadn't he wondered what her motives were in coming to Chicago?

She had mentioned looking for excitement, however. Seth slipped his hand inside his jacket and tried to rub away the knot that formed in his stomach. Was that all this meant to her?

Seth's initial elation vanished. He pressed his lips together. "We'd better discuss this." He nodded his thanks to Mrs. Hammond and led Miss Mayhew to a quiet corner of the tent, making sure they stayed well within public view.

He set two chairs a respectable distance apart and gestured for her to sit. A hint of uncertainty dimmed the light in her eyes, and he knew his brusque behavior was the cause. He moistened his lips and let his gaze drift over her appealing features. *This is never going to work.* If he couldn't keep his thoughts on track during a brief interview, how could he ever expect to work with her on an ongoing basis?

Miss Mayhew smiled at him expectantly. Seth started to speak, but his throat had gone dry. He swallowed hard. "Tell me about your interest in working with these girls. I don't remember you mentioning anything of that kind when we talked this afternoon."

She blinked, and her smile faltered. "Actually, I don't have a bit of experience in doing anything along that line. It's just that. . ."

Seth waited, calm on the outside but his thoughts roiling within. He'd seen the flash of interest in her eyes when they stood talking on the porch that afternoon. If he were going to be painfully honest with himself, that might well have been the thing that fixed her in his mind.

Please tell me this isn't some flibbertigibbet who has decided this would be a good way to get acquainted.

Miss Mayhew looked straight at him and patted her hands together in her lap. "I've never had anything like this happen to me before, but I think God spoke to me tonight. I believe He wants me to work with your girls, so. . ." She spread her hands wide. "Here I am."

Seth steeled himself against the pleading in her eyes. "Are you sure you aren't looking at this as a way to see the sights or get some kind of thrill?"

Her lips parted, but she didn't say a word.

Seth bent forward and rested his arms on his knees. "Miss Mayhew, this is a serious business. These girls are precious souls, and they need someone fully committed to doing the Lord's work. This isn't something you can begin today and let drop a week later. They need someone they can trust, someone who will reflect God's commitment to them." He paused to let that sink in.

She nodded slowly. "I understand."

"I'm not sure you do. The families these girls come from don't live in the best part of town. Far from it. You'll have to learn to expect a certain amount of crudeness in their speech and behavior, and it's possible your personal safety could become an issue. This isn't a decision to be made lightly on the spur of the moment."

He steepled his fingers, ready to press his point home. "If I remember correctly, you haven't been in Chicago one full day. What makes you think you'll be here long enough to win their trust?"

Her slim shoulders straightened under the puffed sleeves of her shirtwaist. She lifted her chin. "I'm starting a job at the fairgrounds in the morning. I've agreed to work there for the duration of the fair, and I'm not one to go back on my word. That means you have a guarantee of nearly four months. Will that be long enough for me to prove myself to you?"

Seth shifted in his seat, trying to stay awake through the session of reports that followed each night's meetings. Dwight Moody himself presided over the gathering, rejoicing in victories won and giving advice when needed.

The great evangelist looked straight at him, and Seth came fully alert. "I understand there is additional cause for rejoicing. Mrs. Hammond tells me you've found someone to help in the girls' work."

"Yes, sir. That's right," Seth managed to say. He still hadn't gotten used to the fact that the man he so long admired knew him by name and considered him a fellow laborer in the Lord's work. "A young lady volunteered at the meeting tonight."

"Excellent!" Moody rubbed his hands together, and his eyes sparkled above his beard. "That was a wonderful idea, to have Reverend Hall announce the need like that. It opened the opportunity to believers who might not otherwise have heard about it."

"Thank you." Seth kept his doubts about Miss Mayhew to himself. No need to let his misgivings spoil an otherwise positive series of reports.

"We must pray that God uses this woman in a mighty way to reach those young people for Christ."

Seth merely nodded. No matter how often he stood in

Moody's presence, he always felt an overwhelming sense of God's nearness.

The discussion moved on to more reports and then to the schedule for the next night's meetings, confirming plans for the various speakers and singers. With everything in order, the rest of the meeting went quickly, and the workers dispersed to go their separate ways and prepare for the morrow.

Seth said his good-byes and hurried to catch his streetcar. When he reached his stop, he walked briskly, keeping a sharp watch for anyone who might be lurking in the darkness. His small apartment was conveniently located for ministering to his little flock, but a fellow had to stay on his toes in this neighborhood.

On the next block, tinny piano music and raucous voices burst forth from a series of saloons. Farther along the street, a door slammed, and a string of oaths and threats split the night air.

His field of service. A place where all manner of evil could happen. . .and often did. He turned his head in time to catch sight of shadowy figures moving out of a doorway on the opposite side of the street. Seth stopped and looked their way, loosening his jacket and rolling his shoulders. The dark forms faded back into the blackness. The danger was past—for now.

Seth let himself relax a fraction but remained watchful. Walking along these darkened streets never failed to remind him of the crying need its inhabitants had for the Light of the world.

He had worked hard among the people here. Though he still had a long way to go, he took comfort in the knowledge he'd managed to make at least some inroads. His group of boys, for instance. Ornery and rough around the edges as they were, he had seen some small measure of success with them and their families. If only the girls in the area could be reached in the same way!

And that brought his thinking back around to Dinah Mayhew and her wide-eyed eagerness. What would she think of these surroundings?

Her probable reaction gave him a grim sense of satisfaction. The area could provide excitement, all right, but not the kind she was looking for. And that should take care of the problem of Miss Dinah Mayhew without any intervention on his part.

Once she had a taste of the place, she wouldn't last long.

CHAPTER 5

*I*s there any place in Chicago that isn't overrun with people? Dinah edged forward in the waiting line.

Crowds seemed to sum up her experience in the city thus far—the mass of people at last night's meeting, the pedestrians she passed on her walk to the fairgrounds this morning, and now the teeming swell of people waiting to pass through the turnstiles at the Fifty-seventh Street entrance to the grand Columbian Exposition.

Caught up in the crush, Dinah held her straw boater in place with one hand and tightened her grip on her reticule with the other. She placed one foot carefully in front of the other, not wanting to risk losing her balance and falling underfoot. The mass of jostling bodies carried her up to the gate, where she held out her employee's pass for the ticket taker's inspection, then pushed through the turnstile, feeling like a cork popping free of a bottle.

Dinah stood stock-still on the broad pavement, still holding on to her hat and staring at the magnificent sight before her. A young couple with three small children in tow bumped into her as they passed. The impact jolted her back to the moment.

Dinah settled her hat firmly in place, then adjusted the box pleats of her forest green skirt. She must get herself in hand and not look like some simple country rube. She was now a resident of the city of Chicago, a bona fide employee of the World's Columbian Exposition, and she needed to act like she belonged there. It was time to get to work. It wouldn't do to be late, especially on her very first day.

But where to go? She had corresponded with Mr. Thorndyke's office several times over the past few weeks. She knew a bit about what her new position entailed, enough to feel sure she could handle the work. She knew the name of the person she was to report to and the name of the building. But somehow, details of the building's location had never come up.

Why hadn't she thought to ask? Tension knotted her stomach, and she pivoted in a slow circle. She had seen plenty of county fairs and had even been to the state fair in Lincoln several times. Armed with that background, plus having read all the accounts of the exposition she could find, she felt sure she had a reasonably accurate picture of its size and expanse. . .but she had been wrong. So wrong.

Now if she could just keep herself from gawking.

One thing was for certain: She wouldn't make any progress toward her goal if she remained rooted in one spot. She set off at a brisk pace until she reached a crossroads, noting the names of the buildings that stood on each corner: Minnesota, Nebraska, South Dakota.

Where to try next? Dinah turned left and followed the road that curved to the northeast, encountering still more buildings, each labeled with a state's name: North Dakota, Kansas, Arkansas. Her steps dragged to a stop. This didn't seem to be getting her anywhere.

Dinah took stock of her surroundings. Buildings dotted the landscape as far as the eye could see. People milled about her, speaking in a multitude of tongues. Atop the buildings, flags snapped in the morning breeze that carried with it the heavy scent of Lake Michigan. Together, they produced a holiday feel, an assault on the senses. And she was going to be a part of it all. A surge of joy swept through her, and Dinah felt herself on the brink of tears.

But standing here like a dithering ninny wasn't accomplishing anything. She had to find the Administration Building.

She retraced her steps to the crossroads, then continued south past the buildings erected for Washington and Colorado until she stood before a large structure built in the style of a Spanish mission. A sign reading CALIFORNIA curved above the central archway. Beneath the arch, she spotted a man in uniform, and her heart quickened. She had read about the Columbian Guards, who made up what amounted to the fair's own police force.

Dinah walked over to him, feeling her palms grow suddenly moist. *What should I say?* The thought of approaching a total stranger felt utterly foreign to her. But she would be working on the fairgrounds, too, she reminded herself. That practically made them coworkers. Besides, he was her only hope at the moment. If she continued trying to locate the Administration Building on her own, it might take hours, and she only had. . . Dinah glanced at the watch pinned to her blouse and gasped.

She quickened her pace and cleared her throat when she was a few feet away from him. "Could you direct me to the Administration Building?" Dinah asked. "The quickest way, please. I need to report to work, and it's my first day on the job."

The warmth in his smile made her jitters melt away. "Welcome to the White City. You've picked a wonderful day to arrive. The weather couldn't be more pleasant. But you're interested in getting on your way quickly, not in a weather report." He pointed toward the south. "The Administration Building is nearly all the way to the far end of the fairgrounds. Follow this walkway to the lagoon."

His finger moved to the left, where Dinah could see a glittering expanse of water. "Stay to the right of the lagoon and continue on until you reach Terminal Station. The Administration Building is right across the Grand Plaza. It's the building with the great golden dome. You can't miss it."

Dinah thanked him and set off once more with a renewed sense of optimism. She glanced up at the golden dome on a massive building to her left. No, that one was labeled ILLINOIS. When she reached the north tip of the lagoon, she paused to check her bearings again.

The sights and sounds of the crowds faded, and Dinah simply stared, taking in the lavish display spread out before her. *No wonder they call it the White City.* Glittering white edifices lined both sides of the lagoon, and she could see more in the distance.

Remembering the guard's instructions, she followed the walkway that skirted the right-hand side of the lagoon. Dinah scanned the structures as she passed: the Woman's Building,

Horticulture, Transportation. Not a golden dome in sight.

She trudged onward, going over the guard's directions in her mind. "The far end of the fairgrounds." It sounded so simple when he pointed her in the right direction. But just how far away was that? It seemed as though the long line of buildings would never end.

Dinah took another glance at her watch and picked up her pace even more. Thank goodness her years of working outdoors on the farm had given her strong muscles and good wind.

A narrow craft sailed by, skimming the waters of the lagoon like a swallow on the breeze. *A gondola?* Dinah drank in its graceful lines, trying to watch its progress and dodge pedestrians at the same time.

And over there on the far side of the lagoon—impossible to imagine in the midst of the mighty city—a crew of fur-clad men propelled a kayak.

Dinah tingled with excitement at the thought of exploring the fair and discovering more of its delights. But she was a workingwoman now. When would she ever find the time? Up ahead, a brass band struck up a Sousa march. The lively melody revived Dinah's mood and lightened her steps.

A train whistle caught her attention, and she hurried ahead, buoyed by relief at the realization she was nearing Terminal Station at last. She stepped into an open area and felt her nose twitch at the rich scent of chocolate borne on the morning breeze. Sniffing like one of Uncle Everett's hounds on a scent, she located the source of the delectable aroma, a small building dwarfed further by the mighty structures surrounding it. The sign over the entrance read MENIER CHOCOLATE COMPANY.

Dinah promised herself a visit to sample the Menier wares

after she received her first pay. Assuming she ever found the Administration Building so she could start her job in the first place.

With a renewed sense of urgency, she looked past the Menier Pavilion. . .and there it was.

"Oh my!" Dinah stumbled to a halt and tipped her head back as far as she could to take in the full scope of the lofty edifice before her. Four square pavilions formed a quadrangle at the base, each rising to an impressive height. From there, two more levels soared upward, surmounted by an octagonal golden dome.

The realization that she would spend her days surrounded by such splendor made her knees wobble. *No time to get all starry-eyed now,* she admonished herself. If she hurried, she could still make it to work on time. Barely.

She spotted another guard near one of the recessed entrances of the building. Emboldened by her earlier success, she marched across the plaza and strode up to him.

"Could you tell me where to find Mr. Thorndyke's office, please?"

The dark-haired guard smiled kindly and pointed to the farthest corner pavilion. "He's on the third floor, miss. You can take the elevator."

Dinah smiled and thanked him and crossed the rotunda, trying to look like someone to whom riding an elevator was an everyday event. She managed not to gasp when the operator put the car in motion, even though she felt as if she'd left her stomach back on the rotunda floor.

When the elevator door slid open, she stepped out and glanced around until she saw Mr. Thorndyke's name on one of the heavy oak doors. Glad she hadn't needed to climb the two flights of stairs, she patted her hair in place, took a deep breath, and pushed open the door.

A girl about her own age gave Dinah a friendly smile. "May I help you?"

"I'm Dinah Mayhew. I'm supposed to start work here today."

A middle-aged woman looked up from sorting a stack of papers on the far side of the office. "I'll handle this, Millie," she told the receptionist.

Dinah fought down a sudden wave of panic as the woman crossed the distance between them and gave her an appraising glance. She held her chin high and hoped she would pass muster. The other woman's features were stern, but her eyes held a kindly expression.

"I'm Mrs. Johnson, Mr. Thorndyke's assistant," she said in a no-nonsense tone. "Before I explain your duties, have you spent much time on the fairgrounds? Have you had a chance to become familiar with the way it's set up?"

Dinah shook her head, feeling more out of place by the minute. "I only arrived yesterday."

"Step over here. It's easier to show you than to explain." Mrs. Johnson led her to a window and pointed to the scene below. Dinah sucked in her breath and stared, fascinated by the bird's-eye view of the spot where she had stood only moments before. Scores of people scurried to and fro, reminding her of a swarming colony of ants.

"This will give you a good idea of the general layout. This building stands in the middle of the Grand Plaza." Mrs. Johnson indicated the broad, open area Dinah had crossed. "The plaza is bounded on the north by the Mines and Electricity buildings, and on the south by Machinery Hall. Behind us on the west is Terminal Station.

"Just below us is the Columbian Fountain." A dreamy smile flitted across Mrs. Johnson's face. "In the evenings, streams of colored water spurt a hundred and fifty feet into the air. It's a sight you won't want to miss. Behind the fountain, the Grand Basin stretches out to the Peristyle on the east. You can see the columns in the distance. And beyond that, of course, is Lake Michigan."

Dinah's lips parted as she stared at the enormous reflecting pool flanked by beveled lawns and glittering white buildings. Her mind tried to take in the wonder of it all and the fact that she wouldn't be a mere visitor—she was going to be a part of it!

"And that's only the beginning." Mrs. Johnson's manner became brisk again. "More than six hundred acres of exhibits, an absolutely mammoth undertaking. And the business life of the exposition is centered here in this building."

She turned back to Dinah. "Mr. Thorndyke is one of the administrators. As you can imagine, in a fair of this magnitude, keeping everything running smoothly requires an enormous amount of attention to detail. This office sends and receives numerous memoranda to the superintendents of the different departments on a daily basis.

"In addition, we receive requests about additional needs and sometimes complaints or disputes that arise between one exhibitor and another. Mr. Thorndyke has to deal with all of these and more. And all of them have to be dealt with in a timely manner.

"Mr. Thorndyke likens this office and its duties to being the lubricant in a well-oiled machine." Mrs. Johnson smiled at her

56

little joke, then led Dinah to a desk near Millie's.

"You'll be collating and filing the reports and making sure Mr. Thorndyke is made aware of anything requiring his immediate attention. You will, of course, pass that information to him through me."

"I've had experience filing." True enough, although the little she'd done during her summer job at Elliott's Pharmacy hadn't been on a scale anything like this. "I'm sure I can—"

The door slammed open, and a slender, blond girl braced herself against the doorway. Dinah took in her stunning hair and fine features. She was probably extremely attractive when she didn't have her face twisted in a murderous glare.

"How many more times am I going to have to trek around these fairgrounds before this exposition ends?" the newcomer demanded.

Millie smiled and went back to her work. The blond's gaze rested on Dinah and sharpened. "Who are you?"

Dinah smiled hesitantly. Mrs. Johnson spoke before she could respond. "This is Dinah Mayhew. She's taking Sarah's place. As soon as you've delivered those reports, I want you to show her how our files are arranged. Then you'll need to check with Mr. Skiff in Mines and Mining to see if he has his information ready."

The girl followed along in Mrs. Johnson's wake, her eyes bulging. "I just got back from the Manufactures Building. I really don't want to. . . ." Her eyes lit on Dinah, and her mouth curved in a smile. She hurried after Mrs. Johnson. "Perhaps Dinah would like to check on Mr. Skiff's progress."

The door to Mrs. Johnson's office closed behind them, and Dinah turned to see Millie grinning at her. "What just happened?" Dinah inquired.

Millie leaned over her desk and lowered her voice to a whisper. "That's Lila Dawson. She's none too pleased at having to spend so much time out of the office. If she isn't here, she can't do anything to catch Mr. Thorndyke's notice, if you know what I mean."

This place grew more puzzling by the minute. "I'm not sure I do."

Millie sniggered. "He isn't so bad looking for an older man. He must be forty if he's a day. But it isn't his looks Lila cares about so much as his bank account. Once she found out he's a widower, she set her cap for him. And that's why she was so uppity with you just now. Unless I miss my guess, she doesn't want you moving in on her territory."

Dinah's jaw sagged, along with the pride she'd felt in navigating her way across the fairgrounds. She thought the morning's problems had ended with finding the sanctuary of her new office. Instead, it seemed she had a whole new maze to find her way through.

Suddenly, the thought of being outside in the unfamiliar labyrinth took on a new appeal. When the door in the rear wall opened and Mrs. Johnson and Lila reappeared, Dinah stepped forward with a brave smile. "I'd be happy to run any errands you need me to, Mrs. Johnson. Where would you like me to go first?"

Seth gripped the handle at the rear of the wheeled wicker chair and trundled it along the bridge spanning the North Canal. He swerved slightly to avoid a couple of young lads racing down the walkway, but the quick, jerky movement didn't put a dent in the flow of prattle coming from his passenger.

"We never planned to come to the exposition, you see. My husband said he expected it would be nothing more than a lot of fripperies and folderol. But then our oldest son brought his wife and family here and, my! The things he talked about in his letters! 'Sell anything you need to raise the money,' he told us. 'But you simply must come.'" The woman barely paused for breath before continuing.

"And so we took a look at our savings and decided we could make the trip. But this—" She waved her plump arms about. "Nothing could have prepared me for it, not even those letters. My land, if you hadn't happened along, I probably would have been stretched out right there on the pavement. I never dreamed it would take so long just to walk from one end of this place to the other."

"Here's the Electricity Building." Seth rolled the chair to a stop in the shade of a mulberry tree. "Would you like me to wait for you?"

"No, thank you. I'm feeling much more refreshed now. I just pushed too hard, wanting to see everything at once. My husband said I was a goose to try to do so much in one day, and I hate to prove him right, but there it is."

She pulled forty cents from her reticule and handed it to Seth. "I'll take it easier from here on. You've given me a nice tour of the grounds, so I have a better idea of what I really want to see. I'll just meander along and take my time about it."

Seth helped her out of the chair and waited to be sure she was steady on her feet. "I hope you enjoy the rest of your visit. Don't hesitate to call for another chair if you feel the need."

The woman wagged her finger at him playfully. "Do you want to give me another tour, or are you just looking for an excuse to preach a sermon to a captive audience? After meeting you, I can see why these chairs are known as gospel chariots." Her merry laugh told him she wasn't offended in the least. "Thank you for the tour. . .and the talk. You've given me much to think about."

Seth maneuvered the empty chair in a circle, ready to head back to the Rolling Chair Company Pavilion on the lake side of the Manufactures Building. Behind him, a bright voice called, "Hello, there!"

He wheeled around, expecting to find another foot-weary fairgoer ready to avail herself of his services. Instead, he saw the young lady from last night's meeting. She hurried toward him with the glowing smile he remembered so well.

"How do you do, Miss Mayhew? I didn't expect to see you here."

"I told you I was starting a job here today."

Seth smothered a grin at the defiant tilt of her chin. Was she always this much of a spitfire? The light afternoon breeze tossed a stray curl across her forehead. Seth watched, distracted, before he remembered to respond. "True enough. I guess I just didn't expect to see you wandering around outside."

Her hazel eyes glittered. "I am not 'wandering.' I'm looking for the Mines and Mining Building, and when I saw you here, I thought maybe you could help me." She pivoted in a swirl of green skirt and started back toward the Grand Plaza. "I'll go look for one of the guards," she called over her shoulder. "They seem to know where everything is, and they don't mind giving directions."

"Wait a minute." Seth abandoned his rolling chair and caught up to her in a few long strides. "I didn't mean to offend you; I was just surprised. I'll be glad to show you to Mines and Mining. You're practically there already."

"Really?" Her eyes shone with a green light. Their shifting colors reminded him of Lake Michigan in its changing moods. "I know it's just off the Grand Plaza, and it's a big white building. But look!" She swept her arm in a broad circle that encompassed the Court of Honor. "These buildings are all enormous, and every one of them is white!"

Her chin trembled, and Seth felt a pang of remorse for his earlier teasing. "You're right. It takes a while to get accustomed to where everything is. Why don't I escort you there and try to help you learn your way around?" He retrieved the chair from beneath the mulberry tree and pushed it along at her side, trying not to think what his employers would say about taking time away from their paying customers.

Dinah's stiff gait told him she still hadn't quite recovered from her pique. "Please don't bother. I'm quite capable of managing on my own." Her pace slowed a fraction. "Could I ask you something, though?"

"Of course."

"I heard that woman say something about a gospel chariot. What was she talking about?"

Seth chuckled. "A lot of the men working for the Rolling Chair Company are theology students or pastors like me. I guess we've developed a bit of a reputation for turning the conversation to spiritual things in addition to giving a tour of the grounds."

"That explains it!" Her smile returned, and Seth basked in its glow. She glanced ahead to the two massive buildings that stood side by side across the plaza from Administration. "Is it one of those?"

"The one on the left. See, you're learning your way already."

Miss Mayhew looked pleased. "Well, good-bye for now. Maybe we'll see each other around here again. If not, then at my first meeting with the girls."

She set off, head held high. Seth couldn't help noticing the graceful way her skirt swayed when she walked.

Watch yourself! He swung the chair around and turned back toward the Rolling Chair kiosk with a purposeful gait. He would be seeing a lot of Miss Mayhew, working with their respective groups of young people, not to mention any future encounters they might have on the fairgrounds. It wouldn't pay to let his emotions rule his thinking.

He had plenty of experience dealing with other female workers in the Moody campaign and had learned to show himself friendly yet reserved. The ability to keep a wall around his feelings had served him well thus far, but the uneasy feeling in the pit of his stomach told him it might be all too easy for this dark-haired beauty to breach it.

CHAPTER 6

More jam?"

"I'd love some, Mrs. Purvis. These biscuits are delicious." Dinah spooned some of the gooseberry jam onto the edge of her plate, then offered the dish to the woman seated next to her at the dining table.

"Thank you. I believe I will." The woman scooped out a hefty dollop and passed the remainder across the table to her husband. "I'm certainly going to miss this cooking when we get back home to Missouri."

She smeared the jam onto her biscuit and took a good-sized bite, then leaned toward Dinah. "Such a shame we didn't have a chance to get acquainted before we left. If we hadn't bumped into you in the hallway this morning, we wouldn't even have known we had another boarder amongst us. I'm Mrs. Sedgwick, by the way. And this is my husband, and our son, Malcolm." She gazed with fondness on the chubby boy filling his cheeks with biscuits and jam until he resembled a chipmunk.

"We've stayed out late every night, seeing as much of the exposition as we could," Mrs. Sedgwick continued. "Of course, that meant we were so tired in the morning we didn't get down to breakfast at the usual time, so we must have missed you coming and going."

"I only arrived the day before yesterday," Dinah explained.

"Oh, then we really wouldn't have had much opportunity to get to know you, even if we'd all been up and around at the same time. Have you come here to see the fair? All by yourself?"

"Actually. . ." Dinah blotted her lips with her napkin and tried to keep the pride from showing in her voice. "I'm working there. I have a job in the office of one of the administrators."

"Oh, my!" Mrs. Sedgwick paused with a forkful of sausage in midair. "A young girl like you, off on her own?"

"Now, now," her husband cut in. "It's a new world we're living in. We must keep up with the times."

Mrs. Sedgwick chewed her sausage thoughtfully. "You're right, dear. One hears about any number of young girls coming to the city, looking for work or excitement or both. Still. . ."

"Hand me that plate of biscuits, Ma," young Malcolm demanded. "I'm still hungry."

Have you ever heard of the word please*?* Dinah waited for his mother to reprimand his lack of manners. Instead, the woman beamed and placed the plate closer to him. "He has a healthy appetite."

Dinah gulped down a swig of coffee so she couldn't be tempted to respond. Out of the corner of her eye, she saw Mrs. Purvis watching the boy in awe, her unflappable good humor absent for once.

64

Having recovered from the shock of finding Dinah on her own, the Sedgwicks proceeded to fill her in on sights she wouldn't want to miss at the fair.

"You simply must see the grounds at night," Mrs. Sedgwick told her. "So astounding, so inspiring."

"Don't forget the Kimberley diamond exhibit and Edison's new contraption," her husband reminded. "Those are well worth seeing, too."

Dinah nodded, one part of her attention bent on responding to their suggestions, the other focused on Malcolm, who was putting away food with alarming speed. Was it possible for a person to explode from eating too much at one time? If he kept going at this rate, she just might find out.

One sparkling dollop of gooseberry jam remained on her plate. Giving in to temptation, Dinah reached for the last biscuit on the platter, only to see Malcolm sweep it up in a pudgy fist.

"He does enjoy a hearty breakfast." Mrs. Sedgwick beamed.

Mrs. Purvis scooted her chair away from the table and scooped up the empty platter. "I'll get some more biscuits," she said to no one in particular. "Some of the rest of us would like to enjoy them, too."

She paused at the kitchen door, stretched her arm high above her head, and tapped along the top of the doorjamb from one side to the other. Shaking her head, she muttered under her breath and disappeared into the kitchen.

Dinah blinked at the odd behavior. The Sedgwicks exchanged glances, then Mr. Sedgwick leaned toward Dinah. "To be honest, we had planned to stay another week. That sort of thing is one of the reasons we're cutting our stay a bit short. The woman has done the same kind of tapping ever since we arrived."

Mrs. Sedgwick nodded and placed her hand on Dinah's arm. "When we asked her about it, she just mumbled something about her late husband and kept on tapping away. We think she may be a bit unbalanced. And of course, we wouldn't want to place little Malcolm in any sort of danger." She cast a quick glance at her son and lowered her voice even further. "Did you see the look she gave him just before she went back for more biscuits?"

"It is rather a strange thing to do," Dinah conceded. Privately, she doubted that Malcolm was in danger of anything more than a severe case of indigestion. But the tapping struck her as a bit peculiar.

"You seem like a nice young woman," Mr. Sedgwick went on. "I feel it's our duty to warn you so you can be on your guard. Perhaps you might want to consider other lodgings."

"Thank you," Dinah said. "I'll keep that in mind."

She tucked their comment away for future reference but didn't think she would need to act on it. As far as she could tell, Mrs. Purvis was a dear woman, not dangerous in the least. Eccentric perhaps, but she wouldn't be the first person Dinah had ever met who had an odd mannerism or two.

Still…she recalled the methodical way the landlady tapped her way across the doorjamb. It wouldn't hurt to keep her eyes open, just to make sure there was nothing to be concerned about.

Dinah slid the last piece of the morning's correspondence into the proper file and squared the pile of papers into a neat stack. "Is there anything else you'd like me to do before I take a lunch break, Mrs. Johnson?"

Her supervisor glanced at the clock, then peered at Dinah over the top of her half-glasses. "Nothing that can't wait until you get back. You've worked right through the lunch hour as it is. If you want to take an extra few minutes, that will be fine."

Lila looked up from her desk across the room. "As long as I don't have to cover for her if she decides to stay out half the afternoon. I don't want to have to tramp around the grounds at two o'clock to pick up the rest of the reports."

"I'll be back long before then," Dinah promised and hurried to the elevator.

Once downstairs, she took a moment to compose herself before starting off. It was sweet of Mrs. Johnson to allow her some extra time for lunch, and Dinah intended to make full use of it. But not for eating.

She set a brisk pace across the Grand Plaza, brushing past the knot of people gathered near the Columbian Fountain. Unlike the clear blue sky of her first day in Chicago, today was overcast. Heavy, dark clouds rolled in across the lake and hung low, giving the sky an ominous appearance that did nothing to lessen Dinah's own uncertain mood.

After looking forward to this moment for so long, after all the planning and scheming to get herself to Chicago, she found herself beset by sudden doubt. Perhaps she had been as mad as Aunt Dora thought for making this move.

Dinah skirted the west end of the Grand Basin and crossed the bridge over the South Canal. Thoughts whirled through her mind like the gulls swooping overhead. Would he recognize her right away? How would he react when she met him?

And what would she say in response? Panic seized her when she realized her well-rehearsed greeting had faded from her memory like mist from the lake.

Maybe a casual approach would be best. She would simply walk up to the booth like any other fairgoer and take stock of the situation—and him—before deciding how to proceed.

Yes, that would work. Pleased with her decision, she hurried along the colonnaded walk to the building's main entrance. Once inside, she paused to let her eyes adjust to the dimmer light and to get her bearings. She stood in the center of the rotunda, surmounted by its mammoth glass dome. Ahead of her lay the huge exhibit floor with its myriad of booths and displays.

How to find the booth she sought? Dinah started along the central aisle, passing exhibits from Great Britain and Germany. Would even an extended lunch break give her sufficient time to locate it? Another broad walkway intersected with the one she followed, dividing the building from north to south. To her great relief, she saw exhibits from the United States on the south side of the divide and quickened her pace. At least she had narrowed the possibilities down a little.

Why hadn't he given her more specific directions in his letter? Or had he even known the location himself when he wrote to her? She did have the name of the booth, but that didn't tell her where to find it. She looked around and clucked her tongue in irritation. Not a Columbian Guard in sight.

Dinah marched toward the east end of the building. There was nothing else for it. She would walk up and down each aisle on this end, then repeat the process on the west half if necessary.

Scanning the signs of the various exhibits, she had to remind herself to keep up her pace. How she would love to stop and explore some of them in more detail!

But that could wait for another time. Right now, her goal

was the Minnesota Threshing Company exhibit.

She passed the pavilion of the American Sugar Refining Company, which claimed to hold more than two hundred samples of various kinds of sugars. Schall & Company displayed a scene representing the landing of Columbus, all done in gum paste.

Dinah's lips quirked upward. Whoever would have thought of such an idea? Onward she trudged, past exhibits of bee culture, canned goods, and tobacco.

A pair of men rounded the corner, so engrossed in conversation that Dinah barely had time to skip out of their way. The two men walked on, apparently unaware of their near miss.

"Did you see that thresher?" The older man said to his companion. "Fella says it's the newest one on the market. It's supposed to cut our time in the field in half."

Dinah spun around. "Excuse me!" She trotted after the men until she caught their attention. "I heard you mention a thresher. Could you tell me where it's located?"

The speaker gave her a quizzical look, then shrugged and pointed toward the south end of the building. "Back there in the annex, with all the other farm implements."

"Thank you!" Dinah hurried in the direction indicated and found herself in yet another great hall filled with all manner of reapers, threshers, and plows.

Her gaze roamed back and forth from one side of the broad, central aisle to the other, looking for the right sign. Dinah's attack of nerves returned in full force. There it was: the Minnesota Threshing Company display.

She pressed her hands against her skirt to dry the moisture on her palms and slowed her steps, trying to adopt the leisurely pace of any other fairgoer.

Where was he? She sized up the crowd gathered near the edge of the booth. Most showed only a casual interest before drifting off to view the other displays, but one couple stood talking to a plump, pretty woman next to a piece of equipment Dinah recognized as a binder. At the other end of the exhibit area, two men bent over a thresher, deep in conversation with a tall, slender man who appeared to be pointing out its features. All three had their backs turned toward her.

She felt a flutter in her stomach and took another look at the three men. There was something about that salesman. . . . The other two men nodded affably and strolled away. The man attending to them turned so she could see his face.

Numbness crept from the top of Dinah's head to her fingertips.

It was him.

Desperate to blend into the crowd, Dinah fell into place behind a passing couple and eased up to the edge of the booth. She peered past the couple's shoulders, drinking in the familiar features: the long, lanky build, the high forehead, and aquiline nose.

Age had made some changes. His face held more wrinkles than she remembered, and the nose seemed a little more beaked. Silver strands shot through his hair, the same dark brown as her own.

What had time done to her own appearance? Dinah's hand crept up to her cheek, and she ran her fingers along her jaw line. His features were still recognizable, even with the changes wrought by age, but she had been a mere child the last time he saw her. How long would it take him to recognize her? After all, it had been ten years.

The couple ahead of her asked a question, and he responded. The voice, at least, was just the same. Dinah's vision dimmed, and tightness gripped her throat. For a moment, she wanted to run away.

No, she could do this. This meeting had been the focus of her dreams for a decade. She wouldn't turn back now.

The couple moved away, depriving her of their protective cover. Dinah's breath caught in her throat. The big moment had arrived. Hoping her tottery legs would support her, she stepped into his field of vision.

The words of greeting died on her lips the instant their eyes made contact. The smile she remembered so well froze, then slid from his face. His jaw sagged, and his lips parted. From where she stood, she could see them tremble.

"You're the very image of your mother the first time I saw her." His voice was husky when he spoke. "The same heart-shaped face, that tilt to your chin. Even your eyes are exactly the color hers were." His Adam's apple bobbed.

Tears stung Dinah's eyes and pooled along her lower lids. "It's been a long time, Papa."

He reached out and folded her in his arms, pulling her tight against him. Together they formed an island in the midst of the swirling throng. Surrounded by a thousand strangers in an unfamiliar city, Dinah felt a sense of being where she belonged, of finally coming home.

A long moment passed before he stepped back, still cradling her shoulders in his hands. His eyes glistened, but his face wore a broad grin. "My little girl, all grown up. I always knew you'd turn out to be a beauty."

Dinah knew her cup of joy had reached its brim. "I was so

happy to get your letter."

"I should have asked you to come sooner. I never meant to leave you for so long."

With an effort, Dinah pushed back the memories of those dark years when she longed to be with him, to feel like part of a real family again. "It doesn't matter, not anymore. What matters now is that we're finally together again." And if she had her way, there would be no more separations. She would be a part of his life from this day on.

Her father kept staring, drinking in the sight of her. "You're looking well. . .no, wonderful!"

Dinah felt her cheeks grow pink with pleasure. "I've missed you so much."

His eyes misted. "You'll never know how hard it was for me to leave you with your aunt and uncle. I knew it was more important for you to have a woman's care and someone your own age to be with than to spend your growing-up years traipsing along after me."

"It was hard for me, too." Tears threatened again, and she blinked them back. "You didn't even let me say good-bye."

"That was probably a mistake. I can see that now. But I was doing what I thought best for you. . .and maybe for myself, too. I wanted to remember you smiling and happy. Can you forgive me for that?"

The shadow of doubt in his eyes tugged at Dinah's heart. "Of course," she whispered.

As happy as she was at this moment, she could forgive him anything. It would have been hard for him to have a child trailing along on his travels. She could see that now, although living out of a suitcase and sleeping on trains would have been a small price to pay to be able to stay with her father. Nearly anything would have been better than growing up with a cousin like Gladys.

But that was her selfishness speaking. She could put all that behind her now. She was no longer a child who needed to be looked after, but a grown woman who could be a help rather than a burden.

And he realized that, too! Hadn't he shown it by writing to her and asking her to join him? Joy welled up within her. Let the past remain in the past. They were together again, and that's all that mattered.

She reached up to pat his cheek, feeling the need to say the words aloud. "You're forgiven, Papa."

"Ernie?"

Her father started when the quiet voice spoke beside them. Dinah turned to see the woman she had noticed earlier regarding them quizzically. "Is everything all right?"

Her father's face split into a wide smile. "More than all right. Things couldn't be better." He pulled Dinah close to his side and wrapped his arm around her. "Allow me to introduce my daughter, Dinah, all grown up and making her father one proud and happy man."

Dinah nodded politely, resenting the intrusion. She had waited too long for this reunion to have it interrupted by meaningless introductions. They had a lot of catching up to do, after all. She wanted to hear about all the things her father had done in the years since she saw him last. Why didn't the woman leave them alone and go on about her business?

As if sensing Dinah's irritation, the woman hesitated, then held out her hand. "I'm happy to meet you. I'm—"

"Sorry," her father cut in. "I'm so excited I forgot my manners. Dinah, this is Abby Watson. Abby is. . .a good friend and coworker."

Dinah caught the quick look the other woman shot at him but didn't know how to interpret it. Abby stepped back. "Excuse me now. I need to get back to work."

The light in her father's eyes dimmed. "We all do, I suppose." He turned to Dinah and caught her hands in his. "You don't know how much good it's done me just to see you again. How long are you going to be in Chicago?"

Laughter gurgled from Dinah's throat. "As long as you are. When you wrote and said you wanted me to join you, I packed up and left the farm as soon as I could. I'm working right here on the fairgrounds, over in the Administration Building. We'll be able to see each other any time we want."

Her father's eyes flared wide. "I never expected. . .well, aren't you the enterprising little thing? That's quite a surprise. Quite a surprise, indeed. I'm putting in long hours here at the booth, but we'll have to get together for a meal sometime when our schedules allow."

Dinah nodded eagerly. "Of course. We have so much to catch up on. I'd better be getting back myself, but I'll see you soon." She stood on tiptoe and brushed a quick kiss on his cheek. Their visit might have been shorter than she'd hoped for, but there would be plenty of other times to talk and reminisce. . . and make plans for the future.

"When I get through with you, Preacher Man, you're going to

wish you never got out of bed this morning." The face that filled Seth's vision split in a taunting leer, and a quick jab showed that the speaker intended to back up his statement.

Seth dodged the jab and tried to ignore the hoots and catcalls from the circle of onlookers.

"Stretch 'im out, Mac!"

"Put one in his breadbasket!"

Seth kept his fists at chin level and eyed his opponent's movements carefully, watching for the next swing, the one that might take him down. He danced back lightly on the balls of his feet and looked for an opening to throw a punch of his own.

The other man feinted with his left, then caught Seth with his right as he ducked away, landing a blow on Seth's jaw that knocked him to his knees. His opponent moved away, then came back and held out a hand to help him to his feet.

"Aw, come on," called a deep-voiced man on the sidelines of the ring. "You aren't quittin' already, are you?"

Mac grinned. "Afraid so, fellas." He clapped Seth on the shoulder. "I'm about finished for today, and it looks like you are, too."

Seth regained his balance and worked his jaw back and forth. "I won't argue with you. You pack quite a wallop. But then, you always did, even back when we were kids."

Mac's trainer came up and threw a towel around his shoulders. "That's my boy! Keep throwing punches like that next time you get in the ring with the champ, and you can go all the way to the top."

When the noisy circle of admirers moved on to watch the next sparring match, Seth and Mac headed over to where they'd left their street clothes on a bench by the wall of the gym. Seth stripped to the waist and toweled the perspiration from his head and torso, then pulled on a clean shirt.

He touched his chin gingerly. "I ought to make you come teach my boys' class tonight. It's going to be hard to talk if my jaw tightens up on me."

Mac looked around as if making sure he couldn't be overheard. "Those weren't exactly sissy taps you were giving me. I'm going to be feeling that punch in the ribs for a few days, but I didn't want to let on when we were out there in front of everybody."

Seth grinned, regretting the action when his jaw protested. "I knew it wouldn't do you any good for me to hold back while you're in training. Not when you're planning to be the next middleweight champion."

"Yeah." Mac swabbed his forehead with his towel. "If they let me do it my way and fight it clean."

"What do you mean?"

Mac shrugged. "Nothing. Just something I overheard. Forget I mentioned it." He finished dressing quickly and bent to lace up his shoes. "You know, I never have figured it out. You would have done just as well in the ring as I have, maybe even better. Why'd you give it all up just when it looked like things were going your way?"

The compliment warmed Seth. "I guess God had other plans for me."

"Just as well. I would have hated having to face you in the ring for real."

Seth rolled his boxing clothes in a towel and tucked the bundle under his arm. Waving good-bye to his friend, he left the smell of sweaty bodies behind and stepped into the fresh outdoor air.

Acting as a sparring partner for his old friend wasn't exactly the kind of thing most people expected of a man of the cloth, but it gave him the opportunity to mingle with men who would never darken the door of a church. *God does work in mysterious ways.*

He turned the corner and headed toward his small apartment, thinking about what Mac had said about his giving up the ring. At one point in his life, he would have committed every ounce of his focus to reach the point where he saw his name on the marquee of the fighting arena. But then the Lord got hold of him and changed his life for good.

Some of his old cronies thought he was out of his mind for giving up the chance at fame and fortune to become a poor Bible-thumper, as they termed it. At one time, Seth would have thought that a crazy idea himself.

He smiled when he thought of how much his goals had changed since those days. He had no regrets, none at all. Fame and fortune would never be his, but he had by far the better end of the deal.

Sports had been his passion while he was growing up. He loved the challenge of keeping his body in tip-top condition and the excitement of the competition. Not until he neared maturity did he realize the fight game also had its seamy side, one where money often outweighed skill in determining the winner.

That brought his thoughts back around to Mac's offhand comment. What had he meant about wanting to make it a clean fight? Had someone been pressuring him to throw a match?

He knew Mac well enough to know his friend wanted to

win on his own merits as a fighter. He also knew how much pressure could be applied by men driven by greed to make the outcome of a fight go the way they wanted it to.

Seth's jaw tightened. He needed to have a talk with Mac, and soon. Even a championship wasn't worth a man sacrificing his integrity.

CHAPTER 7

H ow did God make everything in just six days?"

"My granny says we're supposed to act like Jesus. So how come when my brother tried to walk on water, he sank plumb up to his neck in the river?"

"If God speaks English, like in the Bible, how can He understand when the Poles and the Italians talk to Him?"

Dinah stood at the open end of the semicircle of nine little girls. She had fixed a bright smile on her face at the beginning of the class and found it took every bit of effort she could muster just to keep it there.

How did I get myself into this? Where do they come up with all these questions?

She had studied the lesson outline Seth had given her and walked into the room filled with confidence and a flurry of anticipation. How hard could it be, after all, to discuss a Bible story with a handful of children? But the moment she stood up

79

to begin her first session with the group, queries flew at her until she felt like she was being peppered with buckshot.

No amount of study could have prepared her for this onslaught.

A little blond near the center of the semicircle raised her hand shyly. Dinah nodded at her. "Your dress is really pretty," the girl said.

Dinah glanced down at the checked frock with its rows of lace trim and smiled. Those late hours spent copying the patterns from Aunt Dora's copies of *Harper's Bazaar* had paid off.

The little girl heaved a sigh. "It must be nice to be rich."

Dinah's eyes rounded. "Rich? Oh no, I—" She broke off and took a closer look at what her class was wearing: dresses that looked clean but were faded and threadbare. On the whole, the clothes were worn out, patched hand-me-downs that looked more like something ready for Aunt Dora's rag bin rather than garments suitable for everyday wear.

"Oh my." She had labored over her new clothes in preparation for her move to the city, wanting to blend in with her new life. But here, the contrast between her clothes and those around her was painfully apparent.

"What are you really here for?" The question came from an older girl who leaned against the back wall.

"I—what do you mean?"

The girl jutted out her chin and fixed Dinah with a belligerent stare. "We've seen your type down here before, prissy ladies in their fancy dresses who waltz in here like they're better than any of us. They say they want to help. But what they really mean is they want to make themselves feel like they're doing something grand and important."

In the center of the room, the semicircle of girls shifted on their chairs and eyed Dinah with uncertainty.

Her interrogator went on. "As soon as the wind changes and they get a whiff of the stockyards up their noses, they're gone." A cynical smile curled her lips. "So how long should we expect you to stay?" She folded her arms across her chest and kept her gaze on Dinah, her eyes full of challenge.

Dinah heard the echo of Seth's comment the night of the tent meeting. *So this is what he meant.* She took a deep breath, knowing she had to regain control of the conversation if she were to have any hope of staying in charge. Allowing a slight edge to creep into her voice, she asked, "Aren't you a little old to be in this class? The other girls are between eight and ten years old."

Her interrogator's eyes narrowed. "I'm fifteen, not that it's any business of yours." She pointed to the girl who had commented on Dinah's dress. "That's my little sister. She wanted to be here tonight. But I've heard some of the things you do-gooders say, and I don't want anyone making her feel like she isn't as good as anyone else just because we live down here and don't have a lot of money. As long as she stays, I'll be here where I can keep an eye on her."

Only fifteen? Dinah eyed the girl's hardened, world-weary features. How did one become so cynical at such a young age?

"I see." She forced the words through stiff lips. "In that case, you're welcome to join us. And now we really ought to begin our lesson."

The class fell quiet, and ten faces looked at her with varying degrees of suspicion. Dinah scrambled through her mind for the points she had so blithely prepared the day before and realized she couldn't remember a single one of them.

What was she going to say? What was the lesson even about? She stared back at the expectant faces, but it was no good. Every detail of the lesson had flown out of her mind.

Dinah sneaked a quick look at the watch pinned to her bodice and wanted to burst into tears. Only five minutes had passed. She still had nearly an hour to endure this inquisition. She struggled to find something, *anything* to say.

A dark-eyed girl raised her hand. "You don't live anywhere around here, do you?"

The question sparked an idea in Dinah's mind. "Why don't we spend some time getting acquainted?" She pressed her hands together and tried to look as though that had been her intention all along.

None of her charges showed much enthusiasm, but no one voiced an outright objection. Taking comfort in that, she said, "I'll start. My name is Miss Dinah Mayhew. I was born near Des Moines, Iowa, but I spent the last ten years on my uncle's farm in Nebraska. I've only been in Chicago for a few days. I'm working at the exposition. Have any of you been to see it?"

The girls shook their heads in unison. *Of course they haven't.* Dinah wanted to kick herself. Admission to the fair was fifty cents per person, twenty-five cents for children. Considering the area where these girls lived and their families' probable income, that would amount to a significant sum. Not something to be squandered on a day's entertainment.

At least they were listening, though. Dinah pressed her advantage. "Let's go around the circle. Please tell me your names and a little bit about yourself."

The girl at the left end ducked her head and shuffled her feet. "I'm Tilda," she said in a voice barely loud enough for

Dinah to hear. "I'm nine years old." Tilda fell silent, apparently having exhausted her supply of information.

"Thank you, Tilda. I'm glad to know you." Encouraged by this small success, Dinah urged the girls to continue, trying to commit their names to memory and wondering how she would ever match the names with their faces.

The girl in the center was Jenny. A little coaxing revealed that her protective older sister's name was Martha. Besides Jenny and Tilda, the group included Rosemary, Anastasia, Laurie, Cleo, Frances, and two Elizabeths.

And Martha, of course. The girl looked as defensive as ever, as if she expected Dinah to make a disparaging comment at any moment.

"Thank you, girls. That will help me remember something about each one of you. You're a lovely group of young ladies, and I'm sure your mothers and fathers are very proud of you."

Jenny hung her head. Tears oozed from beneath the feathery blond lashes. "I don't have a mother," she whispered.

Martha glared at Dinah. "Now look what you've done."

Forgetting to be self-conscious, Dinah ignored Martha's jibe and knelt in front of the little girl. Clasping Jenny's hands in her own, she told her, "I don't have a mother, either."

Jenny raised her tear-washed blue gaze and looked at Dinah in wonder. "Is she in heaven? That's where my mama is."

Dinah nodded, her heart going out to the child. How well she knew the pain that lay behind that simple statement.

"What about your father?" Laurie—or was it one of the Elizabeths?—asked.

"He wasn't around much when I was growing up," Dinah told her.

The girls all nodded as if they understood perfectly.

"It wasn't that he didn't want to be with me." Dinah chose her words with care. "His job involved a lot of traveling. I was too young to be of any help to him, so he left me in the care of my aunt and uncle." *And my cousin.* But she didn't see any reason to mention that.

Martha snorted. "Sounds like a man, all right. Ready to dump you when you aren't of any use."

"But we're back in touch now," Dinah emphasized. "In fact, he's working at the exposition, too, and I expect to see a lot of him from now on."

Dinah pushed herself to her feet. A glance around the semi-circle showed her the girls' attitudes seemed to be thawing. They weren't yet eating out of her hand by any means, but at least their faces had lost that closed look. They were willing to give her a chance.

"I wish my dad would make time for me like that," Rosemary said. "He says as hard as he works, he's just too busy for any kid stuff."

Busy. That's it! Thank You, Lord. Dinah resumed her place at the front of the group and gave her first genuine smile of the evening. "Tonight we're going to talk about a time when Jesus' disciples didn't think He had time for children, either."

The girls leaned forward. Heartened, Dinah launched into her lesson. "One time, Jesus was talking to the crowds, and a group of mothers brought their children to see Him."

Cleo waved her hand in the air. "I asked my mama if she'd take me to see Buffalo Bill." Her expression drooped. "But she said we didn't have the money."

Dinah gulped. "I'm sorry to hear that. But Jesus is much

more important than Buffalo Bill. To go on with our story, the disciples thought Jesus was too busy to be bothered with talking to children, so they told the mothers that they and their little ones should go away."

"Sounds just like my father when me and my brothers start making too much noise," said Frances. The other girls murmured assent.

Dinah raised her voice. "But Jesus told the disciples they were wrong. He wanted to see the children very much. In fact, He sat down and spent time talking to them." She saw the expressions of awe that settled on the group. "Some people do think children should be seen and not heard, but God loves each one of you and wants you to spend time with Him."

"Why?" Rosemary blurted.

"Well," Dinah floundered, "don't you like to be with the people you love? God wants to spend time with you, too."

One of the Elizabeths spoke up. "So when is Jesus coming to Chicago? I'd like to talk to Him, just like those other kids did."

Dinah blinked. "He isn't. I mean. . .you see. . ."

Martha moved away from the wall and edged nearer to the chairs. "What she means is, it's only another story, just like all those other do-gooders tell."

Dinah flinched as though she'd been slapped. "That's not true."

"God doesn't live down here in the slums," Martha informed the group. "He wouldn't like it here any more than we do." She turned her attention back to Dinah. "So if God loves us so much, why did He put us here? Why did He take our mother?" She jerked her head toward the door. "Come on, Jenny. It's time to go."

The other girls got up as if on cue and followed them out. Speechless, Dinah stared after them with Martha's question echoing in her mind: *"What are you really here for?"*

Mechanically, she moved to begin straightening the chairs. She turned when she heard the door creak behind her. Jenny stood in the open doorway a moment, then crossed the room and wrapped her arms around Dinah. "I liked the story, Miss Mayhew. Are you going to tell us more about Jesus next time?"

Dinah dropped to her knees and folded the little girl in her arms. "We'll be talking about Him a lot more. And He really does love you, you know."

Jenny's eyes shone. "Thank you, Miss Mayhew. You're so nice, I bet He loves you, too." She skipped out to the hallway, then her face reappeared in the doorway. "And I love you, Miss Mayhew."

Dinah tried to call out a reply, but she couldn't get the words past the lump in her throat. If she needed confirmation of her call to teach this class, she couldn't have asked for more than Jenny's sweet words.

She finished straightening the chairs and swept up her reticule with a light heart. "Next time," Jenny had said. Yes, there would be another time, and their next class session would go much more smoothly.

She would make sure of that.

Seth shepherded the last of his boys toward the church's outer door and went back to make sure his classroom was truly empty. Last time, Jimmy Eldridge had hidden in a cupboard until everyone had gone, then climbed up to the belfry and set the bells to clanging.

A quick check showed the room was clear. Relieved that he wouldn't have to explain another noisy disturbance to irritated neighbors, Seth pulled the door shut and locked it. Across the hall, Dinah was just closing her own door.

What do you know? She lasted out the whole session. He still didn't expect her to stick it out for long, but at least they hadn't torn her to shreds the very first night.

He waited until she reached him, then held open the outer door for her. "Remember, I'm escorting you home after the meetings. This is no place for you to be out on your own."

Dinah just smiled and walked contentedly at his side. Seth sneaked a sidelong glance at her. No, she wasn't just walking. Her steps had such buoyancy, it was more like she floated along.

Seth studied the surprising woman beside him. He had expected frustration, shock, possibly tears. . .but never this appearance of utter satisfaction. Unable to contain his curiosity any longer, he asked, "I take it your time with the girls went well?"

"It was wonderful! Maybe a little shaky at first, but it ended well."

Seth could see the truth of her statement in her glowing expression and her animated speech. He looked at her with new appreciation. More than most, he knew what the youngsters from this neighborhood were capable of. He had hoped for mere survival of the evening; he'd never anticipated this kind of exuberance.

She wasn't downcast at all—far from it. Her eyes sparkled, and her full lips curved upward in a fetching smile.

"I'll admit it wasn't quite what I expected," she went on, "and I know it's going to be a real challenge in some ways. But they're so precious! I know I'm going to enjoy working with them."

She took a little step—almost a skip—and her arm bumped against his. Seth felt as if a jolt of electricity zipped from his shoulder to his fingertips.

Dinah looked up at him, a soft shade of pink tingeing her cheeks. "Listen to me rattling on like that and not giving you a chance to get a word in edgewise." She raised her eyebrows. "Do you mind if I ask you a question?"

Seth rubbed his arm. "Go ahead."

"The other night at the tent meeting, the speaker spoke of you as Pastor Howell." Her nose crinkled. "I've never known a pastor who spent his time handing out flyers and working with children like these, not to mention pushing people around in a rolling chair at the fairgrounds. Do you have a church of your own, or. . ." Her voice trailed off, and she looked up at him with an expression that made his heart turn over.

Seth walked half a block in silence, trying to compose his thoughts. "I grew up not far from here. I know what it's like to live on these streets. One day, I heard a man preaching on a street corner and stopped to listen. What he had to say made sense, and I turned my life over to the Lord right then and there."

His toe kicked a piece of gravel and sent it rattling across to the gutter. "That preacher must have seen something in me I didn't know was there myself. He saw to it that I got a decent education and solid Bible training. I think he expected me to take the first opportunity to go pastor a church in a more pleasant setting."

"But you didn't."

Seth shook his head. "I felt my calling was to come back and work with the people I knew. Several churches in the city believe in what I'm doing. They agreed to pool funds to support my work. One lets me use their building for my boys' and girls' classes. Two others provide enough living expenses for me to get by."

"That's wonderful."

"It's heaven-sent. Along with that, I'll be working with the Moody campaign for the duration of the fair."

Dinah wrinkled her brow. "Campaign?"

"You've heard of Dwight Moody, of course."

"Who hasn't? I think everyone in the world knows of Mr. Moody."

"Then you know of his great crusades both here and abroad. When word got out about the fair being located here in Chicago, Moody saw its potential to reach souls."

Seth went on, warming to his topic. "Think about it. Not since Pentecost have people from so many nations gathered in one spot. What an opportunity! People from all over the world can hear the gospel message, then go home to share it with their own countrymen."

Dinah stared up at him, her eyes wide. "I never would have looked at it that way! So it isn't just a matter of talking to people who ride in your gospel chariot."

"It's much, much more than that. Workers all over the city have devoted themselves to the full six-month evangelistic campaign. It's a wonderful work, and I feel deeply honored to be a part of it."

He took Dinah's elbow to help her skirt a pile of rubbish some careless soul had tossed in the middle of the walk.

Dinah rested her hand on his arm. "I can understand why you're so enthused."

Again, the electricity sizzled through him. Seth felt as though a band were tightening around his chest. He resisted the impulse to reach out and capture Dinah's hand in his. *You know better than that, you dolt.*

The woman God had in mind for him would have qualities that matched his own devotion to the Lord's work, the kind of total commitment that would make her a fit helpmeet for his ministry. Dinah Mayhew was attractive—no one in his right mind would deny that—but his choice of someone as his lifelong mate would have to be based on a spiritual connection rather than on physical attraction.

The scrape of boot leather on gravel disrupted his musings, and he looked up to see two rough-looking men jump out of the alleyway in front of them.

Dinah squealed, and Seth moved to put himself between her and the danger at hand.

"Hey, Preacher," said the one with the stubbly beard. "We hear you've been talking with your buddy Mac."

Seth drew his body into a fighting stance and didn't answer.

The second tough moved a few feet away from his companion and sneered. "You don't know what you're getting yourself into. You're messing around in things that don't concern you."

Seth's gaze flitted from one thug to the other and back again, waiting for them to make a move. Behind him, Dinah stood so close he could feel her trembling and hear her breath catch in quick little gasps.

The first man hooked his thumbs in his suspenders and spoke again. "Go on back to your preaching and leave the fight game alone. You go sticking your nose where it don't belong, and it's liable to get chopped off." He leaned to one side to peer past Seth's shoulder, and his lips parted in a gap-toothed grin. "And then who'd be around to protect this pretty little thing?"

A red haze clouded Seth's vision. More than anything at that moment, he wanted to reach out and throttle the leering brute. But that would give them the opening they were looking for. More, it would put Dinah at risk. He restrained himself with an effort. "You've delivered your message. Now go crawl back under whatever rock it was you came from."

The bearded man chuckled. "Just so you know, we'll be watching. Don't get any cute ideas." He winked at Dinah, then jerked his head at his companion. Together, the two swaggered off down the alley.

Seth watched until they were out of sight, then turned to Dinah. She crouched behind him in a ready stance, clutching a broken chair leg she must have spotted in the pile of rubbish. His anger ebbed at the sight of her. She looked like she was ready to wade straight into the fray and split a head or two while she was at it.

"They're gone," he said softly. "You can put that down now."

Dinah stared down at her hands, wrapped around the improvised club. "I don't think I can."

Seth followed her glance to the whitened knuckles and the viselike grip. He reached out and gently pried her fingers loose, one by one. The chair leg rattled on the pavement.

At this proximity, he could see she still trembled uncontrollably. He gripped her shoulders to calm her. The face she turned up to his was pale. Unshed tears clumped her lower lashes together. Ignoring the warning voice in his brain, he put his arm around her shoulders and started her moving ahead. "Come on, let's get you home."

She held on to his arm all the way back to Blackstone Avenue. Seth helped her up the steps to the front porch, glad she had quit shaking at least. "Why don't you have a cup of hot tea as soon as you get inside?"

Dinah nodded absently; then her gaze sharpened and she stared at a point behind him.

"What is it?" On the alert for danger after their recent encounter, Seth turned in time to see a curtain drop across a window in the house on the opposite side of the street.

Dinah gave a shaky laugh. "It's only Mrs. Boggs, the neighborhood snoop. I'm sure she thinks we should have had a chaperone accompanying us, especially the way I've been clinging to you."

The door of the boardinghouse swung open, and a bright-eyed, middle-aged woman beamed a greeting. "I thought I heard voices. I hope you've had a lovely evening?"

Dinah shot a weary smile at Seth. "It's been. . .an interesting one, at least. You remember Pastor Howell from the other evening, don't you? Seth, this is my landlady, Mrs. Purvis."

Seth took the hand she extended and suppressed a grin when she pumped his arm up and down enthusiastically.

"Won't you come in? I just took a cake out of the oven."

The offer appealed, but he didn't want to overstay his welcome. "I'd better be going. I think Miss Mayhew has had enough excitement for one night."

He turned as the door closed behind the two women, and he noticed the curtain flutter in the window across the street again.

Agriculture, Electricity, Fine Arts, Fisheries. Dinah divided the day's reports into stacks according to their departments. Her fingers carried out the task at hand with her usual efficiency, leaving her mind free for thoughts of Seth. Would he be pushing his rolling chair over near the Electricity Building again this morning?

Machinery, Manufactures, Mining, Transportation. She slipped the stacks into their respective files, then slid the drawer shut and stood leaning against the cabinet, thinking again about the events of last night. She remembered how frightened she had been when those two ruffians had leaped out at them, and how protected she felt when Seth leaped in front of her and faced them down.

"What are you mooning about?" Millie's voice cut into her daydream.

"I was just thinking about the girls and last night's Bible class." Dinah busied herself with straightening her desk.

Lila sniffed. "I can think of a lot of things I'd rather do with my evenings than spend time nursemaiding a bunch of unruly ragamuffins."

"Hardly unruly." Dinah tried not to let Lila ruffle her feathers any more than usual. "They happen to be very sweet little girls. It isn't their fault they were born into those circumstances. Being around them has really opened my eyes. It makes me very grateful for the ways God has blessed me."

Lila's lips curled in a sneer. Before she could speak, Mr. Thorndyke opened his door and leaned out. "Lila, would you come back here, please? I need you to take some dictation."

"Right away." Lila picked up her pad and smiled at Dinah and Millie. "I guess that depends on your point of view. From the looks of things, I'd say I'm the one being blessed." She spun on her heel and disappeared into the back office.

Millie raised one eyebrow and tapped her pencil on her desk. "Don't think that little interruption got you off the hook. Sweet as they may be, you can't tell me those little girls put that dreamy look on your face. Lila can't overhear anything now, so tell me the whole story and don't leave anything out."

Dinah started to protest, but the opportunity of being able to share her thoughts about Seth was too tempting to pass up. "All right." She cast a quick look over her shoulder to make sure they were alone, then pulled a chair up to Millie's desk.

"His name is Seth Howell," she began.

"You mean the pastor who runs the meetings for those kids?"

"That's him. I can't get him out of my mind. I've never met anyone like him."

Millie's eyes lit up, and she propped her elbows on her desk. "So is he showing any interest in you?"

Aside from protecting me from street thugs? "He hasn't come right out and said anything, but he's been very attentive. He's quite the gentleman, very respectful."

Millie wrinkled her nose. "I guess he'd have to be if he's a preacher." She sighed. "I tend to like a more rugged type myself. It doesn't sound like you've set your sights on any stalwart physical specimen. Let me guess."

Millie pursed her lips. "He has weak eyes and round shoulders from studying all the time. That means he wears spectacles. He has soft, clammy hands, and he quotes scripture at every turn. Am I right?"

94

A picture of Seth standing off the two hoodlums floated into Dinah's mind, and she giggled. "Not exactly."

"Well, maybe not the spectacles, but the rest is close, right?"

Dinah shook with laughter. "Maybe you'll get a chance to meet him someday. Then you'll find out just how wrong you are."

And maybe someday she would find out whether Seth could see her as anything more than a children's Bible teacher.

CHAPTER 8

"The stone hit Goliath squarely in the forehead, and the giant fell to the ground, dead." Dinah watched the way the girls stared at her with rapt attention. Relief washed over her. Finally, she had their complete attention! The hours of study and prayer had paid off.

The feeling of success made her voice light and bubbly. "Who can tell me what this tells us about trusting God?"

The silence stretched out. Dinah felt her forehead pucker. *What's wrong? I know they were listening.*

"Doesn't anyone have an idea?" This time she found it harder to keep the cheery lilt in her voice.

The girls wriggled in their seats and their gazes shifted to the floor, the walls, anywhere but at her. Martha slouched against the back wall, arms folded. A sneer twisted her lips.

Dinah willed herself to keep her smile in place. Her teeth clenched so hard her jaw ached. Maybe a leading question would help. "Do any of you have giant-sized problems in your life?"

Rosemary and Frances looked up at her and gave solemn nods.

"My daddy comes home drunk sometimes and yells at all of us," Rosemary told her. "It scares me when he does that."

Frances bobbed her head in agreement. "Mine, too. And sometimes he loses money gambling and we don't have enough to buy food. Then my stomach feels like there's a giant-sized hole in it."

"Good!" Dinah declared.

The girls' eyes widened, including Martha's.

Dinah waved her hands, wishing she could erase her words and start over again. "No, I don't mean good that you're facing a problem. I mean good that you'll be able to understand what this story means."

Sweat trickled down the back of her bodice, and she wiggled her shoulders to make the itch go away. "Now, I want you to think back to the story I just told you. Think about what David did when he had to face a giant. How does this help us know what we should do when a big problem comes our way?"

Rosemary looked at her doubtfully. "We should always keep some rocks in our pocket?"

Anastasia shot her hand in the air. "My brother has a sling-shot. Maybe he could make one for me, too."

A quiet snicker came from the corner where Martha stood.

Dinah clapped her hand to her forehead. "No, no. That's not it at all." Anastasia glared and Rosemary's lower lip quivered.

Dinah felt pressure behind her eyelids and blinked furiously. She was *not* going to break down and cry in front of these girls. Especially not in front of Martha, who seemed more than willing to pounce on every mistake Dinah made.

She filled her lungs and thought back to the notes she had made on the lesson. "What it means is that David trusted God. He didn't need the armor King Saul offered him. He didn't try to face the problem on his own. Instead, he prayed for God's help and expected Him to answer."

There. At least that came out the way she intended.

"So when problems come our way, we can do the same thing: take them to God, pray about them, and expect Him to answer. Do you see now?"

Anastasia slouched in her seat and muttered, "I still think I'll ask my brother to make that slingshot. A pocket full of rocks wouldn't hurt, either."

Dinah opened and closed her mouth, but no words came out. She had come tonight looking forward to teaching her girls the merits of trusting God in all things. Instead, she had stirred up a group of tiny marauders, ready to stone anyone who stood in their way.

She searched for an appropriate comment and blurted out the only response that came to mind: "Let's pray."

While petitions for the girls' safety and spiritual growth flowed from her lips, her heart sent up a separate plea. *What's going on, Lord? I tried so hard! I studied—You know I did. And I did my best to make Your message plain. But I'm not getting through to them, not at all.*

She pressed her hands tightly together. *Help me get through this evening and do better next time. For their sakes, Lord, help me do a better job.*

Raising her head, she put on her practiced smile. "Time to go home now. Do each of you have someone to walk with? This

98

rough neighborhood isn't safe for little girls to be out alone."

Five pairs of eyes turned on her. At their disbelieving looks, she went back over her words and stifled a groan. In a few moments, Seth would escort her back to her cozy boardinghouse on Blackstone Avenue, but this "rough" neighborhood was the only home these girls had ever known. . .and their families and neighbors were what made it that way. Could she have said anything better calculated to point out the differences between them?

"Wait," she said in a weak voice. "I didn't mean—"

Martha pushed away from the wall. "Come on, Jenny. Time to go home."

Dinah watched the last of the group trail out, her words of protest stuck in her throat. She leaned her forehead against the wall. The pressure from the hard surface made her head throb, but that discomfort didn't compare with the pain in her heart.

She had done it again—taken one step forward, then slid two steps back. Maybe three or four, judging from the stiff set to the girls' shoulders when they left.

Lord, I'm beginning to feel like I have a giant problem of my own. . .and it's me.

Dinah squeezed her eyes shut, wishing she could take back every misspoken word. Would she ever get it right?

When she closed the door of her room, she saw Seth already waiting for her across the hall. It took a conscious effort to square her shoulders, lift her chin, and greet him with a confidence she was far from feeling.

She walked past Seth and headed toward the outer door, knowing he would follow. Her actions were rude, she knew, but she wanted to avoid his questions about the class at all costs.

She paused on the stoop and waited for him to catch up. Seth hadn't voiced any outright objections since the night of the tent meeting, but she felt his doubts about her ability to lead the girls' class from the first. She simply couldn't deal with his questions right now. Maybe she should jump right in and steer the conversation on her own.

When he fell into step beside her, she looked up at him. "How did your class go this evening?"

Seth blinked at her reversal of their usual roles; then his eyes lit up. "It went very well." Enthusiasm infused his voice when he went on. "The boys really picked up on the meaning of the story of David and Goliath. They seemed to know the answers before I even asked the questions, and they came up with some great comments on their own. It's amazing how much truth they're able to absorb, even without a lot of biblical background. How about the girls?"

Dinah sighed. So much for staving off the inevitable. She wondered if the question was a mere formality. It was obvious he had his doubts about her. Truth be told, he probably already suspected how inadequate she was. But she wasn't ready to admit defeat yet.

She summoned up her brightest smile. "Just fine. They really seemed enthralled by the story." That much was true, anyway. In the interest of accuracy, she added, "They might be a little weak on applying the truths of the lesson to their own situations."

Seth's brows knit together. "But that's the whole point of the class, to show them how the Bible relates to their lives."

Dinah's sense of failure intensified. Couldn't he at least say something encouraging? After all, she had done her best. Hadn't she spent the last few evenings studying the lesson up in her room after work? And she'd prayed. . .oh, how she had prayed! But to no avail, it seemed. To have the girls respond as they did was bad enough. To hear Seth's lack of approval made it all the worse. She could feel the tears getting ready to flow in earnest.

Turning her head aside, she dashed the moisture from her eyes. She wasn't about to let him see how miserable she felt. Why was his approval so important to her, anyway? Wasn't she doing this for God, rather than Seth?

God had called her to this work, and she would go on with it, whether she had Seth Howell's approval or not. Hadn't tonight's lesson touched on that very topic? When God called someone to fight a battle, He meant for them to obey regardless of what people around them thought. Seth's opinion shouldn't matter to her one whit.

But it did.

The realization struck her with the force of a blow. What was wrong with her? *I'm supposed to be following God; I don't need to get caught up in whether I meet Seth Howell's expectations or not.*

Seth took her elbow and guided her away from a pile of trash littering the sidewalk. Dinah recognized the heap of rubbish from the last time they walked this way. This was the place where the thugs had jumped out at them.

She cast a longing glance at the pile of debris, wishing for the solid feel of the chair leg in her hands again. Or maybe Anastasia's pocketful of rocks.

The girls had a point. With danger lurking in the shadows of these streets, it was easy to see how they could feel they needed something tangible for protection.

Seth's hand tightened on her elbow, and his face took on an intent, watchful look. So he felt it, too. Dinah bumped against his arm and realized she had unconsciously drawn closer to him.

Seth glanced down, and his face softened. His hand slid down her arm to grip her fingers. "You can relax. They aren't anywhere around."

Dinah returned the pressure of his fingers, enjoying the sense of closeness it brought. She wished she could leave her hand in his. Despite her uncertainty about Seth's feelings for her, she knew instinctively that this was a man she could trust. Everything about him proclaimed a measure of security and strength that drew her to him more with each passing day.

But how could he care about someone as incompetent as she was?

Dinah laced her fingers through the strings of her reticule. Her steps might feel as though her feet were weighted down with lead, but she forced the corners of her mouth to turn up. She would keep the smile in place until she could sort out her wayward feelings in the privacy of her room.

CHAPTER 9

Mrs. Johnson, I want to know who's responsible for this." Mr. Thorndyke stood in the outer doorway leading to the vestibule, clutching a fistful of papers in his hand. His face reminded Dinah of storm clouds over Lake Michigan.

The office supervisor handed a stack of files to Dinah and turned to face him. "Responsible for what, sir?"

"I just missed a meeting with Mr. Palmer and some of the other fair officials. I missed it because it was listed on my schedule as taking place at eleven o'clock instead of ten." Mr. Thorndyke closed the door behind him with a *bang*. "Among the things to be discussed was this report from Frederick Skiff over in Mines and Mining, regarding increased security for the Kimberley diamond exhibit." He waved the papers in his fist.

"I arrived just as the meeting was breaking up. I did manage to add the information they needed from me before it was too late, but I looked like an incompetent, arriving an hour late.

Worse yet, I missed having a say in the decisions that were made, decisions that will effect the smooth running of this exposition."

Mrs. Johnson looked unaccustomedly rattled. "That's dreadful! I have no idea how that might have happened."

"I do." Mr. Thorndyke advanced on the room, directing a stern gaze at Dinah, Millie, and Lila in turn. "Skiff sent the details of the meeting to me days ago, attached to this report. He said he turned the report over to one of the girls from my office. He didn't remember which one, but—"

"I think I know who it was." Lila rose from her desk. Her skirt swayed gracefully as she closed half the distance between her and Mr. Thorndyke. Every eye in the room was riveted on her.

"I hate to point fingers, but Dinah is new and she has made a lot of mistakes since she's been here. I've corrected a number of them myself." She directed a sad smile up at Mr. Thorndyke's stony face. "I'm so sorry I didn't catch this one."

Dinah felt the blood drain from her face. Everything inside her turned cold, as if her veins had become ice. Could she have done such a careless thing? She tried to speak, to find some way to counter the accusation, but she couldn't make her lips move.

Mr. Thorndyke glared at her over his pince-nez. "Is this true?"

"I'm sure it isn't," Mrs. Johnson returned in her normal crisp tone. "When did Mr. Skiff send that report over?"

"It was nearly two weeks ago." Mr. Thorndyke's gaze still bored holes in Dinah.

Mrs. Johnson looked straight at Lila. "That was when you were still picking up most of the reports. . .before you foisted that

104

responsibility off onto Dinah." Turning back to Mr. Thorndyke, she added, "Miss Mayhew has done everything asked of her in an exemplary manner and without complaint. She is one of the best workers I have ever had. I know the handwriting of each of the girls here. All it will take is a quick look at your schedule for me to determine who wrote down the incorrect time."

Lila's eyes widened like those of a panicked horse, and she took a step back. "I'm sure it was an honest mistake. One that anybody could have made."

Mrs. Johnson sniffed. "It wasn't such a trivial issue a moment ago when you were ready to blame Dinah, was it? I'm not blind, you know. This isn't the first time you've stirred up trouble here. Please step back into my office, Lila. We have some rather delicate issues to discuss. Mr. Thorndyke, perhaps you'd care to join us?"

She let the two of them precede her and turned back to Dinah. "Why don't you go ahead and take your lunch break now? It might be best if you weren't here when Lila comes back. You've already had enough unpleasantness to deal with." She followed Lila and Mr. Thorndyke into her office and closed the door.

"Take your time," Millie added with a grin. "I have a feeling the lofty Miss Lila may not be here when you get back."

Unable to speak, Dinah pulled a paper sack out of her desk drawer and fled the building.

Her feet carried her past the Columbian Fountain, where she scanned the grounds, trying to find a place without a crowd. *Ha!* As if such a place existed anywhere in the city of Chicago. Where could she go?

She scanned the length of the Grand Basin, the lawns on

either side packed with fairgoers taking a noonday break. A wisp of air floated in from the lake, and Dinah tugged at her collar to let the welcome breeze cool her neck. Now what?

Not to the north. She covered that ground every day when she entered the fairgrounds by the Fifty-seventh Street entrance and knew it would contain nothing but a solid mass of people.

She started over the bridge that crossed the South Canal, thinking she might go out to the Peristyle or perhaps to the shore of the lake beyond.

At the foot of the bridge, her gaze followed the water flowing underneath. Flanking the Obelisk that stood at the canal's end were long strips of grass, and one stretch at the far end was unoccupied. Dinah hurried along the east side of Machinery Hall and past its columned portico to her newly discovered place of refuge.

With a sigh of gratitude, she sank down on the end of the grassy rectangle nearest the Colonnade, positioning herself to take advantage of the scant shade offered by a potted palm on the balustrade above her.

She unfolded the ends of the paper sack Mrs. Purvis had pressed into her hands that morning just before she left. "Just a few things to tide you over in case you need a snack during the day," the landlady had told her.

A snack would have to do. After the emotional upheaval she'd just gone through, Dinah had no inclination to stand in line at one of the crowded lunch counters. She reached into the bag and gasped in delight when she discovered the "snack" consisted of slabs of roast beef sandwiched between thick slices of bread. Mrs. Purvis had even tucked in a couple of blueberry muffins.

"Bless you, Mrs. Purvis," Dinah murmured, and got ready to enjoy her impromptu picnic.

She couldn't have chosen a better setting. From her vantage point, she had a clear view past the bridge, across the Grand Basin, and along the length of the east shore of the lagoon. The sea green roof of the mighty Manufactures Building stretched into the distance on her right, and farther off she could see one of the Fisheries pavilions and the dome of the Illinois Building.

Just ahead, a gondola glided under the bridge and drifted toward her, its smiling occupants listening to a song from their gondolier.

Utterly charmed by the scene, Dinah bit into her sandwich and closed her eyes, the better to enjoy the savory taste. The tension of the morning began to slip away, and she felt able to think back to the altercation in the office.

What would have happened if Mrs. Johnson hadn't come to her defense? Dinah shuddered at the thought. It only went to prove how uncertain life could be. If Mr. Thorndyke had accepted Lila's account and dismissed her, she would have found herself out on the street in this teeming city. And what would have become of her then?

She chewed on her sandwich and pondered the question, glad she didn't face that dilemma. . .at least not now. Going back to the farm wasn't an option, not now that she had broken free of Gladys. Come to think of it, the way Lila cast blame on her without batting an eye reminded her of her cousin's skill in getting Dinah in trouble for her own misdeeds. Maybe other versions of Gladys existed everywhere—a sobering thought.

Dinah polished off the last bite of her sandwich and dug in the bag for the muffins, her appetite increasing as her nerves settled. She popped a bit of blueberry muffin into her mouth. *Delicious!* At least she wouldn't starve, not as long as she had Mrs. Purvis for a landlady.

She took another bite of the muffin and wondered for the thousandth time how two people as wonderful as Aunt Dora and Uncle Everett could have produced an offspring like Gladys— abrasive where they were gentle, cruel where they were kind, and never missing an opportunity to belittle Dinah for being cast off on their doorstep.

But she wasn't an outcast anymore. Dinah brightened at the thought. She had her father back in her life again, and she didn't plan to lose him this time.

On top of that, she had her job and her supervisor's open approval. Dinah basked in the memory of Mrs. Johnson's kind words and the way she had complimented her work. There, at least, she felt sure of herself.

Unlike in her work with the girls. She dusted the crumbs off her lap and stared out across the rippling water. Was she really the right one for that job? Maybe she only imagined God's voice urging her to take it on, but she'd been so sure. . . .

Dinah trailed her fingers through the neatly clipped grass, its texture reminding her of the pasture Uncle Everett's milk cows kept cropped short. She smiled. That was the only similarity she could find between her old life and this new one. No doubt about it, the environment she had landed in was totally unlike anything she had experienced before.

A puff of wind stirred the tendrils at the back of her neck. Dinah lifted the curls with her fingers to let the breeze do its cooling work. Simple pleasures, her aunt always said, were the most satisfying, and at the moment, Dinah was inclined to agree. She hadn't grown up in the lap of luxury by any means, but she had never experienced the stark existence the girls in her class accepted as their lot.

She watched the clouds shift across the sky, her thoughts floating as aimlessly as the white, cottony puffs. Maybe she wasn't a good choice for working with this particular group. Sometimes it seemed as if she and the girls came from different worlds. With all her heart, she longed to reach out and help them. But she didn't have the least idea how to begin.

When she volunteered for the position, she knew she was stepping into a realm in which she had little experience, but she never expected to have to batter down walls of distrust before they would even begin to listen to her.

Dinah's eyes stung, and the scene blurred before her. She truly did want to help the needy girls; but it would be so much easier if the girls wanted to be helped. And the things they revealed about their families and backgrounds! Some of the things they brought up during the class would have made her cheeks flame if she hadn't learned how to mask her feelings years ago.

Dinah folded the lunch sack neatly and tucked it into her skirt pocket. She still had a little time before she needed to go back. Perhaps a stroll around the canal would help to corral her racing thoughts.

The sun glinted off the water, and she put her hand up to shield her eyes. The dazzling rays made the white staff covering the buildings sparkle like diamonds. What a contrast between the beauty of the fairgrounds and the squalor her girls lived in!

If only they could see this. Dinah could imagine their excitement at getting a glimpse of a world far different than their own. Was there any way she could make that happen? She couldn't possibly afford to pay the admission for all of them, but maybe Mr. Thorndyke would know if there were passes available for something like what she had in mind. The more she thought about it, the more her excitement grew. Perhaps she should talk the idea over with Seth.

Her train of thought jolted to a screeching halt. Seth. No matter what she might be dealing with, he was never far from her thoughts. Dinah leaned against a nearby lamppost, losing herself in memories of the way she felt when he looked at her with his caramel-colored gaze.

She remembered the moment those awful men had jumped out at them and tried to intimidate Seth. Try as she might to hide it, she'd been scared to death. But Seth took it all in stride. The whole episode barely seemed to faze him. Why, he'd seemed like one of the heroes of old, standing firm, ready to protect her.

And once he had routed the villains. . .

Her chest swelled in a gentle sigh. She'd been able to feel his strength when she clung to his arm all the way home. After the first couple of blocks, she had been perfectly capable of walking unassisted, but she had held on to him anyway, just enjoying being near him.

No doubt about it, the way Seth looked at her made her weak in the knees. And there were moments when she was certain he felt a similar attraction. But at other times, his eyes held a hint of judgment, as though she had been weighed in the balance and found wanting.

When he looked at her that way, she felt she would never measure up to whatever standard he held for her. Confused thoughts ran through her mind in a jumble. If she were back home, she'd go out to the field and talk to Uncle Everett. He would be able to give her a man's perspective on the situation. Dinah smiled at the way he'd never complained about serving as a substitute father during all the years hers was unavailable.

He's available now. Dinah chortled aloud at the joyous reminder. She didn't need a substitute father anymore. Hers was right there in the building next to her. He could help her sort out her chaotic feelings.

Dinah hurried up the steps to the west entrance of the Agriculture Building, then made her way to the annex. How she had missed being able to run to her father with her problems!

At the booth, she saw Abby showing a model of a corn binder to a cluster of inquirers on the far side of the display. That suited her just fine. She didn't relish the idea of another interruption from her father's coworker. She gazed around the display area until she spotted her father, down on one knee next to a little girl with chestnut curls.

Dinah smiled at the charming scene. It almost looked like a conversation between a father and daughter. *She's just about the age I was when he left.* A wave of nostalgia swept over her. Wouldn't it have been wonderful if she could have gone with him then? But he was right; it would have been much too difficult for him to travel and conduct his business with a child in tow.

She crept closer, not wanting to startle them. The girl spoke with animated gestures, and Dinah's father showed every sign of listening intently. Perhaps the child was lost and he was trying to help find her parents. A few steps more, and she was close enough to overhear what the little girl was saying.

"It's just up there in the main part of the building, Ernie. They're showing how they make chocolate, and then they're going to give out samples. Can I go watch?"

Ernie? Dinah moved closer, easing behind a pillar so she wouldn't be noticed.

"I'll bet there will be a big crowd, though," the little girl went on. "It sure would be easier to see if you could come along and hold me up. But you're probably too busy, right?"

Dinah's father grinned and swept the child up in a bear hug. "I'm never too busy for my best girl. Come on, let's go watch them make chocolate." They walked off toward the main building.

Dinah stood rooted to the spot. What just happened? Abby continued her demonstration, apparently unconcerned about being left to take care of business on her own. And who was the little girl? Dinah could still see the pair threading their way through the crowd, her father's hand tenderly wrapped around the child's fingers. Exactly what Dinah had longed for him to do when she was that age.

It isn't fair! A sob tore from her throat, drawing startled glances from a couple passing by. Dinah pressed her fist against her lips and tried to force her welter of emotions into submission. She had to leave. There were no answers here. . .only more questions.

She pushed her way through the crowd, barely able to breathe until she burst out into the open air again. Clasping her hands against her waist, she waited until she got her breathing under control, then started toward the Administration Building. She needed to get back to a place where she was valued, a place where she could count on things being done in a predictable order. Not

112

like the maelstrom the rest of her life had become.

Crossing the bridge, she saw a man pushing an empty rolling chair along the east side of Machinery Hall. Even from that distance, she recognized Seth.

Dinah wavered. How she longed for the security of his presence! Seeing his face light up at the sight of her would be balm to her wounded spirit. But what if he gave her that disapproving look instead, the one that made her want to shrivel up and blow away like a dry leaf before an autumn wind?

Dinah veered across the Grand Plaza and headed straight to the Administration Building. She simply couldn't take that chance. Not right now.

Seth sketched a wave to the attendant at the rolling chair kiosk and ambled down the greensward on the lake side of the Manufactures Building. The wind ruffled the water into tiny waves that teased the shore and carried with them a scent that reminded him of the times he went fishing with his grandfather as a young boy.

He ambled toward the edge of the sand and stood, lost in childhood memories. A dozen sea gulls wove in and out along the damp shoreline. For a moment, Seth felt tempted to pull off his shoes and join them. He grinned. The boys in his class would have jumped at the opportunity without a second thought.

The sun stood barely past its zenith. Seth moved back into the narrow strip of shade to stroll along the eastern side of the quarter-mile-long building. The hour was far earlier than his usual quitting time, but an eager theology student wanted to take a turn at manning one of the chairs, and Seth couldn't find it in his heart to curb the young man's enthusiasm.

He rolled his shoulders to loosen the stiff muscles. He might not be able to spend as much time as usual at the gym during the course of the fair, but trundling matrons around the vast fairgrounds made for a pretty good workout.

The center doors of the Manufactures Building yawned before him. Seth ducked inside and cut through the building, stopping at one of the lunch counters long enough to buy a bottle of root beer. He carried the frosty drink outside to a spot where willows draped their leafy arms over the lagoon.

Propping one foot on the railing that ran along the water's edge, he took a swig of his root beer and let the cold, bubbly sweetness trickle down his throat. What a perfect way to cool off and take a break before he had to get ready for the meeting with the church board to report on his progress with the children's Bible classes.

He leaned forward, resting his elbow on his knee, and indulged in his favorite pastime of people watching. With the mass of humanity streaming along the walkways, he had plenty of subjects to choose from. As always, he wondered where they came from and where they were going, not only here at the exposition, but in their everyday lives, as well.

What would things be like when they left the fair and returned to their regular existence? What made them happy? What burdens did they carry? And above all, did they have any real hope?

That young couple, for instance. They looked so happy, strolling along the Wooded Island without a trace of care on their countenances. But if they hadn't made their peace with God, that happiness would only be temporary. *Lord, draw them to Yourself.*

Let their joy be eternal and not based on the here and now.

He followed their progress until they passed from sight behind a line of trees, then shifted his gaze to the massive buildings constructed for this exposition of a lifetime. Imposing as they might seem to the casual observer, they, too, were only temporary. He, along with thousands of other Chicagoans, had watched their construction and knew the appearance of solid white marble was an illusion created by wood and wire overlaid with a coating of staff. It was all a facade, built for the moment and never intended to be permanent.

While they lasted, though, they stood as a testament to the genius of their architects. From where Seth stood, he could see the clean, white surfaces of the Horticulture and the Woman's buildings. And over the top of Electricity, he glimpsed the tip of the Administration Building's golden dome, dazzling in the noonday sun.

Dinah would be there now, if not out running around carrying those endless missives that seemed to make up a great part of her workday. Seth held the cool bottle against his cheek. If it were nearer her quitting time, he would be tempted to stay around and offer to walk her home. But she wouldn't get off work for several hours yet, far too long for him to wait.

Too bad. He'd like the chance to talk with her again and get to know her better. The woman was a constant puzzle to him. Sometimes he felt a person of considerable depth lay behind that ready smile. At others, her cheerful demeanor seemed a little too pat. Instead of expressing the doubts one might expect from a new teacher, Dinah remained determinedly upbeat. Did that denote remarkable maturity or a lack of sincerity? The answer to that remained a mystery.

It wasn't as if she was the first attractive woman to cross his path. He had been able to turn his eyes and heart away from similar distractions, knowing they weren't right for him. Why, then, did he find himself so caught up with thoughts of Dinah Mayhew?

He tipped his head back for another swallow.

"Are you planning to park yourself here all day?"

Seth choked on his root beer at the sound of the stern voice behind him.

"We do frown on loitering, you know."

Seth wiped the foam from his chin and grinned at the uniformed guard. "How are you doing, Stephen?"

The guard sauntered nearer and leaned on the railing beside him. "Not bad. Just doing my part to keep crime away from the White City."

"To all appearances, you're doing a fine job of that." He nodded at the peaceful scene around them. "Once people walk onto the fairgrounds, it's almost like they've stepped into a fantasy world, where none of their everyday troubles can reach them."

Stephen Bridger nodded. "That does make our job easier. We have our share of petty crime, but for the most part, there are enough of us patrolling the grounds that we keep any major crime to a minimum." He slanted a grin at Seth. "You probably see worse on the way to your Bible studies."

"That's for sure." Seth rubbed the back of his neck. "Just the other night, I was walking one of the other teachers home, and we were accosted by a couple of hoodlums."

The grin vanished from Bridger's face. "Was anyone hurt?"

Seth shook his head. "They were just trying to throw a scare into me. A friend is being pressured to throw a fight, and they

116

don't appreciate me interfering."

"You mean you appealed to his conscience instead of his pocketbook?"

"Something like that. I did have a talk with him. I hope it had an effect." Seth turned the empty bottle over in his hands. He hadn't had time to visit with Mac lately. He prayed his friend hadn't given in and gone along with the crooked scheme. If he had, it would never happen just the one time. Once you opened the door to people like that, they thought they owned you.

"That's a tough one." Bridger took his hat off and wiped his forehead with the back of his hand. "I'll be praying for you. Let me know if there's anything else I can do." Settling the hat back on his head, he strolled off to resume his patrol.

Seth watched him go, feeling better for the encounter. Bridger was a good man, and he was glad they had gotten acquainted during their months at the fair. He was even more glad to be able to call him his friend. The man wore his integrity openly on the surface. A fellow knew exactly who he was dealing with when he talked to Stephen Bridger.

Unlike Dinah Mayhew, who seemed destined to remain an enigma in his mind.

CHAPTER 10

Dinah slipped the last file into its place, then retrieved her reticule from her desk drawer and begun pulling the pins from her hair.

Millie's eyebrows went up. "What's this? Primping on company time?"

"Hardly company time," Dinah laughed.

"Mrs. Johnson and Mr. Thorndyke have been gone for nearly an hour."

"That eases my mind. At least I know you haven't taken Lila's place in line for Mr. Thorndyke's attentions." Millie ducked when Dinah tossed a ball of crumpled paper at her.

"Don't be a goose. I'm going out to dinner tonight, and I want to look my best." Dinah smoothed her hair back into place and replaced the pins, then stood for Millie's inspection. "Do I look all right?"

"You look fine. Who are you going with? Does this have

anything to do with that note that came for you earlier today?"

Dinah nodded, not bothering to conceal her pleasure.

"Ooh! Dinah has a beau!" Millie planted her elbows on her desk and clasped her hands under her chin. "Tell me everything."

"I haven't any beau. It's my father." Dinah gurgled with laughter at Millie's crestfallen expression. "We haven't seen each other for a long time, and we have a lot of catching up to do, that's all." She looped her reticule over her wrist. "I'll see you in the morning."

Dinah stepped out of the elevator to find her father waiting for her near one of the arches, and her heart skipped at the sight of him. Apparently she wasn't the only one to take pains with her appearance. He wore a herringbone jacket over neatly pressed slacks. A warm glow suffused her at the thought he'd taken special pains to look nice for her.

"I thought we'd try the Café de Marine," he announced. "Have you eaten there before?"

Dinah shook her head and smiled. "That isn't exactly part of my regular route. I've seen it when I passed, but I never thought I'd be eating there."

"Then that will make tonight all the more special." He extended his arm, and she took it, feeling like a princess being escorted to the ball. She didn't try to make conversation while they walked, content just to enjoy the moment as they joined the throngs who strolled the length of the lagoon past the buildings housing the transportation and horticultural exhibits. They passed a number of women with their escorts, and Dinah wondered if any of them could be as happy as she.

Delight shivered through her when they neared the restaurant. "It looks like a castle with all those spires and turrets."

Her father laughed at her excitement. A matter of moments

later, they were seated at a small table in the center of the crowded dining room. A waiter handed them their menus before scurrying off toward the kitchen.

Dinah looked around. "I know you must be used to eating in fine places, with all the traveling you do. But I feel a little like a country bumpkin in the midst of all this. I hope I don't do anything to embarrass you."

She opened her menu and took one look at the prices, then gasped and slammed it shut. "Are you sure you want to eat here? This is awfully expensive."

Her father waved away her objections. "This is a special event. I feel like celebrating."

Dinah dared to peek at the list of offerings again, then closed the menu and set it back down on the snowy tablecloth. "Why don't you order for me?"

"I'd be happy to." Her father motioned the waiter over. "My daughter will have the smoked Atlantic salmon." He consulted the menu once more. "I believe I'll have the same."

"Very good, sir." The waiter disappeared, and Dinah smiled her appreciation at her father.

"Thank you. This is a lovely place, isn't it?"

Her father reached across the table and covered her hand with his. "Nothing is too good for my little girl."

Dinah felt her cheeks flush. It was all just like a fairy tale.

The waiter returned and filled their water goblets. Before he could turn away, Dinah's father said, "Just a moment. I've changed my mind. I'd like the lobster à la Newburg instead." The waiter nodded and hurried off to attend to his other tables.

Dinah's father sat back and regarded her thoughtfully. "I must say it was very enterprising of you to leave the farm and

120

find a job right here on the fairgrounds. So tell me all about it. I know you work in the Administration Building, but what is it exactly that you do?"

Dinah leaned back to let the waiter slide a plate of salmon in front of her. "It's a perfect job, really. I help keep track of all kinds of details about nearly everything that goes on at the fair, but I'm not stuck inside the office all the time. I carry messages and memoranda here and there, and that takes me outdoors every day."

She gave a little bounce in her chair. "I can hardly believe I'm being paid to wander the fairgrounds and take in all these marvelous sights! If I were to change anything, I'd like to take more time to really see the exhibits here instead of just dashing past them."

She picked up a bit of the smoked salmon on her fork and sampled it. "This is delicious! Thank you for making such a good choice. Now enough about me for the moment. What is it that you do for the Minnesota Threshing Company?"

Her father pleated the edge of the tablecloth. "I always had to travel while you were growing up. It seems like I was away more than I was at home, if you remember."

Dinah took a sip of water to help wash down the salmon, which had suddenly gone dry. She remembered all too well. Her mother had done the best she could to give Dinah a normal life, but nothing could completely ease the ache of having her father gone so much of the time. Nor could her mother's efforts quell the teasing of neighborhood children and their endless taunts about her father's prolonged absences.

"Then when your mother died, there wasn't anyplace to come home to anymore." Her father's voice grew rough.

121

Dinah pressed her lips together and squeezed his hand. It had been a dreadful time for them both. He had been left without a wife, and she wound up living with Aunt Dora and Uncle Everett.

And Gladys.

He gripped her fingers, then released them. The broad smile she remembered so well creased his cheeks. "But now I've landed the job of a lifetime. Instead of being on the road all the time selling farm implements, they have me in the company headquarters in Minneapolis, training other salesmen. It's like I spent my whole life getting ready for this, and it just dropped into my lap."

"So you're staying in one place now? You're not traveling anymore?"

He shook his head. "I have a house just outside Minneapolis. They sent me here to represent the company during the fair, but once it's over, I'm going back home." He grinned again. "It's nice to be able to say that again after all these years."

The restaurant seemed to spin around them. Dinah pressed her fingertips to her forehead. This was even better than she had dreamed. "Tell me about Minneapolis."

She spent the rest of the meal eating mechanically, her whole attention focused on her father's stories about fertile farmland, lakes and waterfalls, and the big flour mills in town. When her plate was empty, she set her fork neatly on the rim of her plate and continued to listen, drinking in the description of the place she would be going at the fair's end.

She could already picture herself traveling around with him to see the sights. The house he described wasn't large, but she didn't mind. They wouldn't need much space for the two of them. And she would be in her own home again, cooking, cleaning, and caring for her father, making up for all the long, empty years.

The waiter sidled up beside the table and set the bill at her father's elbow. Dinah held her breath. She had forgotten those exorbitant prices in the joy of being with him again.

Her father turned the bill over, examined it carefully, and chuckled. He pulled several bills from his wallet and laid them on the table, then led Dinah outside into the balmy evening. He chuckled again.

Feeling as though her feet barely touched the ground, Dinah tucked her hand into the crook of his elbow. "You seem very pleased about something."

"I am." He guided her across the bridge at the north tip of the lagoon, past the tiny Merchant Tailors Pavilion, and into the shadow of the dome of the Illinois Building before he spoke again. "I made out quite well on that deal."

"Deal?"

A chuckle rumbled deep in his chest. "That waiter. When I changed my order, he never bothered to alter the bill. He charged me a good deal less than he should have."

Dinah stumbled to a halt. "Then we need to go back and take care of it."

Her father patted her hand and kept on walking. "Don't worry your head about it. It isn't my fault if they hire waiters who don't pay attention to details like that."

"But the poor man. Suppose he gets in trouble?"

"Something like this is good for him. It will teach him to be more careful in the future. It's a small price to pay for a lesson well learned." He turned toward the right and stopped. "Do any of your wanderings take you to the Midway?"

He pointed ahead to the crowded boulevard before them,

with the silhouette of the Ferris wheel etched against the evening sky.

Dinah gaped at the sight.

Her father gave a soft laugh. "I thought not. Let's take a tour of the place, shall we?"

He led her past the Irish Village and through the Libbey Glass Works display. Dinah clung to his arm and enjoyed the sights, feeling like a giddy young girl basking in her father's attention.

"That's probably enough for one evening," he announced. "We'll have plenty of other times together, and there's no sense in trying to see it all at once."

They walked back to the main fairgrounds, where they found a bench on the terrace below the Woman's Building and sat watching the lights that outlined every building in the great Court of Honor. Nearer at hand, fairy lights twinkled along the edge of the Wooded Island.

"Quite a sight, isn't it?"

Dinah only nodded. She knew no words to describe this magical moment and wouldn't have spoken them aloud if she did. Why would she want to disturb the perfection of this most marvelous night of her life?

Her father took one of her hands and sandwiched it between his own. "We need to talk about the future."

Dinah turned to face him, wondering if he could see the pure joy radiating from her eyes. This was a moment she had waited for her entire life.

"Actually. . ." He gave a self-deprecating little laugh. "I need you to talk to Abby."

"Abby?" Dinah strained to see his face in the waning light.

"You met her at the booth that first day, remember?"

"Of course, but. . ." Dinah's head whirled and her mind scrambled for anything that would make sense of this sudden change in topic. "What does your coworker have to do with this?"

"Everything." Her father settled back against the bench. He stared out across the rippling waters of the lagoon, and a beatific smile lit his face. "I want you to talk to her, tell her about the good times we had when you were a little girl. Will you do that for me?"

Dinah stared at him, utterly at a loss.

His tone grew reminiscent. "You do remember those grand times we had together, don't you? How I used to carry you piggyback and the picnics we had under the big elm tree. Remember the way you used to come down to the station to see me off? I'll never forget how precious you looked, standing there on the platform and waving like you thought you'd never see me again."

Unease rippled along Dinah's limbs. The piggyback rides ended when she was four or five, and she could recall precisely one picnic, brought about by her own wheedling. As for the times she stood waving good-bye, those memories had long since been shut away in the shadowy recesses of her mind.

"I don't. . ." She swallowed once, then cleared her throat and tried again. "I don't understand what any of this has to do with Abby. Why should it matter to her what we did together when I was a child?"

"I've asked her to marry me, but she has a few reservations. She wants to talk to you before she agrees to anything."

"But I thought when you wrote and asked me to come. . .

you said you wanted us to be together."

"And so we are." He rubbed her hands between his. "I expected more of a brief visit, though. I never dreamed you'd be so enterprising. Seizing the moment and pulling up stakes like you did—that just goes to show you're a chip off the old block." Her father winked. "But it gives us that much more time here together, and you'll have a chance to talk to Abby more than once in case she needs more convincing than I think."

Dinah felt as though a gaping hole had opened up beneath her. "So. . .your reason for asking me to come to you was so I could talk to Abby?"

"She wants to be sure I would be a suitable father for her little girl. Her late husband—Hannah's father—wasn't the most reliable man from what I've heard. She told me she didn't want to make the same mistake twice and had to know I would be able to provide a 'stable home,' as she puts it. I thought if she could meet you and find out how well I did with you, it would make all the difference."

"You want to be a good father for Hannah." The words fell from her lips like stones dropping into the lagoon.

Even in the dim light, she could see his eager nod. "She's a little sweetheart. Reminds me a bit of you when you were that age. We'll make a grand family, she and Abby and I. All I need is for you to put in a good word for me."

CHAPTER 11

N o date tonight?" Millie's bright glance took in Dinah's droopy appearance.

Dinah forced a tiny smile and gathered up her reticule. "No, not tonight."

"How about joining me for dinner and a stroll around the grounds?"

"I don't think so, Millie, but thanks for asking. I'll see you tomorrow." Not bothering to wait for the elevator, Dinah trudged down the two flights of stairs, intent on making her way home for a meal with Mrs. Purvis and an early bedtime.

How could the mere act of carrying on her normal routine be so draining? This evening she felt as if she had climbed mountains all day instead of a few flights of stairs. Millie might see the bright lights of the fairgrounds as a cure-all for what ailed her, but all Dinah wanted at that moment was to crawl away like an injured dog to lick her wounds in private.

She reached the bottom of the stairs at last and stepped out into the rotunda. Involuntarily, she cast a glance over at the arch where her father had waited for her the previous night, before all her dreams had come crashing down like an avalanche of shattered hopes.

Dinah took a second look and blinked.

Instead of her father, Seth Howell stood waiting. When their gazes locked, he smiled and strode toward her. "Good evening. Would you mind if I escorted you home? I'd like the chance to talk with you."

Dinah opened her mouth to object, then closed it and nodded instead. Far easier to go along with his plans than to expend the energy it would take to argue. Besides, she found something infinitely comforting in Seth's presence. . .when she wasn't worrying about falling short of his standards.

Seeming to understand her need for silence, he fell into step beside her, and they joined the crowds strolling the west shore of the lagoon. Seth waited until they were opposite the great golden doorway of the Transportation Building before he spoke.

"I need to apologize to you."

The blunt statement startled Dinah so that she nearly stumbled. Seth cupped her elbow in his hand as they continued along the water's edge. "I haven't given you the kind of support you deserve with your girls' class. To be honest, I had my doubts at first about your ability to handle the task, but that's no excuse for my neglect."

"I'm rather inclined to think your first impression was correct," Dinah admitted.

"That isn't the way I hear it. I've been visiting with some of the girls' families, and I've heard over and over about the way you've kept on going in spite of them baiting you and giving you a difficult time."

Which wouldn't have happened with a teacher who knew what she was doing.

"When you offered to take this on, I told you I didn't think you were the type to stick it out." His smile disarmed her in spite of what she felt sure he was about to say.

"It seems I was wrong. And in more ways than one. I felt so sure you'd turn tail and run at the first sign of trouble that I didn't bother to give you the kind of support I would have given to any new teacher, especially one without any experience."

He paused while they threaded their way through the exit and left the fairgrounds behind them. "What I'm trying to say is that I've been wrong. Totally wrong. I want you to know how sorry I am, and to ask your forgiveness. If you're still willing to continue working with the girls, I promise to help you in any way I can from here on."

Tears filmed Dinah's eyes and blurred the street in front of her. "I never expected. . ." Her voice trailed off, and she swiped at her eyes with her fingertips. Did men ever say what you expected them to? First her father, who she thought wanted her for herself instead of as a tool to win Abby, and now Seth, from whom she expected recriminations and found affirmation instead.

"Here." He pressed a handkerchief into her hands. "I didn't mean to make you cry."

Dinah dabbed at her eyes with the soft cloth and looked up into Seth's face, furrowed with concern. "It isn't you. Well, not completely," she added with a watery smile. "I had something of a shock last night, and it left me rather rattled, I'm afraid."

Compassion shadowed Seth's eyes. He took the handkerchief and tenderly wiped away a lone tear that escaped to wander down her cheek. "Would you like to talk about it?"

Dinah started walking again while she pondered her answer. The need to share her burden with someone overwhelmed her, but could she trust Seth? She looked up at the man beside her, who had just confessed his own failings, and knew the answer.

"I hadn't seen my father in years." She floundered for a moment, trying to find the best place to begin. "He traveled a lot when I was younger. It seemed he spent more time away from home than with my mother and me, and. . .and I always missed having him around." The simple statement gave little hint of the gaping hole her father's absences left in the fabric of her young life. "My mother was wonderful, but things never seemed right unless he was there with us."

Seth said nothing, but his look of understanding encouraged her to continue.

"When I was ten, my mother died." Dinah swallowed hard, trying to keep her voice from wobbling. "Papa came home then and stayed. For a while at least. As much as I missed Mama, it felt so good to have him there all the time. Like I had a real father again."

The Chicago street faded from her view as she called to mind those bittersweet days.

"After about a year, though, he couldn't stand staying in one place any longer. He said traveling was in his blood, and he couldn't do anything to change that. He came home one day with a new valise, and I thought I'd die. Then he told me he'd bought it for me, that we were going to take a trip together." She closed her eyes a moment, reliving the joy she felt at the knowledge she

130

wasn't going to be left behind again. This time, she wouldn't have to stand and wave, a lonely little girl on the platform, wondering when her daddy would return.

"It should have been hard to leave home, but it wasn't. I was going with him, and that was all that mattered. I asked him where we were going, and he just laughed. He said there was a whole world out there to see, but first we'd stop off for a visit with my aunt and uncle in Nebraska. I'd met them a couple of times before. Aunt Dora and Uncle Everett had always been nice to me, but then there was Gladys."

"Gladys?"

"My cousin. She and I are the same age, only ten days apart, but she never enjoyed having me around. That was all right; I didn't like her much, either. But I knew I could put up with anything for a day or two, and then Papa and I would be off again."

She paused, torn by the memory of what happened next. "But it didn't turn out quite the way I expected."

Seth gathered her hand in his. "What happened?"

"My aunt and uncle were as sweet as ever, telling me how sorry they were about my mother. Gladys didn't like the idea of anyone else getting that much attention from her parents, so I avoided her as much as I could. One night I went to bed, but I couldn't sleep."

She'd nearly been asleep, though, lulled by the comforting sound of the voices of her father, aunt, and uncle drifting up the stairwell to her room on the second floor. Then the tone of their voices changed, jarring her back to wakefulness. Unable to relax again, she slipped out of bed and crept along the hallway to the top of the stairs, where she huddled into a tiny ball on the top step and settled down to listen.

"You can't just up and take off like this." Aunt Dora's voice held a warning note. "It wouldn't be fair to Dinah to be without either of her parents."

"It isn't fair to expect her to live out of a trunk, either." Dinah recognized her father's persuasive tone. "Always being on the move—that's no life for a child."

"Then settle down and raise her," Uncle Everett put in. "It's about time you started thinking about someone other than yourself."

All three of them flinched when Dinah burst into the room like a miniature avenging Fury.

"My father told me he'd been thinking about our situation, how as much as he wanted to, there were some things he couldn't teach me. Things I could only learn from a woman." For a moment, she felt a sense of helplessness wash over her, just as it had done on that long-ago night. Seth drew her hand into the crook of his arm and held it there, giving her the courage to go on.

"He reached out to me and pulled me into his lap." Dinah remembered how she had tottered over to him on stiff legs, sick with dread at what she feared was coming. "He told me life wasn't easy for a traveling man, spending long hours on trains, moving from one hotel to another. It wasn't any kind of life for a young lady, he said. I begged and I pleaded and told him I could be a help to him. I'd find some way to be useful."

Dinah squeezed her eyes shut, as if doing so could shut out the pain that still lingered after all that time. "He told me it would be better for me to stay where I could have a woman's touch. And someone my own age to spend time with. I cried myself to sleep in his arms. I remember him carrying me upstairs to bed, and when I woke the next morning, he was gone."

132

Seth's fingers tightened on hers. "And you stayed on with your aunt and uncle."

Dinah nodded. "And Gladys." She shuddered in spite of the warmth of Seth's touch.

The corners of Seth's mouth quirked upward. "You make her sound like something out of one of Edgar Allan Poe's tales."

"Worse." Dinah managed a wobbly smile. "Poe could have drawn inspiration from Gladys. Square face, a jutting jaw, and a voice like fingernails scraping across a slate."

Seth threw back his head and laughed. "That's pretty awful, all right. She didn't improve with age?"

"Just the opposite. She always felt my coming to live with them ruined her life and blamed me for it. We were both thrilled when I said good-bye and came to Chicago."

"Ouch. I can see how living with her would have been a trial for you." They turned onto Blackstone Avenue and headed north. The laugh lines still lingered around Seth's eyes, but his tone held only compassion. "Did you see your father often after that?"

Dinah's spirits plummeted again. "I didn't see him at all until I moved here. He's the reason I came. He wrote and said he wanted to see me again, that we needed to talk about the future. I didn't realize until last night that he's planning to remarry."

Seth's pace slowed. "So you'll be moving away to live with him once the fair is over?"

The heaviness returned and settled around her heart. "I don't know."

Seth accompanied her up the steps to Mrs. Purvis's front porch, and she suddenly realized she didn't want their conversation to end. "Would you like to come inside?"

The laugh lines crinkled at the corners of his eyes. "I'd like that very much."

Dinah turned to smile up at him. Beyond his shoulder, she could see the lace curtain flutter in the neighbor's front window. Without taking time to consider her actions, she stepped past Seth, gave a broad grin, and waved. The curtain dropped abruptly.

She turned back to see Seth gaping at her and couldn't stop the giggles that rose in her throat. "It's Mrs. Boggs again. That woman doesn't miss a thing."

The laughter buoyed her spirits, and she walked into the parlor with a far lighter heart. "Mrs. Purvis!" she called. "I've brought someone home with me."

Seth followed her as she peered about the empty room, then peeked into the kitchen. "That's odd. She's always in here fixing supper when I get home."

Footsteps clattered down the stairway, and the landlady appeared in the parlor doorway, her iron gray curls bouncing like coiled springs. "Here I am. I was upstairs and didn't hear you come in." Her eyes lit up when she spotted Seth. "Well, look who's here. If it isn't Reverend Howell."

"Why don't you call me Seth?"

"That's a lovely idea. It makes us seem like family, doesn't it? You two sit down and make yourselves comfortable. I'll bring a little snack." She bustled off toward the kitchen, pausing on the way to tap along a section of the baseboard with the toe of her shoe.

Seth leaned toward Dinah to whisper, "Does she always add in that little extra touch?"

Dinah stifled another round of giggles. "Always. Or some

variation of that. I haven't figured it out yet, but it seems to be part of her routine."

Mrs. Purvis hurried back in, bearing a tray of lemonade and sugar cookies. "Just a smidgen to tide us over until mealtime. Supper's going to be a bit late, so this won't spoil our appetites." She perched on a balloon-back side chair and beamed at the two of them, her bright-eyed expression reminding Dinah of a benevolent sparrow.

Dinah bit into a cookie to hide her smile. She had made the right choice in talking to Seth. Sharing her burden helped to lift the heaviness that had weighed her down ever since her talk with her father the night before. With Mrs. Purvis's antics further lightening the mood, she felt almost festive.

Mrs. Purvis brushed a curl back from her forehead and smoothed her apron. "I hope you'll stay and have supper with us," she said to Seth. "It won't be too much longer until the meat's ready to come out of the oven, and I do make a nice pot roast, if I do say so myself."

Seth grinned back at her. "You've talked me into it. A good pot roast is hard to find."

Mrs. Purvis planted her hands on her knees and pushed herself to her feet. "Then I'll set another place at the table. I do apologize for being late tonight, but I got a new boarder today, and I'm completely discombobulated."

"What a shame," Dinah said. "It wasn't someone you were expecting, then?"

"*I* wasn't." Mrs. Purvis shot an odd look her way. "Although I don't suppose it will come as much of a surprise—" She broke off and stared through the parlor doorway toward the foot of the stairs. "Here she comes now. I'll go get supper on." She darted

135

through the kitchen doorway.

Startled by the abrupt departure, Dinah stood, intending to follow to make sure she was all right.

"Well, there you are. I thought you would be getting home soon."

Dinah froze at the sound of a voice she thought she'd left behind for good. Beside her, Seth rose, a bewildered expression on his face. "Are you all right? You're white as a sheet."

Dinah shook her head, feeling like she might never be all right again. Composing her features as much as she was able, she turned slowly to face the woman framed in the doorway. "Hello, Gladys."

"I must say I expected a warmer welcome. You don't seem very glad to see me." Gladys leaned against the walnut chest of drawers and crossed her arms.

Dinah returned her scrutiny, wondering how she had managed to get through supper with her mind a total blank. Whether Mrs. Purvis's pot roast lived up to its reputation, she couldn't have said. They might have been eating cardboard, for all she knew. Seth left at some point, promising to walk her to the girls' meeting the following night. She thought she managed to give him a civil good-bye, but she really couldn't remember.

Now she stood in Gladys's room—thankfully at the opposite end of the hallway from her own—trying to force her mind to catch up with the events of the past hour.

"What are you doing here?" She saw no reason for subtlety in the current situation.

A sly smile creased Gladys's face. "You managed to shake the dust of the farm off your feet. I didn't see any reason why I shouldn't do the same. Mother was totally against it, of course, until she received all those letters from you, talking about how involved you've become with spiritual things."

Dinah's mouth went dry. "I only told her about going to the tent meeting."

"And your work with those girls in the slums." Gladys snorted. "You painted quite a picture of missionary zeal. It certainly had the right effect on Mother, though. She went around singing your praises until I thought I'd be sick."

Dinah pressed her hand to her stomach, hoping the pot roast would stay where it belonged. "You mean my letters are the reason she let you come?"

"When she heard about Mr. Moody's work during the fair, she decided there must be some sort of marvelous spiritual awakening going on. If it made that kind of difference in you, she figured it ought to be safe for me to be here, too." She looked in the small mirror propped up on top of the dresser and smoothed her hair. "You know how hard it is for them to tell me no."

"How long do you plan to be here?" Dinah calculated rapidly. If Mrs. Johnson would give her some time off, she could give Gladys a tour of the highlights of the fair and have her on her way back to Nebraska within two or three days, a week at the most.

Gladys's thin lips pressed together until they all but disappeared. "Why, I'm here to stay, dear cousin. Aren't you glad?"

"What do you mean? How can you possibly support yourself? I'm not about to help you find a job on the fairgrounds."

"You don't have to. I have already found employment elsewhere."

Dinah stiffened and dug her fingernails into her palms. "You couldn't possibly. . ." Seeing her cousin's insufferably smug expression, her voice trailed off and she whispered, "Where?"

"At Marshall Field's downtown. I've been in correspondence with them ever since you left. Everything is all arranged. I just needed to wait until the time was right. My job is a permanent one, by the way. Not something that will fade away in another few months when the fair ends." She favored Dinah with a smile that made her want to grind her teeth.

With an effort, Dinah forced herself to adopt a casual tone. "And once the fair is over and you no longer have me around to torment, what then? You don't plan to work there forever, do you?"

"Hardly. Have you forgotten that in another month I'll collect my share of the inheritance from Grandmother Winslow? By then I'll know my way around the city and I'll be ready to live in fine style."

Dinah's lips quirked upward in spite of her tension. "I'll be getting my own share right after you do. We both know how much Grandmother Winslow left us. It's hardly enough to keep you in grand style for any length of time."

"But it will let me move in the right circles long enough to find someone who can."

"That's the reason you came to Chicago? To find a wealthy husband?"

"Don't tell me it isn't exactly the reason you came here yourself." Gladys traced the stitching line on the comforter with a blunt finger. "Why else would you pack up and bolt off like that?"

Don't make me list the reasons. Dinah lifted her chin. "That isn't it at all. I came because my father is here." She had the satisfaction of watching her cousin's jaw sag.

"Uncle Ernie? Here?" Her pale brown eyes glittered and took on a calculating gleam Dinah knew all too well. "I'll have to pay him a visit and tell him what I think about him foisting you off on us like that. Where do I find him?"

Too late, Dinah realized her mistake. She never should have let Gladys know her father was anywhere nearby. No telling what kind of turmoil she could insert into a situation that was already more than Dinah wanted to deal with.

"That's something you'll have to figure out on your own, I'm afraid. Good night, Gladys. I have to go to work in the morning."

She fled down the hall to the sanctuary of her room, wondering what else could possibly go wrong. She dressed for bed with lightning speed, blew out the lamp, and curled up between the crisp, white sheets, ready to escape into the arms of slumber.

At least Gladys had no idea where to find Dinah's father, and Dinah didn't plan on dropping any hints as to his whereabouts. The fairgrounds was huge, Chicago even more so. Even Gladys, with her proven ability to ferret out secrets, would find it hard to locate him without help.

A small comfort, but at the moment, it was all she had.

CHAPTER 12

Who can tell me what that verse means?"

Dinah looked out at the faces before her, hoping against hope someone would have an answer. Any answer.

The girls—only five of them tonight—stared at the scuffed floor and refused to meet her gaze.

What's going on, Lord? Seth said I'm doing a good job, but how can that be if the girls don't even show up, much less listen and respond?

Even Martha wasn't there to smirk at her from the back corner. Hoping to generate some conversation, she turned to Jenny. "Where is your sister tonight? It isn't like her to let you come alone."

Jenny shrugged and pushed a wayward strand of hair off her forehead. "She didn't come back from the market when she was supposed to. My aunt told me to come by myself and

Martha could pick me up when it's over."

Silence fell again like a leaden blanket. At the moment, Dinah would have welcomed even Martha's sniping. Keeping her smile in place, she said, "Let's look at that verse again. Listen to me read it, and then we'll talk about what it means." She held her Bible aloft and read from Paul's second epistle to Timothy: " 'For God hath not given us the spirit of fear; but of power, and of love, and of a sound mind.' "

Still no response.

Why couldn't she get through to them? There seemed to be a wall around them—one she couldn't breach. Much as she cared about the girls, much as she prayed for them and longed to share the truths of the Bible with them, that wasn't going to happen until they and their families trusted her.

Until then, she was doing little more than marking time, no matter what Seth might say. There had to be a way to reach the families of these girls, to win their confidence so the girls would feel free to respond to her. But what?

A glance at the watch pinned to her dress confirmed the hour. "It's time to dismiss, girls. Be careful walking home. I look forward to seeing you next time."

If there is a next time. She tried to chase the gloomy thought away, but the dwindling attendance told the tale. If she didn't do something to turn the situation around—and soon—she wouldn't have a class left to teach.

"Jenny, I want to be sure Martha is here before you leave." Gathering up her reticule, she followed the little girl out into the hallway. No Martha awaited them. "I don't understand. Didn't you say she would be here to meet you?"

Jenny twisted a strand of hair around one finger and nodded, her little face pinched and taut. Then she pointed to a woman walking toward them. "That's my aunt Alice." Jenny scampered toward the woman while Dinah followed along at a more sedate pace.

"Hello, I'm Dinah Mayhew. Is everything all right? I expected Martha here to see Jenny home."

"Don't ask me where that girl's gone off to." The thin-faced woman pushed her hand through her hair. "Off lollygagging instead of doing the marketing, if you ask me, and leaving the rest of us to carry her load as well as our own."

"You mean she's not back yet?" Jenny's face twisted into a mask of worry. "But she never stays that long."

"Do you think she's all right?" Dinah asked.

"She won't be when I get hold of her," Jenny's aunt said, but Dinah could see the concern that shadowed her eyes. "I've got too many things to handle to be coming all the way down here just because this one wants to listen to stories." She gave Jenny a light cuff on the shoulder. "Come along now. I've wasted all the time here I'm going to." Without so much as a good-bye, she turned on her heel, taking Jenny with her.

Dinah watched the outer door close behind them. She should have offered to pray with them, she thought belatedly. Seth would have done it without a second thought.

Her earlier dejection returned full force. Another opportunity to win their trust, and she had missed it.

He watched while McGinty counted the bills into his hand. The tingle he felt at the sight of his hard-earned cash almost equaled the thrill he experienced while the game was in progress.

Almost, but not quite. Nothing could match the exhilaration of enticing his victims into the high-stakes game of wits where success and failure hung in an exquisitely delicate balance.

He smoothed the bills and tucked them inside his wallet, resisting the urge to wipe his hands along the side seams of his trousers. He could cleanse himself of McGinty's touch once he returned home.

"Got that last load together pretty quickly, didn't you?" McGinty knocked an inch of ash off his cigar, then leaned back in the shabby wooden chair and eyed him with an expression that made the skin tighten across his shoulders.

He nodded, watching the Irishman through narrowed eyes, the way he would watch a snake. "Things went very smoothly."

McGinty pursed his lips and rolled the cigar from one corner of his mouth to the other. "We won't be ready to send out another shipment for several weeks."

"That isn't a problem. I'll wait until I hear from you."

McGinty's eyes seemed to bore a hole into his soul. "You don't seem very concerned about the delay." He stubbed out the cigar without shifting his gaze. "You wouldn't be having another source of income, would you? A connection with my competition maybe, or plans to strike out on your own?"

The air squeezed out of his lungs. He steeled himself not to look away and kept his voice level. "Not at all. I've learned to live within my means, that's all. I wouldn't think about double-crossing you."

"See that you don't." McGinty dropped his voice to a thin whisper. "I'd hate to find out later on that you lied to me."

"Not a bit. Just let me know when you're ready for me to

start collecting again." No point in letting McGinty know he'd already begun. He hadn't planned on starting in again quite so soon, but this last one practically fell into his lap, and who was he to argue with fate?

One of McGinty's henchmen glanced at his hands. "Those are some pretty bad scratches you've got there. You been tangling with a cat?"

He smiled. "My hat blew off and rolled into a rose bush. I had a devil of a time getting it out." He pocketed his wallet and got to his feet. "If that's all then. . ."

"I'll send word when we're ready to start again. One more thing." McGinty's voice pinned him just as he reached the door. "Don't cross me. Don't ever, *ever* cross me."

He stepped outdoors, anxious to distance himself from the ramshackle building in the warehouse district. He stroked his hand over his pocket, running his fingers along the bulge his wallet made. Who would have thought a few short months ago that a chance encounter in Muldoon's pub could have opened the door to such a lucrative—and enjoyable—enterprise?

Enjoyable in most respects. His most recent acquisition, simple as she was to lure in, had fought like a wildcat before he managed to close the cubicle door. He tugged his cuffs down to cover the red marks on his wrists. He had learned a valuable lesson, though. Next time, he would give the powder plenty of time to work and not be tempted to rush the process.

But overcoming these little challenges was part of what made the game so pleasurable. That and the ample remuneration he received. Clever of McGinty to come up with the idea of shipping girls back East instead of selling them to one of the brothels down in the Levee. Less likelihood, as McGinty explained it to him, of the girls escaping and being able to find their way back home.

Between McGinty's connections and his own ability to draw girls from the better classes into their web, they were able to command a higher price, a most satisfactory business arrangement all around. And the time between shipments left him free to pursue his own, even more profitable endeavors.

What would McGinty think if he ever learned of those? He grinned, knowing that would never happen. He knew quite well how to keep the two parts of his life separate. It was a skill that had served him well over the years, the thing that made him so successful at what he did.

CHAPTER 13

Dinah stood in front of the squalid brick building and pressed her handkerchief to her nose to lessen the stench of a dead dog lying in a nearby alleyway. She checked the address against the list she pulled from her skirt pocket. This had to be the right place.

It wasn't any better than the other places she had visited that day. At least it was the last stop she planned to make. Soon she would be out of that neighborhood and on her way back home.

Home. The word would have evoked a far warmer picture in her mind a few days ago, before the reappearance of Gladys in her life. Now, instead of having a cozy chat with Mrs. Purvis after returning from work or Bible class, she slipped up the stairs like a ghost, often as not skipping the evening meal.

At least Gladys hadn't decided to trail after her to the girls' meetings, as she had feared at first. Her cousin made it clear she wanted nothing to do with Dinah's charity work, as she called it.

"If you're vying for sainthood, have at it," she sneered. "That isn't the reason I came to Chicago, no matter what my mother might think."

Dinah scanned the street and took note of the two men slouching on the top step of the stoop of the building next door. She tried to ignore their stares as she mounted the rickety steps. The sooner this visit was over, the better. Already the sun dropped farther toward the horizon. She wouldn't want to be out on these streets alone in another hour.

She didn't want to be out here now, for that matter. But it would be worth it if her self-imposed task had the results she hoped for.

This was the last stop, she reminded herself. She could do this. Pushing down her jitters, she knocked on the door.

The woman who picked Jenny up at the last meeting answered. She raked Dinah up and down with a look full of suspicion. "What do you want?"

Dinah forced a smile. "I'm Dinah Mayhew. We met the other night after Jenny's Bible class, remember?"

"I remember. I figured it wouldn't be too long before you wanted something from us. Well, you're wasting your time. We don't have money for Bibles, if that's what you're selling." She started to swing the door closed.

After getting the same response throughout the long, weary afternoon, Dinah was prepared. She held up her hand to block the door. "Wait. That isn't my intent at all. I was hoping to speak to Martha, or perhaps Jenny's father, if he's home."

"Her father's still at work. As for Martha, we still haven't seen her."

Dinah caught her breath. "She hasn't come home yet?"

Jenny's aunt leaned against the door. "Why else would I be here taking care of my brother's kids when I've got plenty of my own work to do?"

"I guess you're the one I need to talk to, then." Dinah tried to inject a pleasant tone in her voice.

The woman sighed. "And you won't give me a moment's peace until you get what you want, will you? I guess you may as well come in." She pulled the door open to admit Dinah into a dark, stuffy room smelling of boiled cabbage and unwashed bodies.

"Is Dinah home?" Seth asked Mrs. Purvis. "Mr. Moody is speaking at a special meeting tonight, and I thought she might like to go with me to hear him."

The landlady's eyes rounded. "Isn't she with you? She said she was going to see her girls after work."

The air left his lungs in a *whoosh*. "She was going to see her girls? You're sure?"

Mrs. Purvis nodded. "I assumed that meant she had a Bible class tonight." She tilted her head and looked up at Seth, a hint of worry in her eyes. "If she didn't go with you, what could she be doing?"

"I don't know." He tightened his lips. "But I'm going to find out."

"So what is it you want? Speak your piece and be done with it."

148

Realizing there would be no need for small talk or social amenities, Dinah plunged into her explanation. "I'm inviting Jenny and the other girls in my group to tour the fairgrounds with me this Saturday. It would be a wonderful opportunity for them to see exhibits from all over the world."

Before she could finish, the half-closed door to the kitchen swung open and Jenny burst into the room. "Really, Miss Mayhew? That would be so exciting! Can I go, Aunt Alice? I'd really like to."

Her aunt sniffed. "And where do you think we'd get the money? We can't afford no tickets."

"That isn't a problem," Dinah told her, wanting to erase the crestfallen expression from Jenny's face. "A donor provided passes for all the girls." Silently, she blessed Mr. Thorndyke for his generosity.

The thin woman still looked skeptical. "We've already had her sister run off. What good will it do to fill her head with fancy notions? After seeing all that grand folderol, she'll never be satisfied with anything we can give her."

Jenny clasped her hands and ran over to her aunt. "Please, Aunt Alice. I'll do extra chores to make up for Martha being gone. I promise."

At the reminder, Dinah furrowed her brow. "Is anybody searching for Martha?"

Alice huffed out a sigh. "If I'd had the chance to get out of this rat hole for a while when I was fifteen, I would have jumped at it. She's probably staying with a friend somewhere. I can't blame her, I guess, but her pa's going to tan her hide when she decides to come home, I can tell you that."

A lanky boy a couple of years Dinah's junior sauntered into

the room, leaving the door standing open behind him. "I checked with some more of Martha's friends, Ma. No one's seen her."

"Or they aren't admitting it if they have." Alice scrubbed a work-worn hand across her face. "You'd think the girl would at least let us know she's all right, wouldn't you?"

The boy suddenly took note of Dinah's presence. He ducked his head in a quick nod and kept on staring, his gaze dragging down the length of her body and back up again. Dinah felt her cheeks flame under his scrutiny. He noticed her discomfort and grinned.

Through the open door, she could see the way the shadows were lengthening. She turned back to Jenny's aunt. "I really must be going. Will you allow Jenny to go to the fair with me?"

Alice shot a look at the little girl's pleading face. She lifted one shoulder. "Might as well. She won't give me a minute's peace until I give in."

Jenny squealed and clapped her hands.

Dinah felt like doing the same thing. "That's fine. I'll come by to collect her at nine in the morning, and I'll bring her back here myself." She smiled at Jenny. "See you then."

She turned to leave, glad to find Alice's son had filtered out of the room while they were talking. He might be only a youth, but it had been a long time since she had met anyone whose mere gaze made her feel so uncomfortable.

Dinah descended the steps and checked the sun's position. Talking to each of her girls' families had taken far longer than she expected. It would be getting dark before long.

She passed the building next door, where the two men still lounged on the stoop. Out of the corner of her eye, she saw them stand when she passed. Her pulse fluttered in her throat, and she picked up her pace while trying not to let her sudden fear show.

At the corner, she cast a furtive glance behind her. The two men were now ambling her way. Dinah's breath caught in her throat. It took all her effort to keep from breaking into a headlong run. Wanting nothing more than to put this frightening neighborhood and its dangers behind her, she turned back just in time to see Alice's son step into view.

He straddled the walk, blocking her path. His lips twisted into a brash grin. "Hello there, pretty lady."

Seth strode along at a rapid clip, wishing for the first time that he had the means that would allow him to keep a carriage at his disposal. He reached the corner and broke into a jog, concern for Dinah outweighing his reluctance to draw attention to himself.

What did she think she was doing, haring off on her own like that? If he hadn't talked to Mrs. Purvis directly and heard the news with his own ears, he wouldn't have believed her capable of such foolishness.

Had he planted the seed for this scatterbrained idea with his comment about visiting the girls' families? Guilt vied with his irritation. It was one thing for him to make the rounds here, knowing the area and its people as he did. Quite another for a lone woman to go traipsing around that neighborhood, especially without an escort. What had she been thinking?

When he reached the area where the girls lived, he kept a close watch on the street ahead of him and peered down each alley he passed, praying he wouldn't miss her. Surely she was all right.

151

She had to be all right.

Lord, let me find her before it gets dark. Enough problems could arise in that area in broad daylight. Once night fell. . .

Seth rounded the next corner and spotted a knot of men at the far end of the block. Nothing unusual about that, but something about the way they stood, shuffling ahead to converge on the space between them, reminded him of a pack of feral dogs closing in, ready to chew a cat to pieces.

He couldn't see into the middle of their little circle, but something told him he had found what he was looking for. Seth put on a burst of speed.

CHAPTER 14

W hat've you got there, Billy?"
Dinah whirled away from the taunting face of Alice's son to find the men from the porch steps closing in behind her.

"Yeah," called the second man. "We don't get many of her kind in this neighborhood."

Dinah backed away and slammed against the building behind her. She pressed closer against the rough brick wall, as if by some miracle she could disappear right into it.

Billy moved a step nearer. "She came to visit my little cousin, but she doesn't seem too friendly towards me."

Dinah dug her fingers into the brick and felt her breath tear in and out of her lungs in ragged gasps. She darted her gaze between the faces of the three men, feeling like a doe surrounded by wolves. How had she gotten herself into this mess? Why had she ever thought she could do anything to help people who so obviously didn't want to be helped?

"Look at them fine clothes. Pretty hair, too." The nearest man reached out to finger a curl next to her right ear. Dinah jerked away, and a whimper gurgled in her throat.

"She smells good, too," he went on. "Why, I'll bet—"

He broke off, a look of astonishment on his face. Dinah watched him slam against the brick wall and bounce off it onto the ground.

Seth stood over him, breathing heavily and flexing his fingers as if longing to wrap them around the throats of the other two.

They jumped back and gaped at him. The sight would have been comical had the situation not been so dire.

Seth edged between them and Dinah, taking on a protective stance. "Why don't the two of you collect your friend and go back to holding down those porch steps?"

Billy and the other man moved to comply.

Seth remained on the alert. "Billy, you ought to know better than this."

"I didn't mean nothing by it." The youth shot a baleful look at Dinah. "Besides, she ought to know better than to come wandering down around here alone." He and his friend hoisted their fallen comrade between them, and the three of them shuffled off.

Dinah clamped her hand over her mouth and sagged back against the building, not trusting her legs to support her. She closed her eyes, trying to rid herself of the image of the trio closing in on her. She sensed Seth moving closer to her and opened her eyes. "I was so scared. If you hadn't come along when you did. . ."

"What were you thinking, coming down here on your own?"

Dinah shrank back from the anger blazing in his eyes. "I wanted to visit the girls and get to know their families. It was awful, Seth. It's bad enough to see these places from the street, but actually going inside and seeing the way they live. . ."

Seth's expression didn't soften. "I know the way they live. Why do you think I told you never to come down here alone?"

His anger sparked her defiance. "It wasn't just idle curiosity. I've come up with a plan. I arranged for passes for all of them to come to the exposition this Saturday. I needed to speak to their families to let them know and get their permission. I could hardly expect them to let their daughters go off with a total stranger, could I?"

Seth stared at her, his chest heaving. "You're taking them to the fair?"

"Yes, I am. Especially after today, I think it's important to give them a glimpse of the world outside, to let them know something exists outside these deplorable conditions."

Seth's lips thinned into a narrow line. "That may be, but you should have discussed it with me first." He drew one step closer and pointed his finger at her. "You cannot come down here on your own again. Do you understand me? I can't face the idea of something happening to you, which it almost did."

"I'll admit I shouldn't have stayed out this late, but—"

"Early or late, it doesn't matter. You are not to come down here alone. Period. If you can't promise me that, I'll relieve you of your position as the leader of their class."

"I'm picking them all up at nine on Saturday morning. They're little girls; they can't be out wandering around Chicago on their own."

"I'll pick them up and meet you at the fairgrounds." Seth's

voice held a note of finality.

"But I already told them—"

"I'll let them know the plan has changed. They know they can trust me. It's either that, or we cancel the outing altogether. That's the way it has to be. Is that clear?"

"Quite clear, Reverend Howell. And since you're so concerned about my welfare, I wonder if you would be willing to escort me home now?"

Dinah didn't know which was worse: being shut out by Seth's cold silence, or trying to keep up with his long, rapid strides.

The exertion cleared her head after her recent scare, something Dinah regretted, since it let her mind roam back over the recent turn of events. Looking back, it was all too obvious she had been in the wrong place at the wrong time. She remembered how frightened she had been, standing there like a deer at bay until Seth appeared and leaped to her rescue.

But his anger at her had transformed her gratitude into humiliation in the blink of an eye. Looking at it from his point of view, she could see exactly why he felt the way he did. She had made a huge mistake in going into those streets on her own, but she wasn't about to admit that to him. Not when he held his jaw set in that stubborn line. Not when she knew she had just fulfilled all his worst expectations of her.

Dinah watched the way he strode along, completely sure of himself in this setting. The contrast between them couldn't have been clearer: He belonged there; she didn't. It was as simple as that.

How am I supposed to do this? her heart cried out. *Why would You call me to work with these girls and then not give me the means to do it?* As many blunders as she had made in her efforts to reach them, she couldn't shake the conviction that this was what God wanted her to do. But she wouldn't be able to do it if Seth relieved her of her position.

And if she didn't have the class, she would no longer have any reason to spend time with Seth. That loss would be as much of a blow as losing contact with her girls.

No, losing Seth would be much, much worse.

She slanted a look up at him. How did he feel about her? One minute he stood up as her protector; the next, he yelled at her as if she were a nitwit.

Dinah choked back a sob. She had made an utter mess of things, no question about it. Creating problems seemed to be the only thing she was any good at. If she had been a better daughter, her father would have wanted to be with her instead of palming her off to be raised by relatives. If she'd only had the sense to talk about this with Seth before setting out on her own, maybe he wouldn't be angry with her now.

Despair welled up within her, and she wanted to wail like a frightened child. Would she ever be anything other than a failure? It seemed as if she had let everyone down—her father, Seth, the girls. Even God.

They had nearly reached the boardinghouse when Seth slackened his pace and let out a deep sigh. "I'm sorry," he said. "When I saw those men closing in on you, it scared the daylights out of me. But I should never have taken it out on you like that."

Dinah nodded, not trusting herself to speak. She had gone limp with relief at the sight of Seth coming to her rescue, then stiff with shock when he turned his anger upon her. Now his

157

tone had changed again, and she had no defenses in place to deal with his concern.

"You've won most of the girls over," he went on. "You're doing a good job with them."

"Then why aren't they coming to the class?"

"Give them time. Think of this as a test. They still see you as an outsider, but once they get to know you—"

"That's exactly what I was trying to do today! To let them and their families know I really do care for them, that they aren't some project I'll abandon later on."

The tenderness in the look Seth gave her turned her knees to jelly all over again. "The idea was fine. The way you went about it nearly got you into big trouble." He caught her hand in his and stroked his thumb along the backs of her fingers. "I'll make you a deal. You come up with all the ideas you want, but talk to me first before you go putting them into action. Agreed?"

"I will." Dinah's steps dragged as they approached Mrs. Purvis's front porch. The way he was looking at her now, the idea of parting from him seemed unendurable. "Would you like to come in and talk some more about my plans for Saturday?"

One corner of his mouth tilted up in the smile she loved. "There's no time like the present. Do you think your landlady would mind?"

Dinah laughed. "I think she'll be upset if you don't. She really seems to like you."

Seth reached past her to open the door. As he did, his shoulder pressed tight against hers. Dinah froze, seized by a sudden longing for him to wrap his arms around her and hold her close. She drew in a shaky breath and raised her eyes to meet his gaze.

His face was only inches away, so close she could see the fine lines etched around his eyes. Dinah's heart seemed to stop beating while she waited for him to make a move.

The lines around his eyes deepened, and he nodded toward the open door. "After you."

With her cheeks ablaze, Dinah stepped inside.

"I thought I heard someone." Mrs. Purvis appeared in the parlor doorway, a damp dish towel still in her hands. "Oh good, you found her. This just seems to be a day when everything is working for the best."

"Would it be all right if Seth came in for a while?" Dinah asked, hoping her humiliation wouldn't be obvious to the others.

"Of course!" Mrs. Purvis closed the door and herded them toward the parlor. "I can't wait to tell you both. I've had the most wonderful news."

Caught up in the landlady's excitement, Dinah found herself laughing despite her embarrassment. "You two go ahead. Give me a moment to run upstairs and put my reticule away." She reached the bottom step and saw Gladys standing at the top of the stairs.

"It's about time you got home. I've been waiting to talk to you."

She could put her reticule away later. Dinah stepped back and turned to follow the others. "I'm afraid it will have to wait. Mrs. Purvis wants to speak to me."

Gladys sniffed. "Fine. Since I'm obviously not invited to this little tête-à-tête, I'll go back to my room and finish my letter to Mother. We'll talk when you aren't so preoccupied."

Dinah didn't bother to reply. She bolted across the entry

hall and fled toward the parlor.

"Why don't the two of you sit here?" Mrs. Purvis waved them toward the gold damask settee. Dinah lowered herself onto the stiff cushion, suddenly aware of how little room was afforded by the settee's narrow confines.

Seth didn't seem to mind, though. He leaned back and propped his ankle on his other knee as though he felt right at home. Dinah tried to emulate his relaxed air despite the fact they were sitting so close she could feel a tingle whenever his arm brushed against hers.

Mrs. Purvis pulled up a side chair and sat opposite them. She pulled a letter from her skirt pocket. "I got the most marvelous news today, and I just have to share it with someone. You'll never guess what it is." She looked at them expectantly.

Seth laced his fingers around his knee and grinned, obviously getting into the spirit of the game. "A long-lost uncle went to his eternal reward and left you his entire estate?"

Mrs. Purvis gurgled with laughter. "Nothing like that. My dear Randolph provided quite well for me with this house. . . and more, if I can ever find the rest of it. But that's neither here nor there." She smoothed the envelope on her knee and beamed at Dinah.

"One of my former boarders just wrote to tell me she's getting married."

"How nice." Dinah exchanged a quick glance with Seth, who looked as confused as she felt.

"It's most satisfying, you see, because I had such a hand in bringing it about."

Enlightenment dawned. "The engagement, you mean?"

Mrs. Purvis simpered. "I recognized the potential for romance

160

the moment I set eyes on the two of them together. I knew from the first that it was meant to be." Her bosom rose and fell on a deep sigh. "Annie is such a dear girl, and Nicholas is a fine figure of a man, especially when he's all decked out in his Western garb. He was a rider with Colonel Cody's Wild West Show, you know." Her face took on a dreamy expression. "She'll be Annie Rutherford now. Isn't that wonderful?"

Seth's brows drew together. "Rutherford? Big, brawny fellow who wore a fringed buckskin jacket?"

"That's Nicholas to a T! You know him?"

Seth leaned forward and rested his forearms on his knees. "I took some of my boys on a tour of the Wild West Show. Nick Rutherford spent some time with them, and then he and I had a talk while they were seeing the rest of the grounds."

He smiled. "I remember him telling me about a woman he hoped to marry. He seemed like a fine fellow. I'm glad to hear things have worked out for him." He stared at his hands as if lost in thought. "It seems like he mentioned an uncle, as well."

Mrs. Purvis's eyes misted, and she stroked the envelope with a tender touch. "Ah, yes, his uncle Silas. A remarkable man. Truly remarkable. For a time, I thought. . . But it wasn't meant to be. Apparently my gift for matchmaking extends to others but not to myself." She darted a quick glance at Seth and Dinah and resumed her perky expression.

"But I do have a gift. I see that now, and I feel it is my calling to recognize young love and help bring it to fruition." She bestowed a benevolent smile on the pair of them, then hopped up from her chair. "Well, I have things I must be doing. I'll leave the two of you alone to chat."

Her sudden exit left Dinah feeling even more awkward than

before. She shifted uneasily on the horsehair cushion and slid a sideways glance at Seth. To her amazement, he was grinning broadly.

"Do you think the last part of that little speech was directed at us?"

Dinah sputtered with laughter, despite the heat that flooded her face. "She isn't exactly subtle, is she?"

Seth turned toward her, putting himself in such close proximity she could feel the warmth of his arm through her sleeve. "Maybe not subtle, but perceptive." His eyes darkened, and he stretched his arm along the back of the settee, letting his fingertips brush against her shoulder. "Definitely perceptive."

Dinah's throat went dry. So she hadn't imagined the surge of attraction at the front door. She felt Seth's hand cup her cheek and let her eyelids flutter closed, the better to focus on the sensation of his thumb trailing across her temple.

"I thought you were talking with Mrs. Purvis." Gladys's strident voice broke into the tender moment.

Dinah sprang back. "She just left. She had some news she wanted to share with both of us."

"You didn't seem to have any interest in my news."

Dinah gritted her teeth. "I'll be available in a few minutes. Reverend Howell and I have a few things to discuss."

Gladys plumped down on the chair vacated by Mrs. Purvis. "I'll wait until you finish."

Seth got to his feet. "I don't guess we have too much more to talk about tonight. Let's plan on my picking up the girls and meeting you at the entrance at Terminal Station on Saturday morning. Does that sound all right?"

Dinah rose to stand beside him. "Yes, that would be fine. I'll see you to the door." Out in the entry hall, she whispered, "I'm sorry. My cousin doesn't seem to have any understanding that other people's business might be as important as her own."

"It's all right." Seth's smile took away the chill of disappointment. "We really didn't need to say much more about Saturday. I just wasn't ready for our talk to end."

The tingle was back again. "I'm glad you think taking the girls to the fair is a good idea."

"It's a wonderful idea. You're wonderful, as a matter of fact." Seth's eyes darkened, and he leaned forward. Dinah's head tilted back of its own accord, and she watched his face draw nearer.

Heavy feet stumped across the hallway floor. "Aren't you finished yet?"

They sprang apart as though they'd been scorched. One corner of Seth's mouth quirked up in a rueful smile. "I'll say good night now." He opened the front door and gave Dinah a conspiratorial wink. "I think I'll go home and brush up on my Poe."

Amusement warred with frustration as Dinah closed the door behind him. "All right, Gladys, what's your big news? Are you having problems at work?"

"My job is going quite well, thank you. I've already made quite a number of sales. But my news is about something quite different." Gladys struck a pose. "I thought you might like to know that I have a beau."

"A beau?" Dinah tried to keep the skepticism out of her voice. From the anger that flared in Gladys's eyes, she apparently failed.

"I should have known you'd be jealous. You arrived here before I did, but you haven't managed to attract the interest of anyone besides your penniless street preacher."

163

It took all Dinah's effort to ignore the barb. She leaned back against the door and studied her cousin. "You've been here such a short time. Where did you meet this person?"

Gladys's mouth pinched until the corners turned white. " 'This person' has a name: Alan Saunders. He came into the store looking for a necktie. One of the other girls started to wait on him, but he moved over to my station and started talking." She pressed her palms together and sighed. "It was like fate stepped in and took a hand."

"You met him at the store? No one introduced you?"

Gladys bristled. "He's a regular customer. The other girls have seen him plenty of times before."

Dinah shifted uneasily. "But Gladys, what do you really know about him?"

"Everything I need to. We had a very nice conversation that first day, enough that he realized he wanted to get to know me better." Her lips parted in a triumphant smile. "If you were home more in the evenings, you'd know I haven't been frittering away my time sitting here alone."

Alarm bells started clanging in Dinah's head. "He's been here?"

"Only to pick me up." Gladys looked around the entry hall with disdain. "Do you think I want to entertain him in that dingy parlor? Or have our batty landlady come knocking on the walls while I'm trying to carry on a conversation?"

"So Mrs. Purvis hasn't met him? This doesn't sound right. I hardly think Aunt Dora and Uncle Everett would approve."

"I'm not looking for their approval or anyone else's, especially not yours." Gladys's chin trembled. "I just thought you might be happy for me."

"And you think taking up with a perfect stranger is a wise thing to do?"

"How well can you say you're acquainted with your preacher friend? Do you really know anything about him, other than that he works in the slums and hasn't been able to find a position at a respectable church?"

"At least I know his ministry is recognized by Mr. Moody and his coworkers." Dinah whirled and headed to the foot of the stairs. "I have a headache, Gladys. Please tell Mrs. Purvis I won't be down for supper."

Gladys mounted the steps right behind her. "Don't be so dramatic. You just don't want to admit I've managed to attract a suitable beau when you haven't." She dogged Dinah's steps all the way down the hall. "He's quite handsome, too—hair the color of fresh-churned butter and eyes like a clear sky on a spring morning. . . ."

Dinah fumbled with her doorknob. "I need to lie down now."

Undeterred, Gladys went on. "A strong, manly chin, and the way he says my name!" She let out a ripple of laughter. "It sends goose bumps up and down my spine just to hear him speak."

"He sounds like a regular Adonis. Now would you please let me have a little time alone?"

"I knew it." Gladys preened herself. "You're jealous."

Dinah's hand tightened on the cool metal of the doorknob. "I am not jealous, believe me. But we aren't back on the farm, either. I don't have to listen to your trumped-up stories if I don't want to—and I don't. Good night."

She could hear Gladys sputtering through the closed door. "You never wanted anything nice to happen to me, Dinah May- hew. But you're going to eat those words. You just wait and see!"

165

Long after the echo of her cousin's footsteps died away, Dinah lay stretched across her bed, staring at the ceiling. What on earth had gotten into Gladys to come up with such an outlandish story?

It wouldn't be the first time, though. Gladys's ability to spin stories about her supposed accomplishments had been one of the thorns in Dinah's side all during their years together.

But her wild tales were usually built upon some small grain of fact. What was the truth in this case? More than likely, Dinah thought, some male customer smiled across the counter at Gladys and then went on about his business. That's all it would take, though. Gladys's fertile imagination was more than able to take over from such a small beginning.

Still, maddening as Gladys could be, it didn't relieve Dinah of the need to guard her tongue and let the love of Christ shine through her.

" 'Out of the abundance of the heart the mouth speaketh.' " The verse she'd been studying for a future lesson smote her conscience. There was no denying that the last words she had spoken to her cousin reflected her innermost feelings. They might be true, Dinah reminded herself, but were they worthy of someone who presumed to teach God's Word to others?

She crawled out of bed long enough to pull off her dress and tug her nightgown over her head. With no more attention to her hair than pulling out the pins and running her fingers through the dark mass of curls, she flopped back onto the sheets. What would Seth think about the way she had spoken?

More important, what did God think? Dinah tossed from side to side, rumpling the sheets into a tangled mass. She should have told Seth to cancel Saturday's outing. Maybe she ought to just give in and quit. How could God possibly use anyone who had so many character flaws?

Dinah moaned and wrapped her pillow around her head. Maybe things would look brighter in the morning.

CHAPTER 15

"I bet I can beat you to the other end of the bridge. One, two, three, go!"

"My rock can make a bigger splash. Watch!"

"Hey, Miss Mayhew, watch how long I can balance on the railing."

"Not the railing, Cleo. Get down from there immediately." A quick check told Dinah the other girls were in no danger to life or limb at the moment, so she let Tilda and Frances race from one end of the bridge to the other and watched Jenny and Anastasia drop their pebbles into the lagoon. She slumped back against the bench at the foot of the Mines and Mining Building, grateful for the clouds that blocked most of the afternoon sun.

"You look like you've had a rough day."

Dinah looked up into the smiling face of the dark-haired guard she had met on her first day at work and managed a weak smile in return. "Running all over the fairgrounds as part of my job is one thing; keeping track of nine little girls is a whole different matter."

The guard looked back at the girls on the bridge. "How did you wind up in charge?"

"Believe it or not, I volunteered for this." Dinah couldn't help laughing at his look of astonishment. "At the moment, I'm not sure what possessed me to do it, but I did."

She waved to Tilda, now down at the far end. "Don't go out onto the island. We need to stay together; Pastor Howell will be here soon."

The girls raced toward them at the sight of her talking to the guard. "Who are you?" Rosemary asked.

"I like your uniform," Cleo told him.

Anastasia edged closer to Dinah. "He's really good-looking, isn't he? Is he your beau?" She dropped her voice to a whisper. "Does Pastor Howell know about him?"

Dinah felt her cheeks flame. "Really, girls!"

The guard inclined his head. Dinah could see the corners of his mustache twitching. "I'm pleased to make your acquaintance, ladies," he said. "My name is Stephen Bridger, and I am one of the Columbian Guards. I'm here to make sure everyone stays safe and happy at the fair. Are you enjoying yourselves?"

The girls erupted into a mass of giggles and scampered back toward the bridge.

Dinah could still feel the heat flooding her cheeks. "I'm sorry."

Stephen Bridger stared after them. "Don't be. That kind of innocence is refreshing." His expression clouded.

"Is something wrong?" Dinah asked. "You seem troubled."

His brow furrowed. "There are reports of girls going missing around Chicago. We've been told to be especially watchful to make sure nothing of the kind happens here on the fairgrounds." His face grew stern. "I intend to do everything in my power to prevent it."

Dinah got to her feet and did a quick head count, as if the girls might disappear right from under her nose. "What is happening to these girls—do you know?"

"It's hard to say. So many young women have come to the city looking for jobs or a new start."

Like me. Dinah shuddered.

"Some of them have probably been so caught up in all the newness in their lives that they've simply neglected to stay in contact with their families. Maybe they've changed lodging houses and aren't really missing at all; they just aren't where their families can locate them, and letters from home are being returned."

"But is that what's happening here?" Dinah felt a chill as if a cloud had moved across the sun.

Stephen Bridger looked somber and shook his head slowly. "Not all the missing girls are from out of town. Some may have wanted to cut ties with their families and dropped out of sight deliberately.

"But some. . ." He paused. "Some of them just seem to have vanished, and nobody has any idea where they are."

Martha's image popped into Dinah's mind. Which category did she fall into? Dinah devoutly hoped the girl's absence was due to her own choice, however misguided that might be.

Fear clutched at Dinah's throat. "I'd better collect my girls, then. I had no idea they could be in such danger."

The guard's face softened. "I didn't mean to frighten you. The girls in your group are younger than the ones who have gone missing. Most of those have been in their late teens or a bit older."

Dinah felt a flicker of hope. Martha was only fifteen. Did that mean she was still safe? *Please watch over her wherever she is.*

Bridger's eyes filled with a warm light. "And it looks like someone is coming along to give you a hand with watching over your young charges."

Dinah turned to see Seth approaching from the direction of the Transportation Building. He smiled at them both. "Are you two just visiting, or did you have to call out the guards?"

Dinah smiled, feeling her tension melt away. "The girls have been fine. Rambunctious, but fine. You might have brought along one of your rolling chairs, though. I feel like I might need it before we get them all home again."

Seth's eyes widened in mock surprise. "Are you saying you've had a busy day?"

Dinah ticked off their itinerary on her fingers. "We visited the Palace of Fine Arts; toured the models of the Niña, the Pinta, and the Santa María; explored the state buildings at the north end of the grounds; and spent a couple of hours in the Fisheries Pavilion. I drew the line at letting them try to catch the fish in the tanks, though. Rosemary and Anastasia were not pleased."

Seth threw back his head and laughed. "I herded a group of my boys through here last month. I understand exactly how you feel. Let's round them up and get them home, shall we?"

With the girls safely delivered to their families, Dinah thought to relax and enjoy the walk with Seth. Instead, her eyes darted back and forth, searching out the shadows for any possible threat.

She had almost come to grief twice in this neighborhood, and both times the danger had been warded off by this unusual blend of man of God and man of action. How many similar altercations had he experienced during his years of living in this area? Yet while she jumped at every shadow, he strode along with confidence. Watchful, yes, but showing none of the fears that beset Dinah.

He knew this place, was a part of it, while she. . .

Try as she might, she would never belong to this setting he fit into so effortlessly. She came from a different world, and nothing she could do would change that. Sorrow wrenched at her heart, and Dinah couldn't be certain whether it was due to compassion for the people of the area or the fact that Seth felt at home in a place where she could not.

Gladys's taunting comment sprang unbidden to her mind. "May I ask you something?" At his nod, she continued, "Why is it you feel the need to serve the Lord in these surroundings? You have such a way with people, such a heart for reaching out to them. Do you ever feel you're wasting your time on those who can't appreciate your abilities?" She held her breath, wondering if she'd been too bold.

"I guess the best answer I can give you comes from something Jesus once said to the Pharisees: It's people who are sick who need a physician, not those who are healthy." Seth's firm tone carried conviction. "The people here need God desperately, but they aren't willing to listen to someone different than themselves. Jesus understood that when He chose to come to earth and become one of us."

172

Dinah nodded. "I think I understand. You're saying it takes someone they can trust to reach the people here. And they don't trust outsiders readily." She gave him a wry grin. "I've learned that the hard way."

Seth grinned at her quip. "That's right. God put me in this place as a youngster and let me grow up here so I would be able to understand what they face from one day to the next. I understand the way of life here, and they know that."

"I see." Dinah's words came out on a sigh. If a person could only reach people from the same kind of background, what did that mean for her? She had no real home now. Would she ever find a place where she could belong?

Once again, she felt like someone on the outside looking in.

"Have you had enough?" Seth bounced back on his toes and waited to see if Mac would be ready to call it quits for the day or throw another jab.

"Yeah, that's probably plenty for today." Lowering his hands, Mac reached for a towel and slung it around his shoulders. "I don't want to overdo it and lose my edge."

Seth followed him across the gym and propped his foot up on the bench against the wall. He lowered his voice so he couldn't be overheard by the others in the noisy, echoing room. "So what did you decide? Are you going to take a fall or give it all you've got and try to win the fight fair and square?"

Mac tossed the towel to one side and looked away. "I may not have to worry about that if the champ is as good as they say."

"That really isn't an answer, is it?"

Mac shrugged. "It's the only one I have right now."

"Maybe you're trying to fight this battle on your own. If you'd let God help, He'd give you the strength to do the right thing."

A crooked grin spread across Mac's face. "If I wanted to hear you preach, I'd go listen to you at one of your meetings. You're the best sparring partner around, but I'm not interested in any of your sermons."

An uppercut to his solar plexus couldn't have knocked the wind out of Seth any more than the blunt statement. "Come on, Mac, you've been my friend for years."

"Let's keep it that way, shall we? Keep me on my toes in the ring, but save the preaching for church." Mac sketched a wave and headed for the door. "I'll see you later."

Seth stood rooted to the spot for a moment, then slammed his fist into a nearby punching bag. The shock that ran up his arm felt good. He hit it again, first with one fist then the other, building up a steady rhythm.

"Hey, Preach, you must have some real bad thoughts inside you to punish that bag like that."

Seth put out his hand to catch the bag and turned to see one of the gym's regulars standing nearby. "Just needed to work off a little steam, that's all."

The other man smirked. "More than a little, I'd say. You looked like you were trying to beat up on the devil, the way you were going at it." He turned toward a set of barbells, then called back over his shoulder, "Just don't chase him clear off. He helps me have a good time."

Seth watched the other man work with the weights, trying to come up with a response and finding none. He threw one last punch at the bag and headed for the door.

When he came from the gym, he usually felt invigorated by the workout and the contact with the people there. Today felt like a big waste of time. Spending hours at the gym didn't go along with the typical routine of most men in the ministry, but he'd always looked at it as a way to develop relationships and win the trust of the men he wanted to reach.

Had he been kidding himself all along? Judging from the responses he'd gotten this afternoon, he would be hard pressed to say otherwise.

He trudged along the dingy street in as sour a mood as he could remember. Dinah's question reared its head and taunted him. Why did he stay on where he wasn't appreciated?

His glib answer about the sick needing a physician might carry a suitably spiritual tone, but if he were going to be honest, he had to admit he'd been struggling with that very issue long before Dinah brought it up.

What would it be like to serve the Lord in a bigger church, one with a salary that would provide for him—and a family someday—instead of his present hand-to-mouth existence?

He had been given the opportunity to receive some of the best Bible training available. He could easily have taken a pulpit in some pleasant church with people eager to receive his counsel. Instead, he had returned to his roots, hoping to help others as he had been helped.

What was the point? Was he wasting his life trying to share God's love with people who only cared about getting by from day to day, with no concern for the eternal?

Maybe this isn't where I'm supposed to be, after all. He picked up a stick and flung it as hard as he could, watching it spiral away, spinning as wildly as his thoughts. *Lord, You know I'm willing to go wherever You want me to. It doesn't matter where as long as I'm certain I'm in the right place.*

But I've got to know, Father. I've got to know.

Dinah lifted her head at the rap on her door. "Come in," she called.

Mrs. Purvis poked her head into the room. "Your cousin asked me to tell you she'd like to see you downstairs."

"Gladys?" Dinah laid her Bible on the desk beside her notes for the next class meeting. "She shouldn't have sent you to get me. Why didn't she come up here if she wanted to talk?"

Mrs. Purvis looked heavenward. "I've given up on trying to understand that one. I'll tell you one thing, I'd never have believed the two of you were related if you hadn't told me yourself."

Dinah smiled at the backhanded compliment and hurried down the stairs, ready to give her cousin a piece of her mind. "Gladys, what on earth—"

"I'd like you to meet someone." Gladys gestured toward a man who stepped out from the shadow of the hall tree. "Dinah, this is Alan Saunders. Alan, my cousin, Dinah Mayhew."

The man smiled and bowed. "I'm pleased to meet you, Miss Mayhew."

Speechless, Dinah could only hold out her hand in an automatic response. She took in his appearance, trying not to gape at the blond hair, neat mustache, even, white teeth, and sky blue eyes. This was Gladys's beau? Amazing. He was every bit as good-looking as her cousin claimed.

Gladys moved beside him and took his arm in a manner Dinah could only describe as proprietary. Dinah studied the handsome, well-dressed man who stood next to her blocky cousin in her ill-fitting waist and tried to imagine what he saw in Gladys.

"Well, this is a surprise."

"Isn't he just as wonderful as I described him?" Gladys practically purred while she reached up to adjust Alan's necktie. Dinah waited for him to frown and edge away, but he smiled down at Gladys, giving every evidence of being equally smitten.

She struggled for something to say. "My cousin told me a bit about the way you met, but I don't know anything else about you. What do you do for a living?"

Bright red spots formed high on Gladys's cheeks. "Dinah, really!"

"No, no," Alan soothed. "She's your relative. Of course she's concerned for your welfare, as am I." He put his arm around Gladys and drew her close, then turned his attention back to Dinah. "I came into a modest inheritance. Nothing lavish, but enough that I don't have to work full-time. I do dabble in several business interests, though. Commodities, that sort of thing." He smiled down at Gladys. "Enough to keep me busy and out of trouble."

Gladys gazed back at him with a look of pure adoration. "He knows everything about business. I love listening to him talk."

Alan glanced out the front window. "Our carriage is waiting."

Dinah blinked. "Carriage?"

"Alan is going to take me out driving. He wants me to see where he lives."

Dinah raised her eyebrows. "You're going to his home?"

Alan smiled. "Don't worry. We're only driving past there. I want Gladys to see the house, but I wouldn't think of us going inside without a chaperone or doing anything else that might put a blot on her reputation."

Gladys giggled. "I told you he was wonderful."

"I think the evening may turn cool," Alan cautioned. "Perhaps you should take a wrap."

Gladys laid her head against his shoulder for a moment, then hurried toward the stairs. "I'll only take a moment."

Dinah laced her fingers together. "Have you lived in Chicago long, Mr. Saunders?"

"Won't you call me Alan? Gladys has told me so much about you, I feel as though we're old friends already." His gaze sharpened, and he closed the gap between them. "You have something at the corner of your eye. Let me get it for you."

Before Dinah could protest, he cupped her chin in one hand and ran his forefinger across her upper lid. "There, that took care of it." He slid his fingers from her chin with a slow, lingering touch.

Gladys reappeared, carrying her shawl over her arm. "I'm ready."

"Then let's be on our way, milady. Your carriage awaits." Alan ushered Gladys out the door and turned back to Dinah. "It was a pleasure to meet you."

Dinah stood like one of the statues that dotted the fair-grounds. When the rattling of the carriage wheels faded into the distance, she raised her hand to her chin. Had there really been something in her eye, or was that only an excuse for Alan to touch her?

The prospect seemed ludicrous, and it had all been over so quickly. Had she imagined that near caress?

She rubbed at her chin, wanting to rid herself of the sensation of his fingers trailing across her skin. Whether or not he had seen something, he had no right to touch her in so intimate a way.

As soon as Gladys gets home, I'll tell her that her beau is not the gentleman he appears to be.

And then what? She could only imagine the scorn with which the accusation would be met and the comments about Dinah's supposed jealousy.

She shivered. There was no point in telling Gladys; she would never believe it.

Was it my fault? Should I have stopped him? No, there had been no time. The whole incident was over almost before she knew what was happening.

Dinah ran upstairs to fill her washbasin and scrub her face, needing to erase the memory of his touch. While she splashed the water on her cheeks, she told herself it couldn't have been as sordid as she made it out to be. Surely she was making a mountain out of a molehill.

But everything within her said that wasn't so.

CHAPTER 16

Willaim Buchanan scanned the message Dinah handed him. "Thank you, Miss Mayhew. If you'll give me about fifteen minutes, I'll put the information together and have it ready for you to take back to Mr. Thorndyke."

Dinah nodded and stepped out of the Agriculture superintendent's office. Fifteen minutes. Not long enough to go back to the Administration Building, but just about enough time to pay a visit to the Minnesota Threshing exhibit. She made her way down the stairs and past the fairgoers lined up to gawk at a model of the Liberty Bell made entirely of oranges.

There hadn't been any contact with her father since the evening he told her of his plan to win Abby's trust. She halfway expected another missive to arrive any day, but she hadn't heard a thing. At first it came as a relief. Now she wondered if she'd been too harsh with him. While his request came as a shock, she didn't want to do anything to sever this new connection between them.

She could just walk by and observe the booth from a distance, then decide whether she wanted to make an approach. If her father was serious about Abby—her mind still had trouble accepting the idea—she needed to know. And what place, if any, she would have in the new arrangement.

Drawing up across the aisle, she found her plans to watch without being seen thwarted when Abby looked her way, then nudged Dinah's father. He turned, smiling, and waved her over.

He gave her a quick hug when she reached him, his smile lighting up his whole face. "How's my girl today?"

At least he seemed happy to see her. "Fine. I'm here on an errand. I had a few minutes to spare, so I thought I'd drop by."

"Wonderful! Things are a little slow at the moment, so it gives us all a chance to get better acquainted. I was just talking to Abby about you."

"Oh?" Dinah glanced at Abby. The other woman wore a tiny smile, but a guarded expression shadowed her face.

"I was telling her how hard it was for us to be apart. Even knowing you had the money and all those letters I sent didn't do much to ease my pain."

"Letters?" Dinah echoed. "I only received two or three in the whole time since you left."

"Why, I sent you one at least every month." Her father paused, and his face took on a stern look. "What about the money? You did get that, didn't you?"

Dinah shook her head slowly. "This is the first I've heard—"

"I can't believe they kept that from you." His brows drew together and his cheeks puffed out. "It's hard to imagine that of Dora and Everett, but you can be sure I'll have some things to say to them next time we meet."

He placed his hands on her shoulders. "I'm sorry, honey. If I'd only known. . ." His voice grew husky. "Let's bring up some brighter memories, shall we? Why don't you tell Abby about the times we did spend together when you were little."

"Yes." Abby stepped forward. "I'd like to hear about that. Can you tell me some of the things you remember?"

A series of memories ran through Dinah's mind, like a mental photograph album with one person's image notably absent. Aware of her father's rising impatience, she took a moment to sort through her recollections and chose her words carefully. "I remember how happy I was whenever Papa came home. It was almost like Christmas to have him there."

Scenes from the past appeared with startling clarity, and her voice took on a faraway note. "I'd watch through our front window until he came in sight on his way from the station. As soon as I saw him, I'd throw open the door and run like the wind to meet him, and he'd sweep me up in his arms."

She blinked back tears and looked up at her father. "Do you remember?"

He wiped the corner of his eye. "Those are some of my favorite memories."

Abby gazed at Dinah thoughtfully. "May I ask you something? If you enjoyed your time with your father so much, why did you choose to live with your aunt and uncle after your mother died?"

Dinah jerked back as if she'd been slapped. "What makes you think—"

Her father's arm encircled her shoulders. "It wasn't an easy decision for either of us. But out there on the farm, she had plenty of room to run and frolic instead of being shut up in a train car or a stuffy hotel room. And of course, she had her little cousin to play with, as well. I really don't blame her for preferring that to life on the road."

A trembling started in Dinah's limbs and worked its way through her whole body. "Papa, I—"

"Look, Abby, we have a customer." He dropped a quick kiss on Dinah's forehead. "I'm so glad you stopped by. We'll get together again, just the three of us. Or maybe it's time you met little Hannah. I know you two are going to get along famously."

"But—" Too late. Her father had already jumped into a conversation with two men looking over their award-winning thresher.

Somehow she managed to retrieve the report from Mr. Buchanan and make her way outside the building. She tottered along on wooden legs, feeling as if she had stepped through the looking glass in Lewis Carroll's famous story and landed in a world where everything she knew had been turned topsy-turvy.

Holding her emotions in check by sheer will, she passed by the columns that fronted the Agriculture Building, grateful for the shade provided by the building's heavy overhang. If she could just make her shaky legs carry her back to the office and deliver the report, she would tell Mrs. Johnson she didn't feel well and ask for the rest of the day off.

Moving mechanically, she crossed the bridge over the South Canal and angled past the bandstand, her thoughts back on what her father had said. The couple in front of her stopped abruptly, and Dinah plowed straight into them.

"Oh, I'm so sorry!"

The gray-haired man turned and tipped his hat. "My fault entirely, I'm afraid. I shouldn't have pulled up short like that, but

183

my attention was caught by. . ." He gestured toward the Columbian Fountain. "Disgraceful, simply disgraceful." He bowed to Dinah and led his wife away, shaking his head.

Disgraceful? Dinah had always admired the beauty of the fountain and its elaborate sculpture. She walked toward it to see what the man could possibly have found so objectionable.

Slender columns of water rose into the air in delicate arcs, surrounding the stone representation of a graceful ship in the same way it had done every day since she came to work at the fair. But over to the left. . .

Dinah drew up short and gasped.

On the far side of the fountain, a man and woman stood in a close embrace. Copper-colored ringlets spilled down the woman's back as she tilted her head to accept her companion's kiss. Dinah stared, appalled, yet unable to tear her gaze away from the public display.

The man tightened his hold on the woman, then released her and looked around as if suddenly aware of their surroundings. The woman laid her hand along his cheek, and the two of them laughed and strolled off toward the Manufactures Building.

Recognition of the man's butter-colored hair and trim mustache crashed over Dinah like a wave. There was no possibility of misreading the situation this time. Alan Saunders had been kissing a woman right out in public.

And that woman most definitely had not been Gladys.

Dinah crossed the entry hall, hoping she wouldn't intrude on Mrs. Purvis's supper preparations if she slipped into the kitchen to make herself a pot of tea. After the series of shock she had weathered that afternoon, she needed something soothing to settle her nerves.

A grating voice drifted out the doorway, and Dinah realized Gladys had Mrs. Purvis cornered in the parlor. She pivoted and tiptoed toward the stairs, hoping she could reach them unnoticed and avoid her cousin until suppertime.

"Dinah, is that you?"

Too late. She dragged herself into the parlor. What a shame she didn't have a meeting with her girls until tomorrow night. She was anxious to see how the trip to the fair affected their attitudes, and it would make a wonderful excuse not to have to spend the evening with Gladys.

Not only that, but she needed to talk to Seth. Perhaps he could help her make sense of the muddle her world had become.

Gladys cleared her throat. "I was just telling Mrs. Purvis what happened at work today."

"Yes, and a very interesting story it was. But now I need to get back to the kitchen. That pork roast will be ready to come out of the oven any minute." With an apologetic look at Dinah, the landlady scuttled out of the room.

Dinah bowed to the inevitable and sank into an armchair, wishing even more for that pot of tea. "Have you had a difficult day?"

"Hardly. As a matter of fact, I did quite well for myself. The head salesclerk told me to restock some shelves in the back. I informed her that wasn't my job, and I wasn't about to ruin my clothes, handling all those dusty boxes. That's what the stock boy is for."

Dinah's eyes widened. "What happened?"

Gladys's lips curved in a feline smile. "She backed down and called the stock boy after all. Everybody on the floor saw what happened. If she doesn't watch out, I'll be promoted and wind up taking over her position."

Dinah pressed her hand against her forehead. "No, if *you* don't watch out, you'll get yourself fired, behaving that way. Have you ever considered that?"

Gladys toyed with the edge of the crocheted antimacassar on the arm of the settee. "Actually, that doesn't concern me at all. If I lose that job, it won't be the end of the world."

"What are you talking about? There's a recession going on, in case you haven't heard. Do you know how hard it will be to find another position without a reference?"

A faint smile played across Gladys's face. "Maybe I'm not worried about finding another job."

Hope raised its head. "You mean you're planning to go back home?"

"Of course not." Gladys dismissed the notion with a wave of her hand. "I just meant that Alan has an income sufficient to support us both. And he's a genius when it comes to financial matters. Once we add my inheritance to his and he can start investing it, we'll be set for life."

"Alan? What does he have to do with this?"

Gladys gave her a pitying look. "Haven't you seen the way he looks at me? He hasn't actually proposed yet, but he's certainly dropped enough hints. We're practically engaged."

Dinah gasped. "But you hardly know him!"

A dreamy look spread over Gladys's square features. "Our hearts connected the first time we met. I feel like I've known him all my life."

186

Dinah snorted. "Enough to know the kind of husband he'd make? I hardly think so."

Gladys's eyes glittered. "What would you know about the kind of man Alan is?"

"More than I want to." Dinah felt a surge of compassion, knowing she was about to shatter her cousin's dreams. She scooted forward on the edge of her seat, wishing she could soften the blow. "I didn't want to tell you this, but your Alan isn't the wonderful man you believe him to be. Just this afternoon, I saw him on the fairgrounds." Her cheeks warmed again at the memory.

"He was kissing another woman, right in full view of everyone there. And it wasn't a friendly peck on the cheek, either. Quite frankly, I was embarrassed even to have seen it."

Gladys's nails bit into the damask cushion. "It must have been someone who looks like him. Alan would never do such a thing."

"Wouldn't he? He came near to taking liberties with me the day we met, while you were upstairs getting your wrap. I hate to be the one to break it to you—"

Gladys jumped to her feet and loomed over Dinah. "You aren't sorry at all. I know exactly what you're up to. You can't stand the thought of me finding such happiness, and you're bent on destroying my future." She jabbed a blunt finger at Dinah's nose. "Well, don't think it's going to work. I'm not about to let your jealousy come between me and the man I love."

"Please, Gladys, I'm only trying to help."

"Help?" Gladys's face contorted, and her voice went up half an octave. "You have no interest in helping anybody but yourself, Dinah Mayhew. Go play at teaching those street urchins if you

187

want to pretend you're out to do good." She whirled to exit the room, then pulled up short in the doorway. "But heaven help them if they follow any example you set for them. That so-called Christianity of yours is nothing but a sham!"

CHAPTER 17

Light flickered from the small lantern and sent shadows in a wild dance across the basement walls. He set the tray of food on the rough wooden table and placed the lantern beside it.

Drawing a key from his pocket, he inserted it into the lock on the only occupied cubicle and edged the door open. The girl inside lay listless on her cot, just as he hoped. He retrieved the tray, set it just inside the door, and nudged it across the floor with his foot. She could reach it from where she lay when she got hungry enough.

He stood quietly, watching the rise and fall of her chest. He had jumped the gun with this one; he might as well admit it. At the time, he thought it would put him one step ahead. Simple enough to keep her there a bit longer than usual until McGinty gave the word to start collecting again. He hadn't reckoned on her fighting spirit and having to use a higher dose of the laudanum for a prolonged period.

Satisfied with her current state, he stepped out of the tiny room and locked the door behind him. If luck favored him, he would be able to keep her in acceptable condition until he heard from McGinty again. If not. . .

He looked over at the unfinished part of the basement. Its dirt floor had already solved more than one problem for him. If need be, it could hide yet another secret. As any businessman knew, investments didn't always pay off as planned. While this one looked promising at the beginning, it might be better to eliminate the liability, cut his losses, and move on.

Picking up the lantern, he made his way up the stairs and swung the bookcase back in place. Thank goodness he knew better than to put all his eggs in one basket. Having a range of investments, that was the key to success in business. And if his new venture continued as well as he expected, he wouldn't have to depend so much on McGinty. In fact, he might be able to drop that little enterprise altogether before too much longer.

The game would still go on, but in a slightly different form. And with much more to gain.

CHAPTER 18

S o you're saying your father out and out lied to this woman with you standing right there?"

Dinah matched her steps to Seth's as they turned the corner onto Blackstone Avenue, wishing she could find a way to pull herself out of her gloomy mood. Nothing this week had turned out as she'd hoped. After the wild success of their visit to the fair, only four girls showed up at tonight's meeting. Concern over their lack of interest continued to weigh her down. Coupled with her confusion about her father, it all added up to more than she felt she could cope with.

"Maybe it wasn't a lie, but his version certainly didn't line up with the memories I have. And when he talked about sending me money and all those letters, I didn't know what to think."

"What are your aunt and uncle like? Could they have kept the money for themselves, as he implied?"

Dinah shook her head. "I never would have considered such

a thing until he brought it up. I know the only picture you have of them is through meeting Gladys. . . ."

Seth chuckled. "That does tend to color my thinking a bit."

"But they're nothing like her. They do have a blind spot where she's concerned, as if she can do no wrong, but I honestly can't imagine them defrauding me like that."

"In that case, would your father be capable of making the whole thing up?"

"That's why I'm so confused." Dinah breathed out a tired sigh. "I never would have expected it, but after listening to him go on letting Abby think I was the one who made the choice to stay with Aunt Dora and Uncle Everett, I—I just don't know." Thoughts of the incident with the waiter at the Café de Marine drifted into her mind. "Maybe he's not the person I always thought he was."

Seth stopped between the pools of light cast by the street lamps. "And if he isn't, whose fault is that?" He cupped her shoulders in his hands. "It isn't yours, Dinah. Don't try to take that upon yourself."

"But he's my father. He's the whole reason I came to Chicago." She resisted the urge to reach out and cling to Seth's jacket. "Now I don't even know if I have a place to go when the fair ends."

Seth's hand brushed against her cheek. His thumb found a tear and wiped it away. "Your earthly father may not be all that you dreamed of, but your heavenly Father is in charge, and He loves you very much."

Dinah laced her fingers together and clamped her hands tight to keep them under control. "Thank you. You're a good friend." How she wished he could be more! With Seth, she felt warm and protected, secure in a way she had never known before. Did that have anything to do with his feelings for her or merely reflect the loving compassion of the God he served?

She let him take her arm and guide her back into the light, wishing she could read his heart and find the answer.

The door flew open before they mounted the steps. Mrs. Purvis burst onto the front porch, hands fluttering and gray curls askew.

"Thank goodness you're home. I hope I did the right thing."

Dinah gripped Seth's arm and held it tight. "What's wrong? Did the right thing about what?"

Mrs. Purvis moaned and wrung her hands. "She's gone."

Dinah felt the world spinning madly out of control. "Who's gone?"

"That cousin of yours—Gladys. Two men brought a note she signed and came to take her belongings away. I didn't like turning her things over to total strangers, but I didn't know what else to do, seeing as how they had her signature."

Dinah could see splotches of dried tears on the landlady's face. She hurried up the steps and put her arms around Mrs. Purvis. "I'm sure you didn't do anything wrong. What did the note say?"

Mrs. Purvis dug in her apron pocket and produced a crumpled sheet of paper. "Here you are. I've been reading it over and over and hoping I haven't made a terrible mistake."

Dinah took the proffered note and read:

Dear Mrs. Purvis,

I find I can no longer stay under the same roof as my cousin. Please see that my things are packed and turn them over to the men bearing this message. They will deliver them to me. Enclosed, please find the funds to pay for my lodging to date.

Yours truly,
Gladys Turner

Seth came up beside them and looked over her shoulder. "It's her signature?"

Dinah nodded and squeezed Mrs. Purvis. "I recognize her handwriting. I don't see that you had any other choice."

"That doesn't make sense." Seth's brow furrowed. "She just up and left?"

A heaviness settled in Dinah's chest. "Apparently. And it seems I'm the cause." She hugged Mrs. Purvis again. "I'm sorry you've been so distressed, and I hate your losing income from her room."

Mrs. Purvis waved her hand. "That's the least of my concerns. I'm just happy to know you approve."

Taking a deep breath, she resumed her normal cheery demeanor. "Now that we have that settled, why don't you both come in out of the night air?"

Dinah hung her hat and reticule on the hall tree, her irritation mounting. Her heart ached for what Mrs. Purvis had been through. How like Gladys, taking off like that without so much as a by-your-leave. And that spiteful note! Its implied accusation still stung. Out of habit, she cast a furtive glance toward the stairs when she crossed the entry hall, then reminded

194

herself she didn't have to avoid Gladys anymore now that she was gone.

Gone. The realization finally sank in. Gladys was well and truly out of the picture. No more confrontations, no more malicious jibes. Dinah's step grew lighter, and she smiled up at Seth. She was free again.

Mrs. Purvis led the way to the parlor. "I hope you'll pardon me for saying so, but I'm none too sorry to see her leave. That sounds hateful, seeing as how she's your cousin and all, but I've seldom met anyone who carried such a cloud of ill feeling around with them." She slid a sidelong glance at Dinah as if fearing she had said too much.

Dinah patted her hand. "If you want to know the truth, I feel exactly the same way. I spent ten years under the same roof as Gladys, and one of the happiest moments of my life was the day I climbed on the train to Chicago and knew I'd left her behind forever. I never dreamed she'd turn up like that."

"In that case, let's pray it doesn't happen again." Mrs. Purvis clapped her hand to her mouth and looked at Seth. "If you don't think that kind of prayer will offend the Almighty."

The tension ebbed from Seth's shoulders at this lighter turn in the conversation. "Prayer is just talking to God, and He already knows what's in your heart. Go ahead and tell Him all about it, and then let Him choose how to work things out for the best."

Soft creases formed in Mrs. Purvis's cheeks when she smiled. "You're absolutely right. I've always found Him to be very good at—would you mind stepping over a bit?"

195

Seth scooted to one side. "Of course. Was I standing on something I shouldn't?"

"No, no." Mrs. Purvis walked over to study the floorboard where his foot had rested. "Does that look the tiniest bit out of alignment to you?"

"I'm not really sure." Seth watched Mrs. Purvis place the toe of her shoe onto the board in question, then bounce gently up and down.

He looked at Dinah, who appeared as mystified as he felt. "Are you all right?"

Mrs. Purvis quit her bouncing, gave the board a sharp rap with her heel, then shook her head and sighed. "No, I guess not."

"You aren't all right?"

"No, I mean it isn't there."

Between Dinah's look of consternation and the landlady's peculiar behavior, Seth found himself hard pressed not to smile. "Were you looking for something in particular?"

Mrs. Purvis planted her hands on her hips and glared at the floor. "My husband's hiding place."

Seth felt increasingly out of his depth. "Your husband is hiding?"

"No, no. Randolph's been gone to glory these past ten years. I mean the hiding place he left, here in this house."

"All right. What did Randolph hide?"

Mrs. Purvis raised her hands in a show of exasperation. "I won't know that until I find it, will I?"

Seth nodded. "I see."

Dinah stepped forward and rested her hand on the landlady's arm. "Would you like me to make a nice pot of tea?"

"Why don't we all go back to the kitchen and I'll put the

196

kettle on?" Mrs. Purvis suggested. "Something about puttering around in there calms my nerves. After the wreck I've been today, I could use something to relax me."

With the kettle filled and on the burner, they gathered around the kitchen table.

"You were telling us about your husband and a hiding place," Seth prompted.

Mrs. Purvis propped her chin on her hands. "We'd lost two homes to fire, you see. One of them nearly burned down around our ears. Randolph was determined we would never face a complete loss like that again. When he built this house, he told me he and the architect had come up with a plan to keep that from happening. I don't know what he had in mind, but he said we would have a safe place to go in case we ever got caught in another fire. And he told me he'd found a way to be sure I would always be provided for should something happen to him."

She stared off into the distance. "But he died before he could tell me where this place was. . .or what he hid in it. I've been looking for it ever since."

"Couldn't you go back to the architect? Surely he would tell you."

"He might if he was still around, but he left town before Randolph died. I don't know how to reach him, and I don't have a set of the plans." She spread her hands wide. "So I've been on my own personal treasure hunt for the past decade."

Dinah's brow crinkled. "So long? That must be very discouraging."

Steam puffed from the kettle's spout, and Mrs. Purvis got up to pour the tea. "After all this time, it's become a habit. I've been at it so long, I'd hardly know what to do if I found it."

She loaded the tea cups onto a tray and carried it to the table. "What would I do with my time then?"

Seth accepted the cup she offered him. "Are you're sure it's here, inside the house?"

Mrs. Purvis stirred a lump of sugar into her tea. "That's what Randolph told me. I guess I've tapped and stomped on every inch of this place several times over, but I haven't found a thing."

Seth took a long sip and considered the size of the house. Like others in that neighborhood, it extended much farther back than first appearances would lead one to expect. It would take quite a bit of tapping and stomping to cover it all.

He chuckled. "It's a little like the Christian life—we know we have it, we just haven't discovered all its benefits yet. But that doesn't mean we give up on learning what they are."

A smile lit Mrs. Purvis's face. "Oh, I'll keep looking until I find it, but thanks for the encouragement." She got up from the table and picked up a clean dishcloth. "Now I'd better put things to rights before I go to bed."

"And it's time I took my leave. I have an appointment with Reverend Hall in the morning." Seth rose and carried his empty cup to the counter. "Thank you for the tea and the conversation. I'll be praying for your search to be successful."

Dinah walked him to the front door. In the quiet of the entry hall, Seth studied her face. "Are you going to be all right?"

She nodded. "I think so. Finding out what Gladys did and listening to Mrs. Purvis's story helped me remember that other people have problems, too. Mine don't seem quite so big anymore."

"At least Gladys is a distant problem now. That's one less

thing for you to worry about."

"That's right. I think I'll go upstairs and write a letter to my aunt. I've been putting that off far too long."

"Are you going to tell her about her daughter's grand exit?"

An impish grin lit Dinah's face. "No, I think I'll let Gladys do that herself." She stood on tiptoe and brushed her lips against his cheek.

Seth stared at her. "What was that for? Not that I'm complaining, mind you." He loved the way her cheeks pinked at his comment.

"It's for helping me see that things aren't as dark as I thought and for being so sweet to Mrs. Purvis. She really is a dear, you know."

"She isn't the only one." He meant to say the words under his breath, but her reddening cheeks told him she'd heard them. The spot where Dinah's lips had touched his face still tingled. If being kind to Mrs. Purvis meant getting this kind of treatment, he'd have to start bringing the woman flowers at every visit.

He lifted his hat from the hall tree and turned it in his hands. "I guess I'd better go now." *Before I do something I'll regret.*

Dinah stepped back without taking her gaze from him, as if she, too, was unwilling to break the connection between them. "Good night, then."

Seth nodded and let himself out. Touching his cheek, he broke into a whistle and jogged down the steps.

CHAPTER 19

Dinah rested her sheaf of papers atop the railing that edged the veranda of the Woman's Building and watched an electric launch glide by on the lagoon. Its waters looked cool and inviting, a decided contrast to the muggy morning.

She had already visited the Palace of Fine Arts and the Woman's Building as part of her morning rounds. She still had stops to make at Horticulture and Transportation. But surely a few moments under the sheltered archway wouldn't hurt. Dinah drew her handkerchief from her sleeve and dabbed at her throat and forehead.

On the terrace below, a group of youngsters sped by, squealing and laughing. The sight brought a pang when she recalled the day she spent touring the grounds with her girls. So much for her grand idea to bind them together as a group and convince them of her goodwill. All the girls seemed to enjoy their outing well enough, but apparently their enthusiasm only lasted until the day ended.

Class attendance continued to dwindle; at the last meeting she had only Jenny and Cleo. At any moment, Dinah expected Seth to tell her he planned to suspend further class meetings until he could find someone more suitable to carry on.

A light breeze wafted from the lake. Dinah lifted her head to take advantage of every moment of sweet coolness it had to offer.

Except for her success at her job, her whole stay in Chicago had turned into a dismal failure. The fiasco with Gladys was proof enough of that. And instead of bringing relief, Gladys's sudden absence had only added one more headache. Dinah's plan to let her cousin tell her parents about their parting of the ways hadn't worked out as she hoped. Aunt Dora had written several days ago, wondering why she hadn't heard from Gladys.

Forced to break down and let her aunt know about their row and Gladys's subsequent departure, she admitted she had no forwarding address nor any idea of Gladys's current whereabouts.

Yesterday's mail brought another letter, this one sounding rather frantic. They still hadn't heard from Gladys, Aunt Dora wrote. She begged Dinah to try to come up with some ideas as to where their daughter might be. "Perhaps you could go to Marshall Field's and talk to her there—or at least leave a message telling her to write."

Braced for another confrontation, Dinah had made a quick trip downtown last evening, only to find that Gladys's supervisor had no idea of her whereabouts and had terminated her for not reporting to work since the day of their argument.

If she had her way, Dinah would just as soon take the whole mess and chuck it into the depths of the lagoon. How was she going to tell Aunt Dora and Uncle Everett about Gladys's latest irresponsible act? *That's just like her to put the burden for cleaning up her mess on my shoulders.*

A clock chimed in the distance, reminding her that Mr. Samuels awaited her in Horticulture. She made her way down the wide staircase to the terrace level, wishing she could talk it all over with Seth. He had a way of being able to sort things out and help her see them in a new, clearer light.

Face it, I'd want to see Seth even if I didn't have a worry in the world. True enough. He had become a central part of her life without her ever realizing it, and now she couldn't imagine being without him. She dodged a couple of sightseers and went on.

He had never again alluded to her quick kiss on the cheek the night Gladys left. Was that good or bad? She wasn't sure what he'd thought of her impulsive act. He didn't seem put off, but he hadn't responded in kind, either.

What would have happened if Seth had put his arms around her and kissed her back? A string of goose bumps prickled up her arms, and warmth spread throughout her body.

She scanned the walkways, looking at every rolling chair that entered her view and wishing she could spot him right this instant. If she only had a moment with him. . . .

"Dinah?"

She broke into a glad smile and spun around. "I was just— oh, it's you."

Her father strode toward her. "I checked at your office. They told me you would be out this way, so I decided to take a chance and come looking for you."

Dinah watched him approach, wishing his presence filled

her with joy instead of disappointment. This was the first time she had seen him away from the booth during the day. It must be something important for him to take time off to come looking for her.

He caught up to her and smiled as though she were the most important person in his life. "May I walk with you? Carry those for you, perhaps?" He reached out for the sheaf of papers in her arms.

Dinah pulled them closer to her. "No, thank you. Mr. Thorndyke holds me responsible for them." She studied his face. "Why were you looking for me?"

"I need to talk with you." He took her elbow and steered her toward the little round building on their right. "Why don't we sit here in the shade?"

"I really don't have time right now."

Her father continued to propel her up the steps to the veranda that encircled the tiny White Star Pavilion, where wooden deck chairs afforded weary fairgoers a respite from the sun. "It's all right. I told them back at your office I'd only take a few minutes of your time if I found you."

"You told Mrs. Johnson that?" Dinah's knees buckled, and she plopped down onto one of the chairs. She squared the papers on her lap and sat erect on the edge of the seat. "What did you need to talk to me about?"

He sat on the chair next to hers and leaned forward, looking as eager as a boy. "I was wondering when you and Abby and I could all get together. Maybe an evening out where the two of you can have a long talk and get this whole situation ironed out once and for all."

Dinah looked down at her hands. "I'm not sure when I'll

have a free evening anytime soon."

Her father pressed his fingers to the bridge of his nose. "It's been hard on me since your mother died. I just don't want to be lonely anymore. I think Abby could make me very happy, and you're the one who can convince her that this is the right thing to do." He patted her hand, then wrapped his fingers around hers. "You wouldn't mind doing that for your old dad, would you?"

When she remained silent, he tipped her chin up to look at him. She could read the pleading in his eyes. "I'm not getting any younger. It's time for me to settle down, don't you think?"

Dinah's throat contracted. "I thought it was time for you to settle down ten years ago."

He tightened his grip on her fingers. "I know, and I would have liked nothing more. But I was still a traveling man back then. I didn't have a job that let me stay in one place." His look of longing tugged at her heart. "What do you say, honey? You'll always be welcome to come visit. And you'll have the little sister you always wanted. What do you think about that?"

Dinah slipped her fingers out of his grasp and stood. "I really can't say right now. I'll think about it and let you know." She gathered the sheaf of papers tight against her chest and hurried off toward the Horticulture Building, trying to find her way through the haze of tears that filmed her eyes.

Seth paced another lap around the interior of the Administration Building rotunda. The intricacies of the mosaic floor underfoot did nothing to hold his interest; neither did the murals in the dome overhead. His attention was focused on the elevator doors, waiting for the moment when Dinah would step out.

Could she have left early for some reason? He should have let her know he was coming. But how could he, when he hadn't made the decision until the last minute?

He had bombarded heaven with his prayers the past few days, sending up pleas for the strength he needed to fight his growing attraction to Dinah Mayhew. After struggling with his feelings like Jacob wrestling with the angel, he had finally come to a momentous conclusion.

To his great surprise, the Lord didn't seem to share his reservations. In fact, Seth had the distinct feeling he was getting some kind of divine nudge.

And that opened up a new dilemma. He had apparently been given permission to pursue a deeper relationship with Dinah. But how did she feel about him?

Seth stopped before a sculpture titled *Diligence* and pretended to study it. He sensed a certain attraction on Dinah's part, but that didn't guarantee she would be interested in the kind of lifelong partnership he had in mind.

He bounced on his toes and jingled the change in his pocket, earning a look of suspicion from the Columbian Guard who walked past. Seth pulled his hands from his pockets and tried his best to appear at ease.

The irony of the situation struck him. He had preached at several of the tent meetings, spoken to a crowd of hundreds without a qualm. But now the mere thought of baring his heart to one lone woman made him feel as though he were being turned inside out.

Was he doing the right thing? A single man living on a shoestring didn't have any business thinking about marriage.

How could he hope to support a family on his meager income? And if he and Dinah were married, he would want to shower her with every convenience.

Seth pulled up short and tried to rein in his runaway imagination. What was he thinking? If today went the way he hoped, it would only be a first step, a testing of the waters, so to speak.

On his eighth circuit around the floor, he heard the elevator doors slide open. Heart pounding, Seth hurried over and felt his whole body relax when Dinah came into view.

A brilliant smile of welcome lit her face, then faded to a look of concern. Seth wiped his palms against his trouser legs and crossed the rotunda, berating himself for letting his anxiety show. *Smile, you dolt. You're scaring her.*

He forced his lips to turn up. "I've been waiting for you. Would you care to walk a bit?"

"Of course." Dinah's smile held a hint of reserve.

They passed under one of the great arches that formed the four entrances to the rotunda and stepped out into the waning sunlight. Seth hesitated, then walked straight ahead toward the Grand Basin.

They strolled along, looking like any of the other couples that filled the walkways. *Except we aren't saying a word to one another.* What was wrong with him? Now that he had Dinah to himself, he couldn't seem to summon up the courage to speak.

But how did a fellow go about putting something like that into words? *"I think you may be the one God intends as my helpmeet. Do you feel the same way?"* Not likely.

He had to do something to break this silence, though. He opened his mouth but couldn't force any utterance past his dry

206

throat. He swallowed and tried again.

"I wanted to talk to you."

Dinah looked up at him expectantly.

"I've given this a great deal of thought and spent a lot of time in prayer. I wanted to make sure God was in this and I wasn't just acting on my own feelings."

Her eyes shadowed. "You're going to tell me to step down from teaching the girls' class, aren't you?"

"What? No, not at all. You're doing a fine job there. I know you've been worried about the attendance, but we all have our setbacks from time to time."

Dinah nodded as if digesting the information. "Then what is it?"

When had the afternoon turned so warm? Sweat prickled under his collar and ran down the back of his neck. This was not going at all the way he'd planned. After struggling to reach this decision, he assumed the rest of the process would be easy. This was anything but.

Dinah watched him closely, waiting for him to speak. But how could he, with so many people milling around? Whatever made him think this would be a good place to tell her what was on his heart? For that he needed privacy. He needed. . .

A narrow craft skimmed past them and pulled to the boat landing, where it discharged its passengers.

Inspiration struck. "Would you like to go for a gondola ride?" The childlike delight in her eyes told him he'd finally said the right thing.

He handed Dinah down into the boat and stepped back to talk to the gondolier.

The boatman accepted the fare Seth slipped into his hand.

"The *signorina* is very beautiful. You want a private ride, just the two of you?"

"Yes, please." Seth felt in his pocket and pulled out a little more to add to the fare. "Could you give us a tour of the lagoon? A very slow tour?"

The gondolier gave him a broad wink and touched the brim of his flat-crowned straw hat. "I understand. You relax and let Giuseppe take care of everything, eh?"

Seth stepped into the craft and ducked under the canopy to join Dinah on the tufted seat. "Where are we going?" she asked.

"Nowhere in particular. I just thought it would be a nice way to relax on a warm afternoon."

A man on the landing untied the ropes that held the gondola fast and used a long pole to push it away from the mooring. The slender boat rocked gently as it responded to Giuseppe's touch on the single oar.

Seth leaned back against the cushioned seat, letting his earlier tension melt away. Beside him, Dinah sat perfectly still as if afraid she might tip them over if she made a sudden move.

"This was a lovely idea," she said. "I've wanted to ride one of these since the day I arrived. I can almost make myself believe I'm on a canal in Venice."

"Ah, Venezia," Giuseppe's voice carried from the stern. "The city of canals. . .and romance. If we were there, I would show you all the sights: the Piazza San Marco, the Basilica, the Bridge of Sighs. Here, I will point out the wonders of this magnificent exposition."

"That really isn't necessary," put in Seth. "We'd just like to—"

"Up ahead is the beautiful Columbian Fountain," their self-appointed guide intoned. "We turn now to the right, where we enter the North Canal."

Seth gritted his teeth. "This isn't the kind of tour I—"

The boatman made a show of pointing overhead as they passed under a bridge. "In Venezia, we have a tradition. When we go underneath a bridge, couples give each other a kiss. A nice custom, no?"

A wave of heat crept from Seth's collar to his hairline. The idea sounded more than a little appealing, but he couldn't very well go grabbing Dinah Mayhew and pulling her into his arms like some cave man. He didn't dare risk a look at Dinah, knowing she must feel as mortified as he did.

Giuseppe navigated them through the canal and steered them away from the huge bulk of the Manufactures Building toward the Wooded Island.

Dinah shifted on the cushion. "I'm glad to have this time when it's just the two of us. I've been wishing I could talk to you."

The simple comment heartened Seth. This idea of a gondola ride had turned out to be a brilliant plan. He should have thought of it earlier. He smiled at Dinah. "Go ahead."

She looked down at her clasped hands and gave a sheepish laugh. "I'm being silly. I've wanted to talk to you all afternoon, and now I don't even know how to begin."

Seth checked their location. Propelled by Giuseppe's sure strokes, the gondola followed the perimeter of the Wooded Island. Scores of people dotted the bank, but none were close enough to overhear them. "I'm here now. Go ahead."

"It's my father."

Of all the things on Seth's mind, that topic wasn't one he had hoped to hear. "What has he done now?"

"He found me over by the Woman's Building today. I was

working, but that didn't bother him in the least. He wanted to talk to me, and he was determined to keep me around long enough for him to do it."

Seth knotted his hands into fists. "What did he want?"

"He's still bent on me talking to Abby. He insisted I set a time for us all to get together so I could tell her what a doting father he was."

The gondola slipped beneath an overhang of willows. The branches arched over their heads to touch the water on the other side, forming a leafy tunnel.

Behind them, Giuseppe murmured, "Is almost like a bridge, eh?"

Seth froze, suddenly consumed by Dinah's nearness. He slid a glance her way. She stared straight ahead, sitting absolutely still. A soft blush tinted her cheek.

Giuseppe sighed. "No? Ah, well."

He pushed away from the island. "I will now show you the North Inlet, where water from Lake Michigan flows into the lagoon." He maneuvered the oar and steered them toward the northeast.

With an effort, Seth pulled his attention back to what Dinah had said. "So what are you going to tell Abby?"

"I don't know." Dinah stared out across the water. "He's my father, and I love him. But I don't want to bend the truth for him. What am I supposed to do?"

Seth offered up a quick prayer for guidance. "Life is full of choices," he began slowly, "but you can't choose your parents. Sometimes you just have to take them as they are, not as you wish they were."

Dinah swung around to face him, her eyes wide. "So you

think I ought to go ahead and do what he wants?"

"No, what I think is that you need to find out what God wants you to do. The Lord expects us to honor our father and mother, but that doesn't mean we should break His other rules to do it."

He watched the buildings on the shoreline slip past. "You're right. You can't lie to please your father."

"If we go any farther," Giuseppe announced, "we're gonna be in the lake. We turn around now and see the north end of the lagoon." Suiting action to his words, he swung the gondola around.

The boat rocked with the quick change in direction, throwing Dinah against Seth's arm. She straightened and gave him an apologetic smile. "Here I've been rattling on, and you said you had something to discuss with me. What was it you wanted to say?"

She looked up at him expectantly just as the gondola glided under yet another bridge. Giuseppe cleared his throat.

Seth heard a grating noise and realized he was grinding his teeth. He turned around and shot their boatman a scorching glare. The way he felt at the moment, he could cheerfully leap over the curved back of the seat and throw the fellow into the water.

Giuseppe assumed a look of utter innocence and began crooning softly: *"Sul mare luccia, l'astro d'argento. . ."*

Seth sat back and listened to the mingled sounds of Giuseppe's singing and the water lapping against the sides of the boat. This was better. Much better. If the boatman would only continue his warbling, maybe he would leave off making comments long enough for Seth to say what was on his heart.

His gaze traced Dinah's features in the golden evening light that captured the last moment between day and dusk. Summoning up his courage, he leaned toward her. "When I first met you, I wasn't sure—no, that isn't right."

He cleared his throat and started over. "When you took over the girls' Bible study, I didn't know. . . ."

A tiny pucker formed between Dinah's eyebrows. Her fingers curled into little balls, and she held her arms tight against her sides as if preparing to ward off a blow.

Seth could have kicked himself. This wasn't going the way he wanted it to at all.

The gondola veered in a wide arc to the right and slid under the bridge that led from Fisheries to the north tip of the Wooded Island. Seth looked around, suddenly very much aware that in spite of all the teeming masses that swarmed the fairgrounds, no one could see them now, under this bridge in the graying light.

He started to speak again, then closed his mouth. Sometimes actions spoke louder than words.

Pulling Dinah into his arms, he covered her lips with his. From the stern, Giuseppe's voice swelled: *"Santa Lucia! Santa Lucia!"*

A long moment later, Seth pulled away, wondering if he had made his point successfully or just committed the biggest blunder of his lifetime.

Dinah stared at him, eyes wide and lips parted. A tiny vein pulsed in her temple. "That wasn't quite what I expected."

"That pretty well sums up what I wanted to say. Did you mind?" Seth braced himself for her answer.

She looked down at her hands, then peered up at him from beneath her lashes. A slow smile curved her lips. "No. I didn't."

Seth took her hand in his and counted his blessings while Giuseppe rowed back across the lagoon.

It had turned out to be a most satisfactory tour after all. When they got back to the landing, he just might give the gondolier a hefty tip.

CHAPTER 20

T his is for you." Mrs. Purvis slipped an envelope from the stack of morning mail and handed it to Dinah. "It looks like another note from your aunt."

Dinah hesitated, not sure she wanted to see what was inside. She hoped against hope that it would bring joyous news saying they had heard from Gladys and all was well.

There's no way to know unless you open it. Bracing herself, she tore open the flap and unfolded the letter within. A quick scan told her that her hopes had been in vain.

"We still haven't heard from Gladdie," Aunt Dora wrote. *"Not a single word. We can't imagine what could be keeping her from writing, can you?"*

Dinah made a face. She didn't want to imagine what Gladys might have gotten into on her own.

"Your uncle wants to go to Chicago and look for her, but his health is only getting worse, and worry over Gladys is taking its toll.

214

I fear he wouldn't be able to stand the trip, and I cannot leave him to come there myself.

"I'm afraid it's up to you, Dinah. You are our only hope, and we pray God will guide you to find her quickly."

Dinah allowed the letter to slip from her fingers and flutter to the top of the dining table.

"Bad news?" Mrs. Purvis hovered at her elbow.

"In a way. My aunt wants me to track down Gladys. They still haven't heard from her." She pressed her hands to her forehead. "But I don't have the slightest notion where to begin! She didn't even leave an address with you."

Mrs. Purvis's head bobbed. "And those men didn't give me any idea where they were taking her things. To tell you the truth, I didn't think to ask."

"I've checked with the store, and none of her coworkers has any idea where she could be." Dinah plopped down in the nearest chair. "I feel like I've hit a dead end, and I don't know where to turn."

Mrs. Purvis sat down opposite her. "What about that young man of hers? Surely she wouldn't have gone away without letting him know."

"No," Dinah said slowly. "I don't believe she would. If I can locate Alan, surely he can tell me where to find Gladys." She sagged back again. "But I don't know where he lives, do you?"

Mrs. Purvis's features fell. "I guess it wasn't such a wonderful idea after all."

Dinah tapped her fingers on the linen tablecloth. "Wait a minute. He took her for that carriage ride the night she introduced me to him." She shoved away the memory of Alan and his distasteful advances. "He said they were going to drive

215

by his home, but where was it?"

"Give me a minute. It'll come to me." Mrs. Purvis bowed her head in an attitude of deep thought. "She couldn't stop bragging about the place when she got back. It was two stories high and made of dressed limestone."

Dinah pressed her lips together. "Anything else?" Chicago boasted hundreds of limestone houses.

"With mullioned windows and a brick walk leading up to the front door." The landlady looked up and grinned. "And a stone lion next to the walk. She was quite taken by that lion."

"That's wonderful!" Dinah wanted to cheer. "But do you remember where it was?"

Mrs. Purvis tapped her lower lip and hummed softly. "Drexel? No, wait a minute. Colter and Cottage Grove. She said it was right on the corner."

Dinah jumped up and gave Mrs. Purvis a hug. "You're a wonder. I'll go there after work today and see what Alan has to say."

At the memory of his fingers trailing across her cheek, she added, "If I can get Seth to go with me."

Not even to ease Aunt Dora's mind did she want to face Alan Saunders again on her own.

"Thank you for coming with me." Dinah accepted Seth's help stepping down from the streetcar. "I appreciate it more than you know."

"I'd planned on leaving the fairgrounds a little early today to go down to the gym, so I'm glad you caught me when you did. I'd much rather be spending time with you than trading jabs with my buddy Mac." Seth smiled at her, then took stock of their surroundings.

"You said it's on the corner of Colter and Cottage Grove. That's only a block or two this way."

He took her hand and tucked it in the crook of his arm. Walking beside him felt so good, so right. If not for all the hullabaloo over Gladys, her world would be perfect.

They covered the distance quickly. Dinah looked at each of the four corner houses and pointed to one on the far side of the intersection. "That must be it. It's exactly the way Gladys described it to Mrs. Purvis."

She studied the limestone exterior as they crossed the street and went up the neat brick walk. The lawn was well tended, with artful groupings of flowering shrubs. Everything about the home spoke of understated good taste, hardly the picture she had formed of Alan after their meeting. Maybe this was part of the inheritance he mentioned. It would be easier to understand if someone else had been responsible for designing this lovely place.

When they reached the front porch, Seth raised the knocker and let it fall against the carved oak door.

Dinah pressed closer to him, resentment flaring at the thought of having to face Alan again. But surely he would have the information they needed. Then they would be just one step away from finding her cousin. When they did, Dinah planned to give Gladys a piece of her mind.

It was one thing for her to act so spitefully toward Dinah. That kind of behavior would be nothing new at all. But what could she be thinking of, to treat her mother and father like that?

217

Caught up in planning what she would say to Gladys, Dinah jumped when the door swung open on silent hinges. A young woman in a black dress and white apron looked at them curiously. "May I help you?"

"We're here to see Mr. Saunders," Dinah said. "Is he at home?"

Confusion washed over the maid's face. "Mr. Saunders? I'm sorry. There's no one here by that name."

Dinah stared at the closing door. "Wait! *Mr. Saunders.*" She enunciated the name with care. "Are you sure he isn't here?"

"I told you, there's no one—"

A voice spoke behind her. "Is there a problem, Marie?"

The door inched open again, revealing a white-haired woman standing in the foyer.

The maid gestured toward Seth and Dinah. "These people—"

Seth stepped forward. "We're looking for Alan Saunders. We were told he lives here."

The elderly woman stepped forward, dismissing the maid with a gesture. "I am Mrs. Harold Bradford, and I have lived in this house for the past twenty years. I'm afraid I don't know anyone by that name. Perhaps someone gave you the incorrect address."

Seth moved as if to leave, but Dinah wasn't ready to give up so easily. "He's in his late twenties, blond, with a neatly trimmed mustache. He's about this tall." She held up her hand to indicate a spot two inches above Seth's head. "Do you know anyone of that description?"

Mrs. Bradford smiled and shook her head. "I'm sorry. I really can't help you." She closed the door with a note of finality.

Back on the sidewalk again, Dinah stared at the house, going over each detail point by point. Everything matched what Gladys had told Mrs. Purvis exactly. "I don't understand. Why would he tell Gladys this was his home when he doesn't live here and no one even knows him?"

Seth wore a grim look that matched her unsettled feelings. "Maybe he just wanted to impress her?"

"Maybe, although that seems a strange way to go about it. But that was my last hope for finding Gladys. What do I do now? Do you think we ought to go to the police?"

Seth considered her question, then nodded. "Let's catch the next streetcar. I know where the nearest station is."

"You say she's been gone how long?" The burly police sergeant puffed at his pipe, sending a thread of smoke spiraling toward the ceiling.

Dinah resisted the urge to wave the pungent cloud away. "Ten days. She left our boardinghouse without giving a forwarding address, and her parents haven't heard from her since. They are very concerned, and they've asked me to help locate her. But we've already tried everything I can think of. I don't know where else to turn."

The sergeant scribbled on the paper in front of him, then leaned back and regarded Dinah with a bleak expression. "I don't want to dash your hopes, but there isn't a lot we can do for you."

He held up his hand when Dinah started to protest. "Ever since the exposition opened, we've been buried under a pile of

219

missing persons reports. This is just one of thousands we've received."

"Are you saying you won't do anything about it?" Seth asked.

"I'm saying I can't." The policeman toyed with the buttons on his uniform and gave another pull at his pipe. "I'll pass along the information you've given us on your cousin, Miss Mayhew, but we have our hands full trying to solve serious crimes. We simply don't have the manpower to track down every person reported missing."

He stood, indicating the end of their interview, and gave Dinah a kindly look. "You'll probably be able to do just as much on your own as we can. The best of luck to you."

Outside the station, Seth slipped his arm around her shoulders and gave her a light squeeze. "That didn't turn out to be much help, did it? What do you want to do next?"

"I'll have to write Aunt Dora and let her know I'm still looking." She leaned her head on Seth's shoulder, drawing from his strength. "I hate having to tell her and Uncle Everett something that will cause them even more worry. If my uncle were in better health, I know they'd both be on the next train, coming to look for her themselves."

Her shoulders sagged under the weight of the situation. "But they can't, and so it's my responsibility."

Seth crooked his finger under her chin and raised her head so her gaze met his. "Not all yours. I'm in this, too, remember?'

Dinah closed her eyes, wishing they were on the gondola again, back in that moment when only the two of them existed and thoughts of her troublemaking cousin were far away. "It seems like we've hit a dead end everywhere we've turned. There's

220

only one person I can think of who might be able to help."

Seth's brow darkened. "Alan?"

Dinah nodded. "We have to find him. But how?"

"Let me check with a friend of mine. Maybe he can help me find something to go on."

CHAPTER 21

S eth watched Mac slip out of an alleyway and saunter up the walk as if he had no particular destination in mind. When he drew near, he looked around with elaborate care and settled next to Seth against the wood-framed building.

"Were you able to find anything?"

Mac pulled his hat down low and nodded. "I asked some of the boys to check around. One of them came up with something I think you'll be interested in."

Seth leaned closer, wishing he didn't feel like he'd just stepped into the pages of a dime novel.

"He's seen a guy answering that description hanging out over near Muldoon's place," Mac went on. "But he doesn't always go by Saunders."

"You're saying that isn't his real name?"

"From what I heard, it sounds like he has a whole raft of them. He may go as Saunders this week and something else the next. And who knows what he was calling himself this time last year? It's a pretty slick idea, when you stop to think about it. It makes him plenty hard to track down."

"We've found that out."

Mac stared straight ahead. "Another piece of news you might be interested in: He may have some connection with McGinty's bunch."

A thin thread of unease coiled up Seth's spine. He knew the tough Irishman's reputation for being involved in any number of sordid activities around the city. Some of which included. . .

He looked over at his friend. "Is McGinty the one who's putting pressure on you to take a dive?"

Mac leaned away and spat in the street. "I thought we had a deal about keeping your preaching to yourself. I'm just trying to help you find this guy Saunders, that's all."

"We still need to know how to locate him. Any ideas?"

"Johnny followed him and saw him use his key to go into a house near Halstead. It's a pretty sure bet that's where he lives."

"I need an address."

"Thought you might." Mac pulled a slip of paper from his hatband and handed it over.

Seth pocketed it after a quick glance. "Thanks. You've helped a lot."

Mac made as if to leave, then paused. "One more thing. He's got a woman with him."

Seth whipped his head around. "Where, at his house?"

"Johnny saw her through the door."

"What did she look like?"

"I don't know. I can ask him and let you know tomorrow."

Seth calculated quickly. The earliest he and Dinah could visit that house would be tomorrow evening. "That would be great. I'll meet you back here around noon."

The street lay quiet in the evening gloom. Dinah pressed nearer to Seth, which didn't bother him in the least. The warmth of her arm against his brought back memories of their gondola ride and the unspoken promise that hung in the air between them.

"Remember," he cautioned, "we're only here to check things out. The man Mac's friend saw fits Alan's description, but there's no guarantee it really is him. We won't know that until we've seen him in person."

"I can't decide whether I hope it's him or not. If it weren't for needing to find Gladys, I would never want to see him again. The day I met him. . .well, the way he acted when Gladys wasn't around made me feel very uncomfortable."

A slow anger started up inside Seth, but he tried to keep his voice calm. "That ties in with what I've heard." He wanted to bite his tongue when he saw Dinah's startled expression. "He doesn't sound like a very savory character, from all accounts. There may be a bit of a criminal connection."

Dinah shuddered. "I hate the thought of having anything more to do with him, but he's our only hope. We'll just ask him if he knows where Gladys is and then leave."

"It may not be that simple." He wished there were some easier way to break the news. "He may have Gladys with him. A woman answering her description was seen in that house."

"Then that could mean. . . . Oh, Seth!" Her fingers tightened on his arm like a vise. "She never told Mrs. Purvis she planned to leave. Everything was based on the note those men brought. What if he forced her to write it? What if. . ."

He wrapped his hand around hers and squeezed it. "Let's leave the what-ifs for now. It may turn out to be nothing like that." His inner conviction told him otherwise, but as distraught as Dinah appeared already, he wasn't about to tell her the rest of what he'd learned from Mac.

"It turns out Johnny talked to one of the neighbors," his friend had reported during their noon meeting. "He said Saunders is an odd duck. He's only lived in that house the past six months or so. He keeps to himself, so no one really knows him. No one in the neighborhood, at least. He has a habit of showing up with a young lady every once in a while, a different one every time from the sounds of it. And he seems to have a lot of visitors late at night. The whole thing just doesn't sound right."

Seth couldn't agree more. Everything about this situation put him on edge. He slowed when they reached the corner and checked the number on the nearest house. "It must be that one." He pointed to a neat, white dwelling three doors down on the far side of the street. "Are you ready?"

Dinah nodded, then grabbed his arm. "Wait!"

She drew him back into the shade of a towering lilac bush. "Look, the door's opening."

A blond man about Seth's age closed the door behind him and trotted down the steps. When he reached the walk, he turned and set off briskly down the street in the opposite direction.

One look at Dinah's white, set face gave him his answer

225

before he could ask the question.

"That's Alan," she said. "Should we try to catch up to him?"

"Why don't we scout around a bit first. Maybe we can find something to show us whether your cousin is there or not."

Dinah's face twisted. "If she is, if he's done anything to her. . ." She drew in a long, shaky breath. "Much as we get on one another's nerves, she's still family. I couldn't stand the thought of having to tell her parents something has happened to her."

"Let's not borrow trouble. The woman Mac's friend saw may not even be there now. Or if she is, it may not be Gladys, after all."

She studied his face, then squared her shoulders. "You're right. Let's go."

Grateful for the clouds that added to the darkness, Dinah followed Seth from shadow to shadow. They flitted up onto the front porch on silent feet.

"What are we looking for?" she whispered.

"Anything that would give us some clue as to what's going on. I was hoping we could see inside, but the drapes are too heavy." He gave her a rueful grin. "I guess I'm not a very good snoop."

His shoulders sagged. "It looks like we should have followed him after all. There's no telling when he'll be back."

"If only the house could tell us something." Dinah reached out and grasped the doorknob. "I wish I could just walk right in there and—Seth, the door's unlocked."

226

"Are you sure?"

She wiggled the knob back and forth. "See?" Temptation seized her. "We can't just walk in, though, can we?"

Seth eyed the door, then shook his head. "Much as I'd like to, I'm afraid we can't. Why don't we wait awhile? If he doesn't come back soon, we can leave a—"

The doorknob rattled under Dinah's fingers. She yelped when the door swung open wide.

Gladys stood framed in the opening, her face a mask of shock. "What are you doing here?"

With a glad cry, Dinah flew at her cousin and enveloped her in a hug. "You're all right!"

Gladys pulled away and stepped back. "Of course. Why shouldn't I be?"

Dinah followed her into the small living room. "I'm so glad we found you. Hurry now. You can come with us. We'll have you away from here before he gets back."

"What are you talking about?"

Dinah glanced around the room, frantic to be on their way. "Where are your things? No, don't worry about them; things can be replaced. The important thing is to get you out of here. Come on." She tugged at her cousin's arm and started toward the door.

Gladys planted her feet. "Have you lost your mind? What do mean by barging in here? And what makes you think I would want to leave my husband?"

Dinah felt as though the ceiling had just fallen in on her. "Your. . ."

"*Husband.*" Gladys enunciated each letter of the word. "Have you lost your hearing, as well?"

The room swam around Dinah. "You're married? To Alan?"

"You're sounding even more simpleminded than usual. I told you he wanted to marry me."

Through her haze, Dinah felt Seth step up beside her and rest his hand on her shoulder. She struggled to make sense of a world suddenly gone mad. "When did this wedding take place? Why didn't you let anyone know?"

"We were married the very day I left. The day after our. . . disagreement. As to why you didn't hear about it, I didn't think you would want to be involved after the way you attacked Alan. And quite frankly, I didn't care to have you there."

The revelation stunned Dinah. "So quickly? But why?"

"Alan proposed as soon as he heard I had left Mrs. Purvis's. He didn't want me to feel adrift, and under the circumstances, he saw no reason to wait any longer. A minister—a friend of his—performed the ceremony right here in this room."

Dinah opened her mouth, but no words came forth. She cast a mute look of appeal at Seth. He squeezed her shoulder and stepped forward, his eyes full of compassion. "You may wish you had waited a bit longer when you hear what we've learned."

Spurred by his comment, Dinah blurted out, "He isn't the kind of man your parents would approve of. His reputation is hardly the best."

To her amazement, Gladys tossed her head and laughed. "Is this another warning like the one you gave me about his so-called philandering on the fairgrounds? Alan told me all about that. It wasn't the way you portrayed things at all, just another instance of your wild imagination taking hold." A sly smile crossed her face. "Like all the times you insisted your father was going to come back to take you away with him."

Dinah pretended to ignore the jibe. Not for anything would she let Gladys see how it stung. "Fine. If you don't want to believe me, that's your choice. But why haven't you written to your parents? They're half out of their minds with worry."

Footsteps sounded on the front porch. Alan Saunders stopped dead in the doorway and stared at the tableau in his living room. A glint of anger flashed in his eyes when he looked at Dinah, followed by the smile that sent chills up her spine.

He stepped into the room and nodded like any gracious host. "Good evening. What a surprise to find you here."

Gladys hurried to stand next to him and hugged his arm. "Isn't it? You'll think it even more of a surprise when you hear the reason why. They've come to rescue me."

A sick feeling twisted inside Dinah's stomach. "Gladys, please."

Alan's face went blank; then he chuckled. "Rescue you? From what?"

Gladys threw a triumphant grin Dinah's way. "They have some wild notion that I've gotten mixed up with some sort of criminal."

Dinah wanted to sink right through the floor. It took all the courage she could muster to meet Alan's probing look. "Gladys's parents have been beside themselves because they haven't heard from her. They asked me to look for her." Remembering the setbacks they had encountered in their search, she added, "We went to the house you showed her when you went driving. Nobody there knew who you were."

Alan played with a loose strand of Gladys's hair, winning an adoring smile. "Perhaps we made a mistake in not letting your parents know right away." Turning to Dinah, he added, "We were going to surprise them with a visit on her birthday, but I guess we didn't think it through very well. We got so caught up in each other, it's been as if nothing else existed." He pulled Gladys into his arms and rubbed his cheek across her hair. "After all, we are on our honeymoon."

Gladys melted against him and smirked at Dinah. "So you see, your meddling has accomplished nothing at all. We already planned our trip back home to announce our marriage. While we're there for my birthday, we'll stop in and see Grandmother's lawyer and make arrangements for my inheritance to be sent to me here, in my new name." She turned within the circle of Alan's arms and beamed at him. "And then we'll come back here to our little honeymoon cottage."

Seth's hand took Dinah's elbow in a loose grip. "It's obvious we're in the way. We'd best be taking our leave."

"But that still doesn't explain. . ."

Seth increased the pressure on her arm. "Good evening to you both."

Dinah hung back long enough for one last appeal to Gladys. "You will write to your parents?"

"First thing in the morning. I'll break the news to them about our wedding and let them know we'll be coming to see them in a couple of weeks. They may be a little miffed about not hearing about it earlier, but once they meet my darling Alan, I'm sure they'll be pleased."

Clinging to Alan's arm, she turned an insufferably smug smile on Dinah. "By the way, aren't you going to congratulate me?"

Dinah managed to dredge the word up past the obstruction in her throat. "Congratulations."

This time she let Seth lead her outside to the street.

CHAPTER 22

I can't believe she would put us through all that worry without letting anyone know what was going on."

Dinah stumbled over a stone in her path. Seth caught her before she could fall, knowing she was so angry she could hardly see straight. Her obvious pain cut him like a knife. More than anything, he wanted to make all her hurt go away. Instead, he walked on without speaking, knowing she needed this chance to get her anger out of her system.

"How could she treat her parents this way? She's always been self-centered, but this reaches new heights, even for Gladys. And what about us? When I think of all the trouble we went through, how much I feared for her safety—and then to discover she's been hiding out here with that man. On her honeymoon, no less!" She spat out the final words, as if trying to rid herself of a nasty taste.

In the moon's soft glow, Seth could see patches of tears on

her cheeks. "It's been an evening full of surprises, all right."

Dinah took a deep breath. "I'm sorry for carrying on so. But to think we've all been so concerned when everything's just fine. She's as happy as a lark. . .even though the thought of her married to that man makes me shudder."

"At least you know she's alive and well." But fine? Seth wasn't convinced of that. Granted, to all appearances she and Alan were just a couple enjoying their honeymoon, utterly wrapped up in one another. But still. . .

Something didn't seem right, yet he couldn't quite put his finger on what made him feel that way. He went back over their conversation with the couple, point by point.

"What did Gladys mean about arranging for her inheritance?"

"Oh, that." Dinah dismissed the idea with a sniff. "Both of us have a small inheritance coming from Grandmother Winslow on our next birthday. It's only a token amount, but to hear Gladys tell it, she'll have enough to set her up for life."

Pieces of the puzzle started falling into place with unwelcome clarity. "Do you think she's told Alan how much she'll really get?"

"Who can tell? I don't know anyone who can embellish a story the way Gladys can." She stopped still, her eyes wide. "Do you think she gave him one of her trumped-up tales? Is that the reason he was so quick to marry her?"

Seth tried to ignore the twisting in his gut. "If he did, he'll find out the truth soon enough."

"And then Gladys will have to face up to the consequences for once. Oh my. If that's the case, I wonder how enamored he'll be once he finds out his 'heiress' really isn't one."

A variety of emotions played over her face. "Well, she's made her bed; she'll have to lie in it. I'm ready to wash my hands of the whole thing."

A cloud passed over the moon, obscuring its light. Their steps echoed on the walk, keeping a steady pace. Seth's thoughts moved at a much faster rate.

If gaining Gladys's inheritance had been Alan Saunders's motive for rushing her into marriage, what would he do when he learned the truth?

Given Mac's description of the man and his associates, Gladys might have placed herself in a highly precarious position. Anyone involved with McGinty. . .

There was more to this situation than met the eye; Seth felt sure of it. Something about Alan Saunders made the hairs on the back of his neck stand on end.

He didn't want to add to Dinah's distress, but he didn't buy the idea of the happy honeymooners for an instant. Men like Alan Saunders didn't marry women like Gladys without good reason. And that reason usually involved profit. If a man like that felt he'd been cheated, what would he be capable of doing?

The answer chilled him more than the cool night air.

Dinah might be ready to walk away from the situation, but Seth knew he couldn't. Not until he had another talk with Mac.

How did they know? Alan Saunders caught sight of his mottled face in the oval, gilt-framed mirror. He turned away and took a series of deep, calming breaths. He had to stay calm. At this point in the game, it was essential not to lose control.

Gladys's arms slipped around him from behind, and he felt his skin crawl. He summoned up a tender smile and turned to embrace her. "Are you all right, my sweet?"

She laid her head on his shoulder and stroked his cheek. "I'm fine. You're the one I'm worried about, coming home to find them here and then learning about those horrible things my cousin said."

He forced himself to press his cheek against her mousy brown hair. "It must have been a terrible shock when they showed up at the door." He paused for effect. "Or did you have an idea they might be coming?"

"Heavens, no!" Her reaction seemed sincere enough. "I haven't spoken to Dinah since the night before I moved out. Why would I want to? If I had my way, I'd never talk to her again. She's done nothing but make trouble for me ever since her father dumped her on our doorstep."

Gladys heaved a sigh. "Our time together has been so sweet. I'd hate for anything she said or did to come between us." She smiled playfully and tugged at his arm. "Come sit with me on the sofa. Would you like to lay your head in my lap?"

Alan swallowed back the bile that rose in his throat. "No, we'll just take a few moments to sit and let ourselves calm down." He let her nestle close to him, with her head resting on his chest.

Good. That way he didn't have to worry about her reading any thoughts reflected on his face. He ran his hand over her head with long, even strokes, and she snuggled closer. In a minute more, she'd be purring. He kept up the even rhythm, glad for the chance to think without distraction.

How did they know? The question ate at him like acid. He

234

had covered his tracks the same way he always did. A new name and change of location every few months made him impossible to trace.

Until tonight.

Where had he slipped up? Maybe he'd been too sure of himself. He hadn't bothered to set up his next base of operations yet. If he had, he'd pack Gladys up, give her some manufactured excuse, and they would leave that very night.

Leave. The thought reverberated in his mind. Maybe he ought to go alone. Maybe he should cut his losses right now and start over, disappear into the night. . . .

He fought off the sense of panic that threatened to overwhelm him and tried to assess the situation logically. *All that has changed is that Dinah and her friend found us. They haven't gone to the police. They don't know about the girl in the basement.* He felt his pulse slow to a more normal rate.

When the two of them left, they showed no indication of being anything but satisfied with his story. Nothing of any consequence had changed. Everything would go according to plan. . .as long as Gladys didn't suspect.

He looked down at her blocky form lying against his chest and felt the last of his anxiety drain away. There was little fear of that. But he vowed to watch her closely after tonight's events. He would leave nothing more to chance.

Leaning over, he brushed her ear with a kiss. "Why don't you go write that letter now? Tell your parents how happy we are and how much we look forward to celebrating your birthday with them."

Gladys stirred and smiled up at him sleepily. "I could stay right here forever, but if that's what you want. . ." She pushed herself upright and touched her lips to his. "When I'm finished, we can have a cup of tea together before bedtime."

He pressed her fingers and held his smile in place while she made her way to the rosewood writing desk in the bedroom. The task should keep her occupied long enough to give him time to think and plan.

And then he'd slip a little laudanum into her tea again so he would be free to attend to his chores in the basement.

CHAPTER 23

S eth helped Ted Murphy gather the last of the songbooks and pushed a row of benches back into place. Ted nodded his thanks. "I'll see you later when we meet with Mr. Moody."

"Not tonight," Seth told him. "I have to see somebody." He slipped out the nearest exit before Ted could ask questions. He had enough reservations of his own about what he was getting involved in; he didn't want to have to justify his actions to his coworker.

If not for being compelled by a sense of urgency he couldn't explain, he would happily drop this whole investigation. He had plenty of other things on his mind at the moment, chief among them his upcoming meeting with the church board. At Amos Hall's suggestion, he had put together a comprehensive overview of his work, along with a request for them to make him a full-fledged member of their ministerial staff.

He still couldn't quite believe he'd had the audacity to deliver the request. Whether or not the church board would agree to go along with it remained to be seen, but at least he had made the effort. His future with Dinah was riding on their decision.

No, not theirs, he reminded himself. God was in control, and He would watch over them and meet their needs.

Behind the mammoth tabernacle, he strained his eyes to see in the dim light that filtered through the canvas walls.

"Psst! Over here."

Seth followed the voice until he could make out Mac against the side of the tent. He hurried toward him but pulled up when he got close enough to see a second figure.

"What's going on? I thought it was just going to be the two of us."

"Meet Johnny. He's the one I told you about who followed Saunders home. I thought you'd want to talk to him in person."

Seth heard a scuffling sound that ended abruptly on a yelp.

"He didn't much want to come," Mac continued, "especially when he found out where we were meeting. But I managed to persuade him." He stepped forward, pushing a small, wiry man in front of him. Seth could see Mac's hand twisted into the back of the other man's jacket. Johnny wriggled like a fish on a hook.

"Settle down." Mac gave him a light cuff with his free hand. "It's like I told you; this is the last place anyone would look for you." He loosened his hold but didn't let go completely.

Johnny shrugged the jacket back into place and gave Seth a dour look. "What do you want to know?"

Seth swallowed back his distaste. "I need to find out every-thing you can tell me about this man Saunders."

Johnny snorted. "Saunders, Evans, Gillespie, take your pick.

238

He changes his name like I change my socks."

Mac's arm jerked, and Johnny grunted. "It seems our friend knows more than he told me the first time. I'll let him explain it to you. Go ahead, Johnny."

The small man wrenched free and glared at Mac. "I can talk better if I have room to breathe." He turned his back on the fighter and looked at Seth. "He's a slippery one; I can guarantee you that. My sources tell me he does some work for McGinty. I don't know what that is, and I'm not about to pry into McGinty's business. I like to stay healthy—you know what I mean?"

Seth held up his hand, stopping the flow of information. "I've heard all this before. What else can you tell me?"

Johnny peered from side to side and lowered his voice. "I have it on good authority he's got something going on the side that McGinty don't know about."

"Any idea what that is?"

"I got a buddy who's known him from way back, like when they were kids. He says this Saunders, or whatever his real name is, has always been the ambitious type with an eye to making a packet any way he could."

Seth exchanged glances with Mac. "Go on."

"One day he shows up with this gal and introduces her to my buddy as his wife. My buddy's surprised because she's quality, not someone he'd find down in the area they came from. But he figures this guy finally got lucky and hit the jackpot."

Johnny continued, warming to his tale. "Only thing is, six months later, he runs into him again, with a different woman this time. The guy pulls my buddy off to the side, tells him he's now going by another name, and then he says he wants to introduce him to his new wife."

239

A sick feeling roiled in Seth's stomach. "Was this recently?"

A match flared, and Johnny cupped his hand to light a cigarette. "Couldn't have been. My buddy was away for a while. Two years to be exact, courtesy of the state of Illinois. He gets out, and who's one of the first people he sees? None other than his old friend, except now he's calling himself Saunders, and he says he's expecting to get married again any day."

"A third time?" Seth could hear his own disbelief echoed in Mac's voice.

"At least." Johnny snickered. "Remember, my buddy's been away for two years. So then my buddy asks him what he's doing with all these wives, and Saunders just gives him the fish eye and changes the subject. That's all I know."

Dread wrapped itself around Seth's heart. "You don't know what happened to any of those women?"

The tip of Johnny's cigarette glowed. "I don't know, and I'm not gonna ask. Like I said—I plan to stay healthy."

Mac took a step toward him. "You're sure that's all?"

Johnny shrugged. "That's all I got. You want more, you're gonna have to find it yourself. Can I go now?"

Mac glanced at Seth, then nodded. "Yeah. Thanks."

Johnny's mouth twisted in a sardonic smile. "My pleasure. Just remember, you didn't hear any of this from me."

The silence stretched out in the pocket of darkness. Finally Mac asked, "Is that what you needed?"

"It may be what I needed, but it's a lot more than I wanted to know. Now I have to figure out what I'm going to do with it." Seth clapped his friend on the shoulder. "Thanks, Mac. I owe you."

Mac grinned. "I'll remember that." He sketched a wave and

walked off into the night.

Seth hunkered down in the darkness, sifting through the information he'd been given. In all the swirl of confusion, one thing was clear: As little as he wanted to, he needed to talk this over with Dinah.

"Try some of these, darling. I made them just for you."

Gladys set the tray of oatmeal cookies on the small marble-top table next to Alan's favorite armchair. She stood with her hands clasped, waiting for him to take a bite and tell her how good they were. To say how much he loved them. . .how much he loved her.

She reached out to comb her fingers through his hair, but he swatted her hand away. "Find someplace to sit, will you? You know I don't like you hovering over me like that."

Everything within her grew cold and still. "Of course, Alan." She curled up at his feet and pressed her lips together. She would not let the tears come. She would not let him see how his sharp words wounded her.

He had been in an edgy mood for the past two days, ever since Dinah and that preacher of hers had invaded their little haven.

Dinah! Gladys swallowed hard. Just the thought of her meddlesome cousin brought the bitter taste of gall to her throat.

What kind of audacity possessed a person to stick her nose in where it wasn't wanted? Dinah had been a thorn in the flesh ever since Uncle Ernie left her on their doorstep and then went his merry way.

From that moment on, Gladys had been forced to share everything in her life with her cousin. Gone were the days of being doted on by her parents, of being the only ray of sunshine in their lives. Dinah's unwanted arrival had marked the end of Gladys's happy existence.

Until she met Alan. The one thing she could thank Dinah for was paving the way for her to leave the farm and come to the city. If she hadn't made that move, she never would have found her beloved.

She lay her head on his knee, tentatively at first, then let herself relax when he didn't resist her overture. The miracle of finding him, of him loving her, still filled her with awe. She longed for him to reach out and stroke her hair as he usually did. But ever since that miserable night, he had become withdrawn, preoccupied.

A wave of anger swept over her, leaving her weak. It was all so unfair for her happiness to be ruined by her cousin's interference. Hadn't she spent years watching men ignore her presence, only to light up the minute petite, winsome Dinah entered the room? Now her moment had come. She had found the man of her dreams at last, only to have meddlesome Dinah dash her cup of joy to the ground.

It couldn't be happening again, could it? Fear entered her heart and set her limbs to trembling.

Surely Alan hadn't become attracted to Dinah.

Why couldn't men see through that shallow exterior? Dinah was nothing. Nothing! Why couldn't men see that? Even Dinah's own father didn't want her around. That ought to tell them something.

Alan's hand rested on her head with a gentle touch. "I'm

sorry I barked at you. I've been a bit distracted, but I shouldn't have taken it out on you." His fingers wove their way through her hair in the old, familiar way. Gladys closed her eyes.

"Will you forgive me?"

Her heart raced. "Of course." How foolish she had been. Her Alan was back, and she had nothing to fear. Tears of joy squeezed out from beneath her closed lids.

She raised her head and let her adoration show in her gaze. "I was so afraid."

The muscles in his thigh tightened, and his whole body grew still. "Afraid? Of what?"

Gladys called herself every kind of fool. His tension had returned, and she was to blame. Why couldn't she learn to weigh her words before she spoke?

She tried to laugh it off. "Dinah. The way she never leaves well enough alone." She saw the muscles in his cheek ripple under his skin and broke off, wishing she had bitten her tongue. The last thing she wanted to do was bring Dinah to his mind, so why even mention her name?

She tried to read his expression, but his face was devoid of feeling. The fear returned. Had she been right after all? Had he decided he didn't love her anymore?

His lips thinned, and his cornflower eyes turned a flat, dull gray. Fear escalated to terror. Something had gone horribly wrong, but what? Her mind scrambled for a way to undo whatever mistake she had made. "I'm sorry, Alan. I didn't mean to upset you. Can't we let things go back to the way they were before and forget that Dinah was ever here?"

His gaze probed hers for what seemed an interminable length of time. "An excellent idea." The gentle smile was back, but the look in his eyes reminded her of hardened steel. A shiver rippled through her body.

"You're cold. Get up off the floor and sit here." He rose and helped her to her feet, then settled her in the armchair. "Why don't you have some of these delicious cookies? I'll go to the kitchen and make you a nice, hot cup of tea."

CHAPTER 24

Dinah sifted through the paperwork collected on her morning rounds. Nothing out of the ordinary except for a request for additional cleaning help from Mr. Collins in Fisheries. She marked it for Mr. Thorndyke's attention and set it aside.

A tap on the door drew her attention. She caught her breath when Seth opened it and leaned inside.

Millie straightened and patted her hair. "May I help you?"

Dinah hurried toward the front. "I'll take care of this." As she passed Millie's desk, she heard her murmur, "Don't try to tell me that's your father. I've already met him." Dinah blushed and tried to stifle a grin.

"I hope I'm not coming at a bad time." Seth held up two paper sacks. "It's almost noon, and I wondered if you were ready for lunch."

"Well. . ." Dinah's nose twitched at the appetizing smells coming from the bags. "I was supposed to cover the office while Millie went out."

"And have me be the cause of you missing out on a picnic? Never!" Millie flapped her hands in the direction of the door. "Go on, get out of here."

Out on the Grand Plaza, Seth led her toward the left, not stopping until they reached the bridge at the far end of the Mining and Electricity buildings. "I thought we could go out on the Wooded Island. We ought to find plenty of shade there."

"Shade sounds wonderful," Dinah agreed. She followed his lead along the main pathway, then down to a bench near the shore of the lagoon under the draping branches of a willow tree. Through the slender limbs, she could see the clean, sweeping lines of the Japanese Building only a short distance away. There, clusters of people moved to and fro, chattering like magpies. But here in their little alcove, they existed in a world apart.

Seth dusted the bench free of willow leaves, then opened the bags and pulled out sandwiches and containers of lemonade. He handed one of the sandwiches to Dinah. "Here you are. It's chicken. I hope that's all right." His light tone contrasted with the grave look in his eyes.

Dinah unwrapped her sandwich, then set it on her lap. "Something tells me you didn't just invite me out here for a picnic."

Seth set his drink down on the grass and turned to her. "You're right. We need to talk."

Dinah sat in stunned silence while Seth outlined what he had heard from Mac and his informant the night before, her heart sinking with every word. When he finished, she clutched his arm. "Then Gladys really is in danger! Seth, we have to get her out of there whether she wants to come or not."

246

She jumped up, tumbling the untouched sandwich to the ground. "Why did you wait this long to tell me? We need to do something now!"

"Hold on a minute." Seth drew her back down on the bench beside him. "Think it through. Alan won't harm her until he has the inheritance."

Dinah leaned against him and buried her face in her hands. "Gladys and that stupid inheritance! Look where her exaggerating landed her this time." She looked up at Seth. "We have to take this to the police."

"And tell them what? We found your missing cousin, but now we think her husband may try to kill her?" Seth shook his head. "We have no proof, nothing solid anyway. At this point, it's all hearsay."

"But this Johnny person—"

"Would not be considered the most reliable source of information as far as the police are concerned."

"Then that means. . ."

Seth nodded, his face somber. "It's up to us."

A numb feeling started in her heart and spread to her fingertips. She watched while a plump duck waddled up onto the bank and pecked at her sandwich. Waving the chunk of bread back and forth like a victorious hero, it carried the morsel back to the lagoon.

Dinah blinked and looked up at Seth. "So what do we do?"

"We'll pay them another visit tonight. I don't have a definite plan; it's hard to know what to expect when you don't know what you're up against. We'll have to take it as it comes. If Alan is gone when we get there, we'll take Gladys with us if I have to carry her out kicking and screaming."

"And if he is there?"

Seth drew a long, slow breath. "We'll cross that bridge when we come to it. I don't want you—or Gladys—getting hurt. Let's hope for the best. If we can get her out without Alan knowing, so much the better. Let's go about the same time we did before and hope going out in the evening is part of his regular routine."

Dinah and Seth huddled once again in the shelter of the lilac bush. Tonight the curtains of the little white house were open, and a lamp burned brightly inside. They watched Alan Saunders walk across the living room to a room beyond their view for a moment, then reappear.

Dinah never loosened her grip on Seth's sleeve. "We've been watching for nearly half an hour, and there's no sign of Gladys." She dug her fingers into his arm. "Do you think we're too late? Has he already—"

"Don't jump to conclusions. We can only see the one room from here. She could be cleaning up the kitchen for all we know."

"How do we find out?"

Seth tugged at her hand and started off down the street, staying away from the circle of light cast by the streetlamps. "First off, we pray this neighborhood doesn't have a Mrs. Boggs."

They crept along the street, melting into the shadows, careful not to make a sound. Slipping across the front yard, they eased up to the right side of the house and pressed flat against the wall. On Seth's signal, they raised their heads cautiously and looked in the side window, where a view of the living room from a different angle verified that Gladys wasn't there.

Seth pointed toward the rear of the house, and Dinah nodded. The windows back there were likewise free of curtains. They peered into a neat little kitchen. Contrary to Dinah's fervent hopes, they saw neither Gladys nor any sign to indicate she had been there.

Fear clutched at Dinah's throat.

Side by side, they slid along the rear wall, past the back door to the far end. "This house isn't very big," Dinah said. "We're running out of places to look."

Seth stopped before she spoke the last word. In the window in front of him, the curtains were closed, but the window itself stood open a few inches at the bottom.

Seth pressed his finger to his lips, then slipped his hand through the narrow gap and eased the curtains apart. No lamps illuminated the small room, but light seeped in from the living room, enough to show them the still form of a woman lying on the bed.

Dinah sucked in her breath. "Gladys!"

She studied her cousin but saw no sign of movement. "She's so still. Is she. . ." She couldn't bring herself to voice the word aloud.

"No," Seth whispered. "I can see her breathing."

"How do we get her out? We can't leave her, but we can't get to her with him in there."

Seth rubbed his hands together. "This is where we get creative. I've never been much for breaking and entering. It doesn't normally fall under a pastor's job description. But under the circumstances. . ." He placed his hands under the sash and tugged. "It's stuck."

"Can't you get it open?" Dinah put her hands alongside his

and pulled with all her might.

"Not without making too much noise," Seth replied. "We need to find some way to distract him." He looked around. "Why don't I go around the front and knock on the door? You can raise the window and get to Gladys."

Dinah shook her head. "I'll never get it open on my own. I'm the one who should go." Before he could protest, she darted around the corner and ran to the front of the house.

When she reached the porch, her feet refused to carry her one step farther. What was she doing? The last thing in the world she wanted was to face Alan Saunders alone. But with Gladys's life at stake, she had no choice. She forced her feet to climb the steps and rapped sharply on the door before she could change her mind.

She didn't have to go inside. All she needed to do was keep him occupied long enough for Seth to gain entrance to the back bedroom, rouse Gladys, and get her outside.

There was no answer from within. Where could he be? And what would she do if he decided to answer? The flaws in her impulsive decision grew more evident with each passing moment. It wasn't a fully formed plan by any means, but as Seth said, they had to improvise, and this was the best she could come up with. The most important thing was getting Gladys out, willingly or not.

Dinah lifted her hand to knock again, and the door opened. Alan's eyes widened at the sight of her, and his face grew very still.

Dinah smiled and prayed for inspiration. "Good evening. Is Gladys home?"

A ripple of irritation disturbed his studied calm, then

disappeared as quickly as it had come. "I'm afraid she has already retired for the night. She had a headache and decided to go to bed early." He put his hand on the door as if to close it.

Dinah strained for any hint of sound coming from the back room. What was Seth doing now? It hadn't been nearly long enough for him to accomplish his mission. She had to give him more time.

Pushing down her revulsion, she slipped inside the room before Alan could swing the door shut. "Oh, what a shame. I was hoping I could see her and apologize for our intrusion the other night."

Alan stepped to one side, blocking Dinah from further entry. "I'll let her know you stopped by."

Dinah stiffened at the sound of a muffled *creak*. "I need to apologize to you, as well. I'm afraid we never got off on the right foot." *Hurry, Seth!* "After all, you're family now, and we must do our best to get along. Perhaps we can start fresh and put the past behind us."

His Adam's apple slid up and down his throat. "What a good idea. Consider your apology accepted." He reached out and took her by the elbow. "Now if you'll excuse me, I was just preparing to turn in myself." He steered her toward the door.

The high-pitched, scraping sound of wood rubbing against wood came from the direction of the back room, followed by a light *thud*. Alan whirled around, white-faced, and charged toward the rear of the house.

"Seth, look out!" Dinah screamed. Bolting forward, she grabbed Alan's arm with both hands and tried to drag him to a stop. Through the doorway, she could see Seth shaking Gladys.

251

He looked up and took a step toward Alan. "She won't wake up. What did you do to her?"

The muscles in Alan's arm bunched under Dinah's fingers. In one fluid motion, he swung his arm forward like someone cracking a whip. Dinah sailed across the room and landed in a heap atop Gladys's inert form. Her cousin let out a soft grunt but didn't stir.

Dinah lifted herself up in time to see Seth leap toward Alan. Their bodies made a hollow *thud* when they collided, and the two men tumbled out into the living room.

She pushed herself off the bed and ran to the doorway, where she saw them locked in a desperate struggle on the floor. Seth's face wore a fierce expression she had never seen before, and Alan's lips curled back in a wolflike snarl.

Rolling back and forth, they crashed into a small table and knocked it to the ground. A vase tumbled unbroken onto the rug. Alan pinned Seth to the ground with one arm and fumbled for it with the other, stretching his fingers to their limit. With a look of triumph, he grasped the vase and held it aloft, ready to bring it down on Seth's skull.

Dinah let out a shriek and dove for his upraised hand. The vase slipped from his grasp and rolled across the rug. Dinah scrambled after it and scooped it up. Holding it tightly in both hands, she whirled to see Alan already on his feet and Seth scrambling to get up. Before she could swing the vase, Alan grabbed her outstretched arm and shoved her into Seth. They landed on the floor in a heap.

Seth pushed himself free of the tangle and sprang to his feet, hands clenched. Dinah struggled to her knees and looked around the room. The front door stood open to the evening breeze, and Alan was nowhere to be seen.

Dinah gasped when Seth started toward the door. "You're not going after him, are you?"

"No, I'm just not in the mood for any more surprises." He closed the door and turned the lock, then leaned against it, heaving in great gulps of air. "Let's go see about Gladys."

Dinah rushed to the small back bedroom and shook her cousin repeatedly. "Gladys? Gladys, wake up!" She looked up at Seth. "I don't know what's wrong with her."

"Do you see how shallow her breathing is? I think he may have drugged her." Seth's expression was grim.

"How are we going to wake her up?"

"Get some damp cloths, and see if you can bring her around. I'm going to find a cab. We need to get her to a hospital." He brushed her lips with a quick kiss. "Put a chair under the doorknob. I'll be back as quickly as I can."

CHAPTER 25

H ow are you doing this morning? You had a long night."

Dinah leaned back against Seth's shoulder. "Yours wasn't a bit shorter than mine." She stared out at the lake, envying the gulls that bobbed placidly on the blue-gray waves. Learning Gladys hadn't ingested enough laudanum to do any permanent damage had been a profound relief, but the long night's vigil at the hospital had left her unutterably weary.

"The doctor wants to keep an eye on her, but he says he'll release her in a day or two." She smiled when she felt Seth slip his arm about her waist. "I wired Aunt Dora early this morning. She's going to come in on the train and take Gladys back home as soon as she's ready to be discharged. She said the news buoyed Uncle Everett up so much, she felt she could leave him long enough to make a quick trip here and back."

She closed her eyes and drew in a breath of the damp air. "It's all so sad. What a horrible way to find out what stretching

254

the truth can lead to. I keep wondering what Gladys is going to do now."

"She'll need prayer, and a lot of it. It's been a hard way for her to learn that lesson."

"I never liked her exaggerations, but I never wanted to see her life ruined like this."

Seth's arm tightened about her, an anchor in the storm her life had become of late. "God can take that rubble and use it to build something new and beautiful if Gladys will let Him. He's willing to give her a second chance and let her start over."

"That's nice to know. I guess we all need a second chance from time to time."

A deep whistle sounded, alerting them to the arrival of one of the steamships that carried visitors from the city to the fairgrounds. Seth sighed. "We might as well go back. We'll be overrun in a few minutes."

They started back along the pier, and Seth laced his fingers through hers. Dinah clasped them tight, wishing she could keep them in her grip always. Better yet, that she could hold on to his heart forever.

Behind them, people walked down the ship's gangplank and swarmed toward them in a mass. Their time of solitude was over.

Stepping off the pier, Seth and Dinah strolled through the dappled shade under the columns of the Peristyle until the Grand Basin came into view. At the end nearest them, the golden Statue of the Republic lifted her arms to the sky. The sun caught the wings of the eagle she held in one upraised hand. At the other end, the dome of the Administration Building glinted in response.

"Quite a sight, isn't it?" Seth's voice held the same sense of wonder Dinah felt.

"You'd think I would have my fill of it after walking around the grounds every day, but it keeps drawing me back." Dinah laughed. "Most people wouldn't dream of going back to their workplace on a day off. I'm just grateful I didn't have to work today. I don't think I could begin to cope after everything that has happened. But I can't think of a better place to let my nerves unwind than out there on the pier. That was a wonderful idea you had. There's something so soothing about watching the water."

Seth angled north toward the Manufactures Building. "Now that you don't have to worry about Gladys anymore, maybe we'll have time to concentrate on more pleasant things."

A delicious shiver of anticipation ran through her. "What did you have—"

She broke off when she saw a tall man waving at her and heading their way. "Oh, no."

Seth came alert. "What's wrong?"

"It's my father."

"Good morning!" Her father exuded a jovial air of goodwill. "Lovely day, isn't it? I'm so glad I ran into you like this."

Dinah's thoughts turned to running of a different kind—in the opposite direction. Since that was out of the question, she forced a stiff smile. "I'd like you to meet someone. Papa, this is Pastor Seth Howell. Seth, this is my father, Ernie Mayhew."

"Good to meet you." Her father tossed off the obligatory salutation and turned back to Dinah. "Look, honey, we really need to get this meeting with Abby under way. I can't keep waiting for you to give me an answer. She's getting nervous, and she doesn't understand why you don't want to talk with her."

"I don't have anything against Abby. It's just that—"

"My chance for happiness is slipping away. You don't want that on your conscience, do you?"

Dinah pressed her lips together and counted to ten. "All right. I'll meet you for dinner as long as Seth can come."

"That's fine. I don't care who else joins us, just as long as you're there. Let's make it the Café de Marine again. Tonight at eight, all right?"

"Tonight?" She looked at Seth, and he nodded. *Might as well get it over with.* "All right, we'll see you tonight."

Seth took her arm. "I need to walk Dinah home now, sir. I hope you'll excuse us."

"Of course, of course." Her father practically glowed. "We'll be looking forward to it."

"Well, at least it started out to be a lovely day." Dinah walked beside Seth up the porch steps.

"And it's going to get better. As soon as my meeting with the church board is finished, I'll come by and pick you up. I should be free by early afternoon. That will give us some time together, just the two of us, before we have to meet your father."

Dinah paused with her hand on the doorknob. "Would you like to come in for a few minutes?"

"I wish I could." The look in his eyes filled her with a melting warmth. "But if I'm going to make it to that meeting on time, I need to go now. I'll be cutting it close as it is." He dropped a light kiss on her lips, sending a bloom of liquid fire clear down to her toes.

"I'll see you then." Dinah closed the door behind her, knowing she would be counting the minutes until he returned. She pressed her fingers to her lips, and her heart quickened. Seth hadn't come right out and declared himself, but that kiss held a promise.

Nearly giddy with anticipation, she hung her hat on the hall tree. What should she wear for their afternoon together? She wanted to look her best. Her mind whirled through the possibilities until she settled on her heliotrope skirt and the matching jacket with leg-of-mutton sleeves.

Dinah grinned and started upstairs to her room. Her pleated cotton blouse with the large bow at the neck would be the perfect accompaniment, and the outfit would serve for their meeting with her father and Abby, as well. All she had to do was press it before Seth came.

She stopped on the landing. Why not take care of that now? With that chore out of the way, she would have time to relax, perhaps catch a little nap before he arrived.

She ran back down the stairs. "Mrs. Purvis, I'm home. Could I use your iron, please?"

No cheery call greeted her. She crossed the entry hall. "Mrs. Purvis?"

Dinah checked the parlor and then the dining room with no success. Perhaps Mrs. Purvis was doing some baking. She pushed open the swinging door and stepped inside the kitchen. "Mrs. Purvis, are you here?"

"No." An arm snaked out from behind her and coiled around her neck. "But I am."

"Hello, Dinah." Panic engulfed her when she recognized Alan's voice. She clawed at his arm around her throat, but he only pulled it tighter until she could barely breathe.

She could feel him fumbling at something with his free hand; then he clamped a cloth down hard over her nose, holding it there until her knees buckled.

Her thoughts clouded. She was dimly aware of being half dragged, half carried back through the parlor and out the front door, where she nearly lost her footing on the porch steps. If not for Alan's tight grip around her waist, she would have fallen to the pavement.

The sunlight hurt her eyes. Dinah tried to raise her hand to shield them, but she couldn't seem to make it move that far. She saw the neighboring houses as a blur while Alan hustled her to a cab that stood beside the curb.

Through the haze, she heard another voice ask, "Is that your sister?"

"Yes, she's very ill, I fear. Thank you for waiting."

Rough hands hoisted her up inside the cab. Dinah slumped against the seat where she landed and felt Alan climb in beside her.

Some deep part of her screamed out a warning. She had to rouse herself, to be ready to fight. Dinah drew in deep breaths, trying to clear her head. She needed her wits about her! What Alan had in mind she could not say, but one thing was clear: She had to get away.

The deep breathing seemed to work. Her mind grew less

fuzzy. Praying for success, she gathered her strength and pushed away from Alan. She scrabbled for the door handle, intent on wrenching it open and leaping from the cab. Better to risk any injury she might sustain in a fall than to remain in Alan's power.

Before she could reach the handle, his arm encircled her waist and jerked her back against him. The cloth covered her nose and mouth again, and she heard his smooth voice in her ear: "Now, now, we can't have that."

She tried to pull away the hand holding the cloth but couldn't find the strength. With a sense of despair, she felt herself slipping into the fog again.

The next thing she knew, she was being roused by a rough shake. Alan stepped across her and jumped out of the cab to pay the driver. He grabbed her around her waist and set her on the street beside him.

Dinah pushed against his chest but found she had no more strength than a kitten. *The driver!* She looked up at him, putting all her effort into making him understand. "Please."

The cabbie touched the brim of his hat. "No need to thank me, miss. I hope you get to feeling better soon." She heard him cluck to his horse and watched her only hope set off down the street at a trot.

Alan took hold of her upper arm, his fingers digging into her flesh like pincers. The pain pulled her out of her stupor enough to be able to put one foot in front of the other. She stumbled along a walk, then up a set of steps, with Alan bending over her in a manner anyone watching would think solicitous.

At the top of the steps, he opened a door and pushed her inside, then turned to close and lock it without ever letting go of her arm. With that accomplished, a cold light entered his eyes, and he abandoned all pretense of concern.

Dinah continued to draw deep breaths. With every intake of air, she felt her thoughts come back into focus. They stood in a small room—Alan's living room. Fear gave her strength, and she tried to pull away. Alan tightened his grip on her arm, and she cried out from the pain.

He propelled her across the room and stopped next to a bookcase that stood beside an open door. Dinah looked through the doorway into the room where Gladys had lain the night before.

She felt as though she would smother. "No! You can't put me in there." She planted her feet and held her ground.

"You're quite right." Alan made a quick move with his free hand, and the bookcase appeared to move away from the wall. Dinah blinked, sure she must still be under the influence of whatever he had given her.

A closed door stood behind the bookcase. Alan opened it with one hand, revealing a dimly lit opening. He pulled Dinah over in front of it where she could see a steep, narrow staircase leading downward.

"Downstairs," Alan ordered. "Now."

With her feet feeling for every step and one hand pressed against the wall, Dinah made her way to the bottom. A lamp sitting on a table at the foot of the stairs offered the only light. They stood in a musty little hallway with two closed doors on either side. Alan opened the nearest door and shoved her inside.

Dinah stumbled to a stop and turned to face him. Instinctively, she took a step back and came up hard against the opposite wall of the tiny space. She planted her hands against its surface and felt bits of the rough plaster crumble off beneath her fingertips.

"Why are you doing this?" She flinched at hearing the near hysteria in her voice.

Alan stepped into the doorway, blocking out most of the light, as well as any hope of escape. "I was a happily married man, Dinah. You stole my wife away and, with her, any hope of gaining her inheritance."

He moved forward. Dinah shrank back against the unforgiving wall. Pinpoints of plaster scored her shoulders through the fabric of her dress.

"But you're going to make it up to me," Alan continued.

"What are you talking about? Gladys will never come back to you."

"I'm not talking about Gladys. I'm talking about you."

Dinah struggled for breath.

"My dear, talkative bride was good enough to let me know that your grandmother left money to you both in equal shares." He tilted his head and clicked his tongue. "What a shame I didn't find out about that before I married Gladys. You would have been much more pleasant to have around."

"I—I don't understand."

Alan stepped forward again until his feet almost touched hers. Outlined by the faint light from the flickering lamp outside the room, he looked like some sort of hulking monster. "It's quite simple. I was patiently awaiting Gladys's birthday and our visit to her family lawyer. I will extend my patience a little while longer and wait for your birthday instead. Yours is only ten days after hers, I believe?"

Dinah felt as if she had entered a nightmare from which she had no hope of awaking. "Why do you think you would get any money of mine?"

Alan brushed his fingers along her cheek, and Dinah fought back a scream. "As my wife, you will sign a document making me the beneficiary of your wealth in the unfortunate event you should predecease me."

"Your wife!" Dinah choked on the words. "You must be mad. What makes you think I would marry you?"

His voice hardened. "Let us just say that if you don't agree to that, your preacher friend will meet an untimely demise."

"But. . .but you're still married to Gladys."

"A mere technicality—one I've managed to deal with before. Reverend Harper, the same gentleman who officiated at the ceremony with your cousin, will be most happy to perform our nuptials, as well."

He was mad; he had to be. "No man of God would agree to that." Dinah spoke with more certainty than she felt.

Alan lifted one shoulder. "*Reverend* is something of an honorary title in his case, but it does look good on legal documents. Gladys accepted him without question. It really won't matter that you know otherwise as long as your name goes on the license next to mine."

Dinah's knees gave way, and she felt herself sinking down to crouch on the dirt floor at his feet. "What then?"

"These accommodations will have to do until I find another suitable place for you to await your birthday. At that time, you will sign the document making me your beneficiary. My attorney will witness it and send a note to the lawyer handling your grandmother's estate, informing him that you regret being

263

unable to handle the matter in person but have given him full authority to take care of the transfer of funds for you."

Alan backed to the doorway, blocking out the light again. "By the way, you might be interested to know that you will be known as Mrs. Phillip Gephart. Alan Saunders will soon cease to exist."

He pointed toward a spot to Dinah's left. "You'll find your bed against the wall. There's a chamber pot underneath. All the comforts of home." He backed into the light of the hallway where Dinah could see the smile that twisted his mouth. "I'll leave you here to think things over. When you get hungry enough, I'm sure you'll decide to cooperate. If not, consider the fate of your friend should you choose to refuse."

He closed the door, leaving her in utter darkness. She heard the *click* of the key in the lock.

"No!" The scream ripped from Dinah's throat. She sprang toward the door and fumbled across the smooth wood surface until her fingers found the knob. She twisted it with all her strength, but it held fast. She knotted her hands into fists and pounded, bruising them against the unyielding surface.

Dinah tipped her head back and let out an anguished wail. This couldn't be happening. Surely she would wake up and find she had been dreaming. But the musty basement smells and the pain in her arm where Alan's fingers had dug into her tender flesh let her know it was no dream.

Her breath caught in great, hiccupping gasps. She had to find a way out. There must be one, if only she could discover it.

Placing her hands flat against the wall, she took a few shuffling steps to the right. Her palms encountered nothing but solid plaster. She reached the corner and turned. The second wall held nothing different.

Dinah started to move on, then froze when she heard a faint sound. Was Alan coming back? Every muscle in her body tensed as she strained to hear the noise again.

Tick, tick, tick. A faint tapping seemed to be coming from the wall she leaned against. Not Alan, then. Relief made her go limp. *Tick, tick, tick.* Dinah rapped against the wall with her knuckles. The tapping ceased for a moment, then started up again. Could a squirrel have gotten inside the wall? Or a rat? Dinah shuddered and fought back a sob. *Please, no. Not that.*

She continued her exploration along the back wall, then turned again at the third corner. Her shin banged against something solid. Using her hands instead of her eyes, Dinah discovered an iron bedstead topped by a thin mattress. She felt her way past the bed, then continued her search until she reached her starting point at the door, finding nothing to give her any hope.

Dinah groped her way back along the wall until she reached the bed, then sank to the floor. Laying her head on the thin, lumpy mattress, she let herself give in to despair.

"God, where are You? Why did You let this happen?" She waited, hoping for some sort of divine answer. Only the heavy stillness greeted her.

The last of her courage crumbled. Sobs wrenched her body, shaking the bedstead so it rattled against the wall. "Where are You?" she shouted into the darkness.

Her voice cracked, and a final cry wrung from her heart: "Do You even hear me?"

CHAPTER 26

The afternoon sunlight shone brighter than Seth had seen it in days. Everything, come to think of it, seemed fresh and lovely, including the nosegay he had just purchased from a street vendor.

He pressed the tiny cluster of blossoms to his nose and sniffed appreciatively. Someday he would buy the biggest bouquet he could for Dinah, but these would do for now. He didn't want to waste one precious minute of her day off hunting down a florist's shop. Not when he had such marvelous news to share with her.

He still couldn't believe it. The church board had not only embraced his proposal but had given him more than he had asked for. Enough to make a decent wage. Enough to support a family. Seth wanted to call down blessings on every member of the board, along with Amos Hall for coming up with the idea in the first place.

What would be the best way to break the news to Dinah? And when? Seth's thoughts moved in tempo with his hurried steps. He had made tentative plans for the evening, contingent upon the board's response to his request. A meal at a nice restaurant, followed by a romantic stroll, where he could tell her all that was on his heart.

But that was before her father sprang his own dinner invitation.

He had it in mind to protest and suggest another night for Dinah to meet with Abby, but then she turned to him with that look of pleading. He knew he couldn't refuse her.

It would work out better this way. With the pressure of dealing with her father's demands lifted from her shoulders, she would be free to hear what he had to say and accept without any reservations.

He hoped.

His next step, then, was to plan a truly special evening, one they would remember for the rest of their days. He was still turning possibilities over in his mind when he loped up Mrs. Purvis's front steps.

Seth tapped on the door, hoping Dinah might answer it herself just as she had the day they met. He would never forget his first sight of her dear face. The door swung open, and he held his breath.

"Did Dinah come back for her reticule?" Mrs. Purvis peered past him. "I found it when I got back from my marketing. I thought it was strange, but then it struck me that maybe you stopped by and the two of you got so caught up in each other that she didn't realize she had dropped it until later." The landlady gave him a wink and nudged him with her elbow.

267

Seth shifted the nosegay to his other hand. "I don't understand. I dropped her off this morning. She knew I was coming back after my meeting."

"How very odd." Mrs. Purvis's forehead wrinkled. "You must have come after I already left."

"I'm surprised she didn't say anything to you about going out. She didn't leave a note?"

"I didn't see anything, but you're welcome to come in and take a look around."

Seth stepped into the entry hall, his mind racing. "Where did you find her reticule?"

"Back here." Mrs. Purvis led him through the parlor and dining room and pointed to a spot just inside the kitchen door. "It was right there."

Seth laid the nosegay on the table. "That doesn't make sense. Where would she have gone without her reticule?"

Together, they walked back to the front of the house. Mrs. Purvis stopped in the entry hall. "Look. I just noticed. Her hat is still hanging there on the hall tree."

"Are you sure she isn't here? Have you checked the rest of the house—looked in her room?"

Mrs. Purvis's emphatic nod set her curls to dancing. "She's not inside, and that's a fact. She simply isn't here."

Seth opened the front door and looked up and down Blackstone Avenue, as if doing so would somehow bring Dinah into view. Unease grew within him like a gathering storm.

Mrs. Purvis joined him. "Do you suppose she went into the backyard for some reason? She might have fallen or twisted her ankle."

Slim as the possibility was, Seth grasped at it. "I'll go check."

Mrs. Purvis twisted her hands and tried to think. Where on earth could Dinah be? It wasn't like her to disappear like that without a word to anyone, not like her at all.

"Ethelinda!" a stentorian voice called from across the street. "Ethelinda Purvis!" Henrietta Boggs descended her front steps with a regal air and marched toward the boardinghouse. "I demand to know what is going on in that establishment of yours."

"Not now, Henrietta. I have a lot on my mind."

"And well you should." Mrs. Boggs wagged her finger under Mrs. Purvis's nose. "I have never seen such goings-on. I really ought to complain to the authorities. Honestly! Girls running around unchaperoned, a constant stream of men going in and out. . ."

Mrs. Purvis blinked. "Why, whatever do you mean?"

"Do you mean to tell me you don't know what's going on right under your very nose? In that case, allow me to enlighten you. That girl who is boarding with you—the one who is supposed to be so smitten with the so-called preacher. How can you put up with her coming home at all hours the way she does? Or do you even notice?"

Mrs. Purvis felt her hackles rise. "She's a hardworking girl, Henrietta. She has a job at the fairgrounds during the day, and she leads a Bible class for young girls in the evening." She squared her shoulders and drew up to her full height, putting the top of her head in the region of Mrs. Boggs's ample chin. "I am proud to know her and have her in my house."

"If that is what you think, then you haven't been doing a

very good job of keeping tabs on her behavior. I saw her walking home with him earlier today. He kissed her, Ethelinda! Right there on your front porch."

"Really?" A joyous smile widened her lips. "Oh, I knew it!" Her thoughts drifted into a happy daydream, called back by her neighbor's strident tone.

"I knew you had gone out marketing, so I watched to make sure he didn't go inside. They parted on the doorstep, but not ten minutes later, she came out on the arm of that fellow the other girl—her cousin, was it?—was so taken with."

Mrs. Purvis put one hand to her head. "What? What's that?"

"It isn't enough for her to have one man fall at her feet. She has to go after more and keep them all on her string at the same time." Mrs. Boggs curled her lip. "I ask you, is that any way for a proper young lady to behave?"

Mrs. Purvis clutched her neighbor's arm. "Tell me about the man she left with."

Mrs. Boggs sniffed. "Now you're interested. It's a little like closing the barn door after the horse is already gone, isn't it? I'm telling you it was that man her cousin has been walking out with. I recognized him easily enough."

"Are you sure it's the same one?"

The other woman bristled. "I'm absolutely sure. I've seen him over here often enough these past weeks. Do you think I made a mistake?"

Mrs. Purvis stared open mouthed, appreciating for the first time her neighbor's keen eyesight and sense of civic duty. "What were they doing? Did it look like she was going with him willingly?"

"Willingly? She was hanging on his arm, practically draped all over him." Mrs. Boggs leaned over until they stood eye to eye. "Truth to tell, from the way she walked, I thought she looked a bit tipsy. I've said it before, and I'll say it again: You really ought to screen your boarders more carefully."

"What happened then? Which way did they go?"

"He walked her down the street and handed her into a cab waiting there. An assignation if ever I saw one!"

Mrs. Purvis threw her arms around her astonished neighbor. "Thank you, Henrietta. You'll never know how happy I am that you told me."

Mrs. Boggs pulled back out of the hug and shook herself like a hen ruffling her feathers. "Well, thank goodness you've finally seen the light. I hope from now on you'll pay more attention to—"

"Not now." Mrs. Purvis picked up her skirts, flew down the porch steps, and rounded the corner of the house, feet churning against the grass. Why, she hadn't run like this since she was a girl!

"Seth!" she shouted. "Seth, I know where she is!"

Darkness, nothing but darkness.

Dinah perched on the side of the cot, her arms wrapped around her middle, and rocked back and forth, trying to ignore the thin, metal edge of the bedstead that dug into her legs.

How long had it been since she had left the cozy warmth of Mrs. Purvis's home? Without light, without any means of reference at all, there was no way to gauge the passage of time.

271

She could see nothing, hear nothing except for the intermittent tapping in the wall.

She drew up her feet and tucked them under her, praying no vermin would find their way out of the wall and into her room. *No, not a room,* she thought dully. *Call it what it is—a cell.* And she was a prisoner.

She continued rocking. How long did Alan intend to leave her there? What if she didn't see him again for days? The light breakfast she had eaten before going out to walk on the pier with Seth had long since worn off. How long would it take to starve to death? Or perish of thirst?

A new thought teased at her mind, chilling her to the bone. What if something happened to Alan? No one knew she was there. No one would know where to look for her. A low moan escaped her lips, and she felt herself sinking into hopelessness again.

She needed something else to think about, something other than her loneliness and fear. From her memory, she dredged up one of the verses she had studied for this week's Bible lesson. "God hath not given us the spirit of fear." She forced the words out through stiff lips, her voice sounding hollow in the tiny room.

She lay down on her side and curled into a ball. The darkness pressed down upon her until she felt she would suffocate. She wrapped her arms around her knees, hugging them against her chest.

"God hath not given us the spirit of fear." A spark of peace began to glow in her heart. Against all her expectations, she felt her eyelids droop, then close.

A key rattled in the lock.

In a flash, Dinah sat bolt upright.

CHAPTER 27

Thanks for meeting me here." Seth watched Mac and the two men trailing him file into the empty lot where he waited.

"I figured we might need some extra help, so I brought a couple of guys from the gym." Mac nodded at his companions. "Meet Fred and Leo."

Seth studied the newcomers. He knew the type, men ready for a rough-and-tumble at a moment's notice whether they had a good reason or not. He wouldn't want to meet either of them in a dark alley. "Glad to have you here."

Fred flexed his fingers. "So where is this fellow? I don't hold with anybody hurtin' women."

"Around the corner." Seth pointed. "The third house down."

"Are you sure he's there?" Mac asked.

"No," Seth admitted. "But I do know he has Dinah, and this is the only place I can think of to look." He steeled himself against thoughts of what would happen if they got inside the house and didn't find her. "If he isn't there, maybe he left some clue inside the house. And if he is. . ."

Leo's eyes glittered when he smiled. "If he is, we'll take care of him."

Seth looked at his band of rescuers and gave a brief nod. "Fair enough. Let's move out." He led off down the block, trying to prepare himself for what would come next.

What would he do if Dinah wasn't there? His stomach tightened. The question had taunted him ever since he sent Mac that plea for help.

What if he didn't find her at all? No, he wouldn't even consider that possibility. Life without Dinah didn't bear thinking about. It wouldn't be a life at all.

Seth waved the group to a stop at a spot where they wouldn't be visible from the windows if Alan should indeed be in the house.

Fred gave the place a long, measuring look. "This is it?"

Seth nodded slowly, beset by second thoughts. "Look, this is my problem. I don't want to cause any trouble for the three of you. Maybe we should just go get the police."

Leo snorted. "Sure, go ahead. And let me tell you what'll happen then. You don't know she's in there for sure, right? So you go to the station and tell them the whole story. They tell you they can't come out without something more to go on, so you've wasted all that time. And even if he is here now, maybe he's flown the coop by the time you get back. Then how are you going to find your girl?" He shook his head and smacked his fist against his palm. "Some things you just gotta do for yourself."

Seth looked at the three of them in turn and nodded. He led them up the steps to the front porch, amazed at how little noise they made. How many times had they done something like this before? Seth pushed the thought away. He had a feeling he didn't really want to know.

He edged over to the window and peeked inside. His heart sank when he saw the empty living room. He swallowed back his disappointment and turned to the others. "It doesn't look like he's here."

Mac rolled his shoulders. "Then let's see if he left some clue inside."

Gingerly, Seth tried the front door. "It's locked."

Fred pulled a slender piece of metal from his vest pocket and nudged Seth to one side. "Not to worry. I can take care of that."

The door of the cell creaked open. Alan lounged in the opening, holding a plate of roasted chicken. "Have you made up your mind yet?"

Picking up a drumstick, he made a show of tearing off a tender bite. He chewed it slowly without taking his eyes off Dinah. "There's another plate upstairs if you'd like some. Of course, you'll have to agree to sign the marriage license like a good girl."

Dinah clenched her fists and gave him a stony stare.

"You need to understand that you are going to put your signature on the marriage license, willingly or not. It will be much more pleasant for you if you cooperate." Alan chewed another morsel. "One other thing to consider—it's some time until your birthday. You could get very hungry by then."

"So. . ." He waved the plate back and forth. "Should I go get the rest of that chicken or not?"

The savory aroma made Dinah realize how ravenous she was. She dug her nails into her palms. "I'm fine." Without warning, her stomach rumbled.

Alan chuckled. "That's what I thought." His smile held an excitement Dinah found more disturbing than his anger.

He finished the last of the chicken and licked his fingers one by one. "We're in luck. 'Reverend' Harper will be coming over this afternoon. He'll bring the license with him."

"He may call himself a minister, but he's no better than you—a criminal."

"Perhaps." Alan seemed unperturbed. "But we have a lucrative little arrangement. We've worked quite well together in the past."

Desperation gave Dinah a boldness she didn't really feel. "You can't hope to get away with this. I'll tell the authorities it was a forced marriage."

The look on Alan's face made her blood run cold. "What makes you think you'll have that opportunity?" He turned to set the plate on the table outside the door.

Seeing her chance, Dinah ran at him with her hands outstretched. If she could shove him off balance and get to the stairs, she might be able to elude him long enough to reach the street. It was the slimmest of possibilities, but it was all she had.

Quick as a striking snake, Alan spun around. His arm lashed out, and his fist caught Dinah on the side of her jaw. She flew across the cubicle and crashed into the cot. Its legs buckled under the impact, spilling her off the mattress and onto the floor.

Alan remained in the doorway, his chest heaving. "Don't—ever—try that—again." He took a slow step toward her. "I could have made things somewhat pleasant for you. But not now."

Dinah froze where she landed, sure the end had come. Seth's image swam into her mind, and regret for what they might have had together choked her.

Alan's shadow fell over her. Dinah pulled her knees to her chest and wrapped her arms around her head. *Oh, God, help me!*

He stopped in midstride, and Dinah peeked up to see him tilt his head as if listening. A look of deep satisfaction spread over his face. "I hear someone at the door. It appears the good reverend has arrived."

He stepped back into the hallway and swung the door toward him. Just before it closed, his lips parted in a parody of a smile. "Better freshen up, my sweet. It's your wedding day."

Fred jiggled the metal strip in the lock again. With another quick flick of his wrist, the door stood open. The four men entered, fanning out across the living room. Seth stood near the front window, wondering where to begin. The room looked just as it had the last time he had been there.

Or did it? He scanned the room, trying to pinpoint what it was that caught his notice. His gaze came to rest on the opposite side of the room. One edge of the bookcase stood out a few inches from the wall.

Seth nudged Mac and started over toward it. Before he got halfway across the room, the bookcase swung out farther, and Alan stepped from behind it.

At the sight of Seth, Alan froze, and his jaw went slack. He took in the other three men, darted a quick glance behind him, then broke for the kitchen door.

"Grab him!" Mac yelled.

Seth sprinted forward, but Leo sailed past him. Wrapping his arms around Alan's knees in a flying tackle, Leo brought him down with a *crash* that shook the house.

Dinah pulled her legs underneath her and put her hand to her throbbing jaw, trying to bring her thoughts into some kind of order. He would be back. She had to think clearly.

She crawled to the door and pressed her ear against the heavy wooden panel. Alan and his spurious minister might come downstairs in a matter of minutes. What was she going to do?

She needed a way to defend herself, something capable of inflicting more damage than she could with her two bare hands. She might not be able to break her way free, but she wouldn't give in without a fight. What could she use? There had to be something.

Dinah crawled back over to the remains of the cot and felt around in the dark like a blind woman. Her fingers encountered the mattress and the shards of the shattered chamber pot, then closed around a broken bed slat. She pulled it out from under the mattress and scuttled back over to the door.

Pushing herself to her feet, she pressed her ear to the door again, straining to hear any advance warning of the men's approach. She had to be ready when they came. The bed slat felt solid in her hands. She ran her fingers along its length, approving of the jagged splinters at one end. She tightened her grip and stood, poised to swing her weapon with every bit of strength she possessed.

So far, all remained quiet. Dinah focused all her being on her sense of hearing, everything within her intent on catching any noise, any shred of sound at all.

She heard a muffled *crash*, followed by faint voices. She squashed her ear against the door. More than one voice; someone was up there with him, then. Dinah held her breath, the better to concentrate. She couldn't tell who was speaking or make out any words, but the tone sounded angry.

Hope stirred. Maybe it wasn't his friend. Maybe something had gone wrong with his plan. And whatever went wrong for Alan might turn out to be good for her.

Dinah dropped the slat and beat upon the door with her fists, hoping to attract the notice of whoever was up there. No good; the wood absorbed the sound. She picked up the slat again and raised it over her shoulder, then swung it against the wood again and again, hoping against hope that someone would hear and come to investigate.

CHAPTER 28

W here is she?"

Leo and Fred hauled Alan to his feet, one holding him by his collar, the other gripping his shoulder. Alan sagged between them, his dapper appearance disheveled for once. His eyes darted between the men like a trapped rat seeking escape.

"Where is she?" Seth repeated. "What have you done with her?"

The old arrogant light returned to Alan's eyes. "Done with who? I have no idea what you're talking about."

Seth grabbed him by the shirt front and pulled him free of Mac's men. With his face mere inches away from Alan's, he ground out, "What have you done with Dinah?"

Alan's lips lifted in a sneer that made the blood run like fire through Seth's veins. "I take it you've misplaced her? What a pity. Such a pretty thing, wasn't she?"

Seth shoved his tormentor to arm's length with his left hand

and smashed his jaw with a roundhouse right. Alan crumpled to the floor like a broken toy.

Seth looked down at his fallen foe. He rubbed his knuckles and gave Mac a rueful grin. "The church board might not approve, but between you and me, that felt good."

Fred pointed at Alan and pursed his lips. "Nice punch. Only one problem. Now he can't tell you where your girl is."

"Maybe he doesn't have to." Seth started toward the bookcase. "Let's see where he came from."

He pulled the bookcase out farther. Behind it stood an open door and a set of stairs leading downward. On a table at the foot of the stairs, a small lamp burned. Seth descended, every sense on the alert. A muffled thumping brought him to a stop. He scrutinized the floor below but saw no one. He continued down, step by cautious step, peering into the dimly lit corners.

At the bottom, he turned up the lamp to give more light. A small hallway lay before him, with two closed doors on either side. The end of the hallway gave way to an open, unfinished area. The thumping continued, seeming to come from the first door to his right.

With his heart pounding in time with the rhythmic thudding, Seth grabbed the doorknob and rattled it. Immediately, the sound stopped. He put his mouth to the door. "Dinah?"

"Seth!" Her faint scream barely penetrated the heavy wood. "Get me out of here!"

Using both hands, he twisted the doorknob, but it held fast. He jumped back and kicked the door, to no avail. Running to the foot of the stairs, he yelled, "She's down here, Mac, but the door is locked. Look and see if he has any keys on him."

A moment later, Mac appeared at the top of the stairs. "I

found a ring of keys on the floor. Looks like he dropped them when Leo tackled him." He tossed the keys down, and Seth snagged them out of the air.

Four keys dangled from the ring. He tried them one by one, praying the right one would be there. The third key turned in the lock. Seth flung the door open. Dinah stood in front of a twisted cot, clutching a splintered board in her hands. She let it clatter to the floor and flung herself into his arms. "Oh, Seth!"

He crushed her to him and buried his face in her hair. "I was so afraid I'd lost you." He cupped her cheeks in his hands and tilted her face upward. Dinah flinched.

"What's wrong?" Seth pulled her out into the hallway, where he could see the light bruising along her swollen jawline. His teeth clenched. "He did this to you?"

"Yes, but nothing more." She touched her fingertips to the discolored area. "Nothing more, thank God! I was so afraid he was going to kill me."

"Thank God," Seth repeated and pulled her back into his embrace.

Footsteps pounded on the stairs and Mac called out, "Everything okay? Fred went to find a cop. Leo's watching Saunders." He stopped abruptly when he spotted Seth with Dinah in his arms. "Oops, looks like you're doing fine."

Seth turned his attention back to Dinah. With infinite care, he tipped her head back again and lowered his lips to hers. Dinah gave a soft cry and slid her arms around his neck. He pressed her against him and held her as if he would never let her go again.

Mac cleared his throat. "I'll see you back upstairs...whenever you get around to it." His steps retreated, then Seth heard him shout, "Hey, watch out!"

Dinah followed close behind Seth as he charged up the stairs. They found Mac dusting himself off next to the bookcase.

"What happened?" Seth demanded.

Mac didn't meet their eyes. "He must have come to and decided to play possum and wait for his chance. When I stepped out here, he jumped up and shoved Leo into me, then took off out the back. Leo's gone after him." He hung his head. "I'm sorry, Seth."

Alan was free? Dinah pressed close to Seth. He took her into the circle of his arm and drew her to his side. A moment ago, it seemed all would end well, and now this crushing blow. When would this nightmare end?

Moments later, Leo stomped through the back door. He glanced at Mac and shook his head. "He got away. There's no sign of him anywhere. That is one slippery character."

Dinah wagged her head from side to side, her whole being screaming in denial. She clung to Seth. "What am I going to do? What if he tries to do this again?"

Seth's arm tightened about her, and he pulled her around so that her head rested against his chest. Cradling her in his arms, he rocked back and forth as though he held a small child. "That isn't going to happen. Fred will be back with the police any minute. With what you have to tell them, they'll have plenty to go on this time."

"But he knows where I live. What if he comes back and tries to hurt me or Mrs. Purvis? You haven't seen him when he's angry, Seth. He's a madman."

Seth's fingers stroked the side of her face, tracing over her bruised jaw with a feather touch. "The police will be looking for him now. His game depended on his staying unseen and unknown, working in the dark. Once the light shines on him, he'll be so bent on staying out of sight he won't have time to think about coming after you."

Dinah leaned her forehead into his chest, wishing she never had to leave the safety of his arms. "I don't think I'll ever be able to draw an easy breath again as long as I know he's out there."

"The police will handle it. Trust God to take care of things. Look what He did today—if Alan hadn't just been coming up those stairs when we came in, we never would have known where to look for you." He ran his hands up and down her arms. "Even the cot breaking worked into His plan. It gave you that piece of wood you used to bang on the door. That was a clever idea, by the way. It was the tapping that led me straight to you. How long had you been keeping that up?"

"Only since I knew there was someone else in the house. I wouldn't have dared to do it if I thought Alan was here alone. I wasn't sure anyone would be able to hear me." A shudder ran through her, and Seth began the soothing strokes on her arms again. "It was so awful down there in that horrid little room, with just a cot over in the corner and not a speck of light. I couldn't even hear anything except something tapping inside the wall. It was like being shut up in a dungeon."

Dinah jerked back and stared up at Seth. "Why would he have a room set up like that? It's as if he planned to keep someone imprisoned." Her stomach curdled. "Seth, there are three other doors down there. That tapping. . ."

She gathered her skirts and hurried down the stairs as quickly as she could. This time it was Seth's turn to follow. "Where are the keys?" she called over her shoulder.

She spotted the ring hanging from the lock of her former prison. Yanking them loose, she moved to the next door. Her fingers refused to cooperate when she tried to sort through the keys. She thrust them at Seth. "Here, you do it."

The second key turned in the lock with a satisfying *click*. Seth pushed the door open. A skinny, bedraggled girl sat on the edge of a cot identical to Dinah's, blinking in the sudden light.

She stared at them as if unable to believe what she saw. Even from the doorway, Dinah could see her lips tremble. "Miss Mayhew? You found me."

If not for Seth's support, Dinah knew she would have fallen to the floor. She looked at the pitiful creature and held out her arms. "Martha!"

Dinah put her arms around Martha and held her close on the serpentine-back sofa. The girl shivered as though she would never be warm again.

Dinah brushed the matted hair away from Martha's forehead. "You've been missing for nearly three weeks. Have you been down there all this time?"

Martha sniffed back tears and nodded. "I was on my way home from the market. I was going to put things away and then take Jenny to class. This man came up and started talking to me there on the street. He said I looked about the same size as his sister, and she had a lot of nice clothes she wanted to give away. He wondered if maybe I could use them.

"I told him I had to get back home. Then he told me he had a carriage around the corner and he could take me to his sister's house to pick up the clothes." Her voice wobbled, then broke. "He said he'd have me back home in no time."

Dinah held her until the sobs subsided. Her own ordeal had lasted less than one day. What untold horrors had Martha experienced in the time she'd been locked away in the basement?

Martha scrubbed at her cheeks with the heels of her hands. "I guess it wasn't very smart of me. Somewhere deep inside, I felt like something wasn't right. But I just kept thinking about those clothes. He made them sound so pretty, like the kind *you* wear, and I thought maybe I'd look like I amounted to something if I could dress like that."

Dinah's heart melted, and her tears mingled with Martha's. "Oh, my dear."

"It was pretty stupid, wasn't it? I know I'll never look as elegant as you do."

Dinah turned the girl so she faced her squarely. "Listen to me, Martha. A person's value isn't based on outward appearances. What God treasures is the person you are inside, where it counts."

Martha sniffed again. "Maybe He really does care about me. Down there in the dark, I kept thinking about that story you told us. The one about the giant. Remember?"

Dinah nodded slowly. "David and Goliath."

"You said it meant we could take our problems to God and expect Him to answer. I kept thinking that maybe this was something too big for even God to take care of." She gave Dinah a watery smile. "But it wasn't, was it?"

Tears threatened to spill over again. "No," Dinah said. "It

wasn't at all. He was busy protecting us both."

"How long have I been gone?" Martha's forehead crinkled. "I've been asleep a lot of the time. It seemed like every time he fed me, I couldn't stay awake, so the last couple of times, I shoved the food under my cot. The room was so dark he never even noticed. Then I'd pretend to be asleep when he came in."

Dinah looked over Martha's shoulder at Seth and mouthed, "Laudanum." He nodded, grim-faced.

"That's how I knew when he brought you in. I heard a little noise and listened at the door. I thought maybe he'd put someone in the next room, so I started tapping on the wall."

Dinah's heart swelled. "I'm so glad you did."

"Is there anybody else down there?"

Seth knelt in front of them. "No, we checked the other rooms." He exchanged glances with Dinah. The rooms had been empty save for the same sparse furnishings Dinah's and Martha's cells held, but both showed signs of being recently occupied. Dinah didn't want to imagine what had become of the unfortunate occupants.

"What kind of monster is he?" she breathed.

Martha nodded vigorously. "Monster, that's a good name for him. He used to talk to me when he thought I was asleep. He'd tell me how he hoped I wasn't too impatient to leave, that as soon as he had enough girls ready for another shipment, he was going to send us all on a trip to New York where we'd meet a lot of men. He kept talking about how my life was going to change, but he said I'd get used to it."

Her face crumpled, and she buried her face in Dinah's shoulder. "But I didn't want to get used to anything like that, Miss Mayhew. I just wanted to go home."

287

The front door scraped open, and Fred entered, followed by a man in uniform. Dinah drew her first confident breath of the evening. "As soon as you tell the policeman everything you've told me, we'll see that you get there."

Alan Saunders ducked into an alley and tried to work out his next move. It had been simple enough to evade the big oaf who followed him out the back door. A few quick twists and turns, and he had been free.

But now what? He couldn't go back to the house, not with that preacher and his friends on the lookout for him. No doubt by now, Dinah had given them all the details of what he'd done and planned to do, enough to lock him away for a good long while.

Had they found the other girl? A metallic taste filled his mouth. He should have gotten rid of her days ago. Never leave a loose end; that had always been his rule, and it had served him well. He had never broken it until today, and look what had happened. Instead of walking boldly down the street, he was reduced to darting down alleys and back streets.

He moved to the mouth of the alley and took a quick look down the adjacent street. In the next breath, he pulled back, cursing his luck. Another policeman. It seemed he saw one every time he turned a corner. So far, he had managed to avoid them, but how long could that last?

He had to do something. His nerves were on a raw edge. Even the common people on the street made him jittery. Every time one of them looked at him twice, he felt like he was going to jump out of his skin.

This was wrong, all wrong. He was supposed to be the hunter, not the prey.

Chicago was no place for him now; that much was clear. But where could he go? The only money he had available was what he carried in his pockets, enough for a couple of meals but no more.

Think. Think! He needed to find someplace where he could take shelter.

The answer struck him like a thunderbolt. *McGinty's.* That would be just the place! He had done good work for the man. McGinty was in his debt. Surely he would protect him, give him a place to lie low for a day or two. When the pressure was off, he could go to his bank and withdraw the money on deposit under the name of Edward Stephens. Once he had those funds in hand, he would be free to travel anywhere he wished, and McGinty and the city of Chicago would never see him again.

But he couldn't go there just yet. Too many people still roamed the streets, not to mention the police. He needed someplace to hide until dark. A safe location where he could stay out of the public view.

There it was, just the place. He trotted down the alley, careful to keep close against the fences, and darted into a broad, open doorway.

CHAPTER 29

Dinah looked up at the turrets of the Café de Marine.

"Are you sure you want to do this?" Concern colored Seth's voice.

"I have to. I gave him my word. And I need to have this over with."

She looked down at her blue-checked dress and adjusted the bow at the front. The heliotrope skirt and jacket hung in her wardrobe, still unironed. A momentary pang of regret assailed her, remembering her plans to look especially nice for Seth.

No matter. In her state of near exhaustion, extraneous things like wearing a particular dress didn't seem to be important anymore. She was alive; she was with Seth. Those were the things that counted.

Dinah put her hand to her mouth to stifle a yawn. Between recounting her ordeal to the policeman—which he assured them would set off a citywide manhunt—and seeing Martha's glad reunion with her family, she'd hardly had a moment to draw a breath. More than anything, she would love to fall into her cozy bed at Mrs. Purvis's and sleep for a week. But that wasn't likely to happen.

"Ah, here you are!" Her father strode toward them, jaunty as ever. "I was afraid you weren't going to make it."

Dinah summoned up a smile. "No, Papa, I told you we'd be here."

"Come on. Abby and Hannah are waiting for us over by the door."

Seth put out his hand. "Mr. Mayhew, before this goes any further, there are some things you ought to know."

Her father jingled the coins in his pocket and darted quick glances toward the restaurant. "Can't we talk about it over dinner?"

"I don't think so." Seth's voice held a note of resolve. "This may cover some things we wouldn't want to discuss in front of a little girl."

"What kind of things? What's going on, Dinah?"

Dinah's hand rose of its own accord, and her fingers brushed the tender spot on her jaw. Surely he couldn't fail to notice the blossoming bruise, even in the waning light.

You're looking at me, Papa, but do you really see me?

Seth slipped his arm around her waist, and she leaned against him, grateful for his support. "Sir, a lot has happened since we saw you this morning. In that time, your daughter has been abducted and held captive by a villain of the worst sort. If not for the grace of God, she would still be in his clutches."

He continued, his voice firm. "I don't believe that sitting in a roomful of people and trying to behave as though everything is normal would be the best thing for her tonight. Frankly, I tried to talk her out of it, but she insisted on coming."

"That's my girl." Her father chuckled. "Always a woman of her word."

The way Seth's jaw tightened told Dinah his patience was wearing thin. "Why don't we find a quiet place where we can all sit down and talk?"

Her father started to sputter out a reply; then he stopped and looked at Dinah. "You're okay, aren't you, honey?"

Would she ever be all right again? "I will be, but Seth is right. I don't think I'm up to being around a lot of people."

Her father patted her on the shoulder. "We can ask for a table in a quiet corner. You still have to eat, after all, and I've made a reservation. What do you say? You'll feel better for having a good meal inside you."

"I really don't think—"

"Come on, Dinah." He used the smooth, persuasive tone she knew so well. "You promised you'd talk to Abby, and I'm counting on you."

"And I will. It's just that. . ." Her voice cracked, and she fought to keep it under control. "Don't you understand, Papa? I have been so afraid today. That man was talking about killing me!"

Her father placed his hands on her shoulders and planted a kiss on her forehead, like he used to do when she was a little girl. "It must have been awful, honey. I'm sorry you had to go through all that." He let out a long sigh. "Okay, okay. Let's go find some benches over by the lagoon and sit there. This isn't the way I planned things, but I've got to have you talk to Abby. She needs to hear what you have to say so she can make up her mind."

"I've already made up my mind." Abby stepped forward from the shadows. "This is your daughter, Ernie, your own flesh and blood. You heard what she's been through today. What's wrong with you? She needs to know you love her, but all you can think about is what you want."

Dinah's father gawked at her. "Abby, I do love her. That's why I suggested we skip the restaurant and find someplace quieter to talk. She knows I care about her, don't you, Dinah?" He stretched out his hand toward Abby. "Go on. Get Hannah and bring her back here. We'll all go sit down and talk this out, the five of us."

"After what I heard, I wouldn't take a chance on you, even if it was just myself and I didn't have a little girl to think about. I have to admit you can be a real charmer when you put your mind to it. Too bad it doesn't go all the way to your heart." Abby tapped her chest with her fingers. "If you treat your own daughter like this, how would you treat me in a few years?"

She shook her head slowly. "Good-bye, Ernie. I'm heading back to Minneapolis." She walked back toward the café, calling for her daughter.

Dinah's father stared after her, his mouth working soundlessly.

Dinah felt the prick of tears behind her eyes. She stepped forward and laid her hand on her father's arm. "I'm sorry, Papa."

"Sorry?" Her father found his voice. "It's a little late for that, don't you think? I brought you here, thinking you could help me out, and all you've done is think about yourself." He turned and watched Abby's and Hannah's retreating figures with a look of longing. Abby never looked back.

"If I've learned one thing over the past few weeks, it's that

293

God can take the very things that cause us the most pain and turn them around for our good." Dinah reached out to him again, but he shook her hand off and fixed her with a look of disdain.

"I wish I'd never sent you that letter. I thought you could help, but you've ruined everything."

Alan Saunders crawled out from under the pile of straw in the back of the livery stable and dusted himself off. Horses whinnied and stomped in the nearby stalls. He slipped down the broad center aisle and out into the alley before the hostler came to see what was causing the disturbance.

His nose crinkled at the stable's acrid smell even after spending two miserable hours burrowed in that dusty straw waiting for night to fall. He ran his hand through his hair. Bits of straw sifted their way past his collar. He cursed and scratched the back of his neck, then set out into the welcoming dark.

It was almost midnight by the time he gave the coded knock on McGinty's door. One of the ever-present henchmen opened it and gazed at him with a flat-eyed stare.

"I need to see McGinty. Now."

McGinty looked up when they entered his office. Alan was not surprised to see him awake and still at his desk. Among those who knew him, the man's ability to go without sleep was legendary. Alan found this capacity to function better in the wee hours a fitting attribute for one of the denizens of the night.

McGinty studied him a long moment before speaking. "What brings you here at such an hour?"

He had worked out his pitch during his hours beneath the straw, knowing it would have to strike just the right note. "I need a place to stay for a couple of days—disappear from the public eye, as it were. I was hoping I could count on you to help me out."

"Were you now?" McGinty tapped his fingertips on the desktop. "And I wonder who you might be hiding from. It wouldn't be the law, would it?"

Alan attempted a light laugh. "It's nothing urgent, just a little misunderstanding. But it's important I stay out of their reach for the next day or two."

McGinty patted his fingers together. "So the police are after you. And you led them here."

The glint in his eyes jolted Alan like an electric shock. He hastened to add, "It has nothing to do with our business arrangement. I swear it."

McGinty picked up his cigar from the ashtray and drew on it. He tipped his head back and blew a series of smoke rings toward the ceiling. "I believe you, Alan. This has to do with the girl you snatched today, the one you planned to force to marry you. Am I right?"

Alan felt his world begin to crumble.

McGinty gave a gentle chuckle. "Did you think I managed to stay clear of trouble the way I do without getting inside information from the police from time to time? I have quite a network of information."

He planted his palms on the desk and stood. "They don't mind looking the other way when it comes to the brothel trade; I pay them well enough for that. But here, dear boy, you're talking outright murder." He clicked his tongue. "You've become troublesome, my lad. I would have been content just letting you hang out to dry if you'd stayed out there on your own. But now you've gone and brought your troubles to my doorstep."

Alan opened his mouth, but no sound came out.

"You're right about one thing, Alan. You do need to disappear." McGinty gestured with his right hand.

Alan looked over his shoulder to see two hard-faced men materialize from the office's dim corners. A third blocked the door. The room suddenly seemed devoid of air. There would be no slipping past these three.

Realization crashed upon him with sickening clarity. He'd been wrong. Letting the police capture him would have been better, after all.

CHAPTER 30

Dinah waited while Seth opened the door and held it for her. Their steps echoed down the empty hallway.

"I don't even know why I'm here tonight."

"Because you're the teacher. You made the commitment. If only one child comes—even if none of them show up tonight—you have to be here. It's that consistency we talked about the very first time we discussed the class. In the long run, you'll be glad you came regardless of who is here."

She saw the challenge in his eyes and looked away. But Seth was right; she had made the choice, and she had to follow through on it.

Dinah marched the rest of the way down the hall to her classroom and paused with her hand on the doorknob. "All right, I'll do it. I may sit out the whole class period alone, but I'll do it."

She took two steps inside the room before her mind registered the scene before her. All nine of her girls sat demurely in their semicircle. The rest of the room was filled wall to wall with their families, and a smile wreathed every face.

Dinah put her hand to her throat and stumbled back. "What's this?"

Jenny rose and tugged her forward. "We just wanted to thank you for loving us."

Her aunt nodded. "Martha told us how you found her and how much that Bible story helped her hold on."

Martha beamed, misty eyed, from her place directly behind Jenny's chair.

Dinah looked around at the gathering. "I—I don't know what to say."

She felt Seth move up beside her. He grinned and leaned close enough for her to hear his whisper: "I told you you'd be glad you came."

Jenny's father cleared his throat. "I got to admit we thought at first you were just doing this to make yourself feel good. But then the things you did for these girls—taking them to the fair, sticking it out and being here whether the girls showed up or not, and then bringing our Martha home—well, we all just wanted to tell you we're glad you're here, and we hope you'll stay." He turned to his neighbors, and the room filled with cheers and applause.

Dinah blinked hard but couldn't stop the tears from rolling down her cheeks. "Thank you. Thank you all so much." She gave a shaky laugh. "I do have a lesson ready for tonight, but I'm not sure I'm prepared to teach it to such a large crowd."

Anastasia's mother waved her hand. "Don't you worry about any lesson. It doesn't matter tonight. We just wanted to come out and tell you thanks for being here for our girls." Murmurs of assent rippled around the room.

"Thank you all for coming." Dinah swiped at her cheeks. "You have no idea how much this means to me."

Alice stepped forward. "One more thing. That story you told Jenny and Martha—the one about the giant? I never heard anything like that before." She looked around, as if gathering courage from the others. "Some of us were wondering if you'd start a class for us women. We'd like to know what you've got to say."

Dinah choked back her sobs, too overcome to speak. She turned to Seth, who winked and squeezed her shoulder. "Are you ready to take on another class?"

Joy bubbled up inside her. Still too filled with emotion to speak, she could only nod. She would teach any number of classes, providing God wanted her to.

Admiration shone in Seth's eyes. "I'm proud of you. You've more than proven yourself to these girls. . .and to me."

As if someone had given a signal, the girls jumped up from their chairs and swarmed around Dinah. She hugged first one, then another, wishing she could wrap her arms around all of them at once. Their parents crowded behind them, offering more words of thanks and encouragement.

Through tear-filmed eyes, Dinah looked at their faces—so hostile in the beginning, so welcoming now—and reflected on the turn her life had taken.

While she floundered trying to understand all that went on, God's hand had been at work in everything, even using her father to lead her—not away from Gladys, but to Chicago, where she could find the place of service He planned for her all along. A place of service and. . .

Dinah looked over the heads of her girls at the man she had come to love. A question rose within her heart, and she thought she saw an answer in his eyes.

"Why are we turning this way?" Dinah tilted her face and looked up at Seth. "I thought we were going back to the boardinghouse."

"Since we didn't stay long at the class tonight, we have some extra time. I thought we might spend it at the fairgrounds."

"You mean walk around and look at it like normal people?" Her lighthearted laugh made his heart sing.

"Something like that." The lights would be on soon, transforming the parklike setting into a glittering fairyland. It would be a perfect night for seeing the grounds. But he didn't plan on spending a lot of time looking at exhibits.

A couple passed them, moving away from the direction of the fairgrounds. Dinah gasped and huddled close to him before shooting a glance back over her shoulder.

Seth wrapped his arm around her shoulders and pulled her tight against his side. "What's wrong?"

"That man." She gave a shaky laugh. "He reminded me of Alan. But he isn't, of course. How silly of me to react that way." She tilted her chin up and made a brave attempt at a smile, but Seth could feel the shudder that rippled through her body.

He drew her aside under the spreading arms of a mulberry tree and let the throng of fairgoers flow past them. "There's nothing silly about it. You've been through a terrible experience. It's going to take time for you to recover from it."

"Of course. It's only a matter of time." Her smile wobbled,

and tears pooled along her lower lids. "But I don't know if I ever will get over it. Not completely, anyway. As long as I know he's out there, I'll always wonder when he's going to show up again." Her voice broke on a sob, and she rested her forehead against his chest. "I couldn't bear it if something like that happened again, Seth. I couldn't!"

"You don't need to worry about him." Seth brushed his fingers through the curls that framed her cheeks and lifted her face until their gazes met. "He'll never bother you again, I promise."

The sad light in her eyes twisted at his heart. "We both want to believe that, but there's no way to know for sure. He'll come back some day—I just know it. I can't get the thought out of my mind. And those poor women he sent to New York! I lie awake at night praying for them and wondering if there's any hope."

"There is." Seth cupped her face in his hands. "The Chicago police are already acting on what Martha told them. They're going to alert the New York authorities to see if any of the women can be rescued. Let's keep on praying they'll all be set free."

Dinah nodded in solemn agreement. "I will. My heart aches for them. Some of them are no older than Martha. How many others is he going to hurt? And how will I ever feel free of him?"

Seth drew his thumbs across her cheekbones with a feather touch. He hadn't planned on bringing up such a dark subject on this, of all nights. Still, the most important thing at the moment was to put her fears to rest. He hesitated a moment more, then made up his mind. "Mac has friends in many places. He came to see me this afternoon. Alan has already been located."

Dinah's lips parted, and her fingers dug into his arms. "When? Where is he now?"

301

"They found him this morning, floating in the Chicago River. He'll never hurt you. . .or anyone else. . .again."

Her eyes widened as the meaning of his words sank in. "The river. You mean someone—"

"More than likely." He pressed his forehead against hers, remembering the question that sprang from his lips the moment Mac shared the news: *"McGinty?"*

Mac had given an eloquent shrug. *"Probably. But they'll never pin it on him."*

Not now, perhaps, but the hoodlum wouldn't go unpunished for his evil deeds forever. That would be a problem for the police to solve, though. Right now, Seth had other priorities. He slipped his arms around Dinah's waist and whispered, "You're free, my love. You'll never have to worry about him again."

Her breath caught. "I'm not sure how to feel now. It will be wonderful not to keep on living in fear. But I almost feel guilty about being so relieved."

Seth shook his head. "Every one of us is responsible for the decisions we make. He made the choices that brought him to this end. It's tragic, but it isn't your fault. Never think that."

He dropped a light kiss on her forehead and led her to the fair's entrance, where they pushed through the turnstiles and made their way past the noisy hubbub of the Midway to the shaded pathways leading to the Court of Honor.

Dinah slowed, her attention caught by something on their left. Seth followed her gaze to the spires of the Café de Marine and frowned at the reminder of the night her father had rejected her.

"Have you heard anything from him?"

Dinah shook her head. "And to think, he was the reason I

came here. When I got that letter, I just knew everything was going to change. All those hopes I had, all the dreams I built up in my mind over the years. . ." Her voice dwindled to a whisper. "That's all they were—dreams."

Seth took her hand and twined his fingers through hers. "You do know it's not your fault?"

She mustered up a smile. "I'm beginning to realize that. It isn't so much that he doesn't care about me. I honestly think he's incapable of caring about anybody but himself, and there's nothing I can do to change that."

He tightened his grip on her fingers. "There's only so much any human can do. We'll keep on praying that God will open his heart." He drew her to a stop.

Dinah looked up at the long, white edifice before them. "We're starting with the Woman's Building?"

"Actually, I had something else in mind." Seth gestured in the opposite direction, where several gondolas lay moored at the boat landing.

The glow on Dinah's face rivaled the incandescent bulbs that outlined the buildings of the Court of Honor. *So far, so good.* He recognized Giuseppe in the nearest gondola and waved.

The boatman spread his arms wide. "Ah, you have returned. You want another tour of the lagoon?"

Seth waited until he helped Dinah maneuver down the small, square step and into the boat, then motioned Giuseppe aside. "No tour, just lots of bridges."

Giuseppe beamed and winked. "I understand, *signore*."

Seth stepped in beside Dinah and patted his jacket pocket to make sure it still held the small parcel he had tucked inside it earlier. He settled onto the tufted seat, and Giuseppe pushed the small craft away from the landing.

Dinah snuggled against him, far more relaxed than on their previous ride. He stretched his arm out along the seat back, and she rested her head on his shoulder.

Giuseppe steered them past the tip of the Wooded Island and sang softly from his position in the stern. The setting could not have been more perfect.

Seth rubbed his cheek against Dinah's hair, savoring the softness of her glossy curls. "It's been quite a week."

Dinah nodded. "When I first came to Chicago, I told myself I was looking for adventure. I never imagined it would lead to anything like what we've been through."

"You've handled it amazingly well."

"It never would have happened that way without God." She shifted and turned to look up at him. "And you."

Looking at her sweet face only inches away, Seth found it hard to fight the temptation to press a lingering kiss onto her full lips. . .and decided he didn't want to resist after all.

When they drew apart, he could see Dinah's eyes sparkle in the moonlight. "I didn't see any bridge."

Seth's heart hammered at her nearness and the sweet, honeyed taste of her lips. "It's okay to break a tradition now and then. Providing, of course, that you begin a new tradition of your own."

Dinah sighed and nestled against him. "I think I like this new one better." They sat in silence while the gondola rippled across the dark lagoon.

Seth looked out across the water at the lighted walkways filled with people and thought of the days he spent wheeling visitors around the vast fairgrounds. The first time he had laid eyes on the wonders of the White City, he had been struck by its inspiring splendor. But mingled with that sense of awe had been the knowledge that, as splendid as this was, heaven would be a place of infinitely more beauty.

Dinah stirred, and Seth looked down at the woman in his arms, grateful that God sometimes chose to give a little taste of heaven here on earth.

"This is so nice," she murmured. "I wish it could go on forever."

"So do I." Seth kissed the top of her head. "The first day we met, I knew there was something special about you. No matter how hard I tried, I couldn't get you out of my mind." He gave a throaty chuckle. "And I have to admit I didn't try very hard."

Dinah sat up and turned to face him. "I could have sworn your first impression of me was that I was a flibbertigibbet."

Seth flinched. "Guilty as charged, I'm afraid. But when I watched the way you dealt with your father and Gladys, your discouragement over the girls' class. . ." He smiled down at her upturned face. "In other words, when I finally took the time to listen to what my heart was telling me, I realized how much you meant to me." Laughter rumbled in his chest. "And after seeing the kind of trouble you can get into, I also learned I can't let you out of my sight."

He held her gaze. "And I don't want to."

Dinah stared up at him. Her parted lips trembled, and her luminous eyes matched the stars for brilliance. Seth brushed back a tangle of curls from her shoulder and let his hand rest against her neck. He could feel her pulse racing under his fingertips, and his own heart quickened its pace in response.

Moving his other hand to cup her cheek, Seth looked deep

into the hazel eyes that captivated him from the moment they met. "Dinah, I love you with all my being. Will you marry me?"

He heard her breath catch. She smiled, but he saw a flicker of uncertainty in her gaze. He slid his hand to her chin and traced her lower lip with his thumb.

"I'm not your father, Dinah. You will never have to worry about when I'm coming home or wonder whether I'll want you with me. There is nothing I want more than to have you beside me, now and always."

Only the sound of the water lapping against the side of the gondola and Giuseppe's gentle crooning met his ears. In the soft light, he could see crystal droplets form along Dinah's lower lids. She studied him for a long moment, then let out her breath on a trembling sigh.

"I know you're not like him. You are God's man, and you reflect His faithfulness in everything you do." She rested her hand on his shirtfront. "I love you, too, Seth. I can think of nothing I would treasure more than to become your wife."

At that moment the gondola slipped under a bridge, enveloping them in shadow. Their lips found each other in the darkness. A gentle rocking told Seth the boat had come to a stop. *Good man, Giuseppe.*

He tightened his arms around Dinah and lost himself in the glory of their embrace.

Minutes—or was it hours?—later, they drifted out from under the bridge again. Bathed in the moon's glow, Dinah's face shone with an ethereal light.

Seth fished in his jacket pocket. "This was my mother's." He unwrapped the small twist of paper to reveal a plain gold band set with a glittering diamond.

He took Dinah's hand and slipped the ring on her fourth finger. "I know how pleased she would be to see you wearing it." He covered her hand with his, enjoying the nearness of the woman to whom he had just pledged his life.

"Is there anyone I need to speak to? Your father?"

Dinah shook her head. "Aunt Dora will be in town tomorrow to pick up Gladys. We can tell her then. I know she and Uncle Everett will be very happy for us."

Seth's mind raced ahead. "As soon as we set a date, I'm sure the church board will be glad to let us get married in the chapel. Provided that's what you want, of course."

Dinah raised his hand in both of hers and held it to her lips. A tiny smile quirked her lips. "If it's all the same to you, I think I know the perfect place to hold our wedding."

CHAPTER 31

Dinah fastened the last button at the back of her fresh, white blouse and patted the folds of the shirred bodice into place. She slipped on the heliotrope jacket and checked her reflection in the mahogany-framed pier mirror. The pale lilac shade brought out the color in her cheeks and made her eyes sparkle.

She took a deep breath. It would do. In the wedding of her girlhood fantasies, she would have worn a flowing dress of shimmering white, but that was one more dream to be set aside. In her present circumstances, she had neither the funds to purchase the materials needed for such an elaborate gown nor the time to sew one.

But she did have Seth. Her lips curved up, and the pink in her cheeks deepened. What did her girlish dreams matter when she had this reality before her?

"What do you think?" she asked Millie.

Dinah's friend cocked her head and pursed her lips. "I guess you'll do." Then she laughed and wrapped Dinah in a hug. "You're gorgeous, white gown or no. Seth Howell is one lucky man."

"*Blessed*, Millie. We're both blessed." Dinah corrected. "There's no such thing as luck."

"Then I hope I get blessed that way, too, one of these days." Millie grinned back at her, unabashed.

"I'm so glad you're going to stand up with me. You've become such a dear friend."

"I'm glad you'll still be working with me, even though you're getting married," Millie said.

"I'll be there until the end of the fair. I gave my word when I took the job, and that's important to me."

"I'd hate to have to get used to someone new," Millie quipped. "Or take a chance on getting another Lila."

Dinah laughed. "It's nice to know I'm appreciated." She picked up her tortoiseshell brush and began smoothing her dark brown curls into place. She found it hard to believe that after becoming such an integral part of their lives, the great fair would come to an end in another two months.

But offsetting that bittersweet thought was the joyful knowledge that the adventure of life as Mrs. Seth Howell was about to begin. In a few short minutes, she and Seth would pledge their love to each other forever.

A wave of excitement left her dizzy. She closed her eyes and took a breath to steady herself. One week from proposal to wedding left her with little time to do anything but walk through the past few days with her mind in a whirl. Theirs had been a far shorter engagement than convention would dictate, but Seth wanted to tie the knot right away, and Dinah had no inclination to argue with him.

"I still can't believe it," she told Millie. "I thought my whole life was in a shambles, but God pulled all those broken pieces together and made something wonderful from them."

Millie fussed with Dinah's jacket collar. "I never knew a preacher's wife before. So what are the two of you going to do after the fair is over—go out and be missionaries to the Hottentots?"

Dinah laughed until tears sprang to her eyes. "Right now, we plan to stay here in Chicago, but who knows what lies ahead? The important thing is that we'll be together."

Together. Even now, she could scarcely believe it. She pressed her hands against her waist to quell the flutter in her stomach.

A quick tap sounded, and Mrs. Purvis poked her head around the door.

Dinah stepped forward for her inspection. "How do I look?"

The landlady studied her from head to toe, and her eyes glowed. "You're lovely. Absolutely lovely. I was wondering, though. . ."

Dinah pivoted and glanced in the mirror. Had she missed something?

Mrs. Purvis slid into the room, holding up a white satin dress.

Dinah caught her breath.

The landlady smoothed her hand over the shimmering fabric. "This was mine. I don't have a daughter to pass it along to, so. . ." She shrugged. "I wondered if you would like to wear it. It's all pressed and ready to put on. I would have brought it to you earlier, but I just finished adding a ruffle around the bottom, since you're a bit taller than I am."

Dinah's cup of joy overflowed. She swooped down on the older woman and gave her a big hug. "Mrs. Purvis, you are a treasure."

Mrs. Purvis laid the gown on the bed and fluttered her hands at Dinah. "Better get changed quickly. Time is getting short, so I'll be heading back downstairs. I want to make sure everything is in place and check on that young man of yours."

Dinah stroked the satiny folds with her fingertips, hardly able to believe she was about to wear such a lovely confection. When Seth saw her in just a few minutes. . .

Just a few minutes! She reached around to the back of her blouse. "Millie, can you help me with these buttons?"

The Reverend Amos B. Hall leaned against the counter in Mrs. Purvis's kitchen and sipped from a glass of water. "That's a fine young woman you're getting, son."

"I couldn't agree with you more." Seth gripped his mentor's hand. "Thank you very much for agreeing to perform the ceremony for us. We feel very honored."

The minister's eyes twinkled. "The pleasure is mine. It's always nice to play a part in furthering the course of young love." He set the glass down and pushed open the swinging door. "I just came back for a swallow to wet my throat. I'll see you out there in a few minutes."

Seth looked at Mac. "Do you have the ring?"

"You've asked me that fifteen times already, and the answer is still the same. It's right here in my vest pocket."

Seth pulled out his handkerchief and used it to wipe his moist palms. He poured another glass of water from the pitcher on the counter and took a deep swig.

"If I was your trainer," Mac said, "I'd say you needed to sit down for a bit."

Seth emptied the glass and set it on the counter. "It wouldn't do any good. My feet want to keep moving." He paced the kitchen, trying to think of something to keep his mind off his nerves. "You have that big fight coming up. Did you ever decide what you're going to do?"

Mac's lips set in a firm line. "I had a long talk with my trainer. I told him I'm going to fight it clean or not at all. I knew McGinty was up to his neck in fixing fights. That didn't seem so bad. But trafficking in women. . ." His mouth twisted as though he'd bitten into something sour. "I don't have the stomach for that. I don't want any part of it, or him. I'm going to make it on my own, fair and square, or drop out of the game altogether."

Seth looked into his friend's face, heartened by the conviction he saw there. "What would you do then?"

"I don't know." Mac shrugged and grinned. "Maybe if I get bored enough, I'll drop into church now and then."

Seth gripped his friend's shoulder. "I'll look forward to that."

The door opened again, and Mrs. Purvis entered. "Everyone is in their seats, and Dinah's almost ready. I'll crank up the phonograph in a few minutes. I just wanted to check on you boys."

"We're fine," Seth assured her.

Mac burst out laughing. "One of us is, at least."

Mrs. Purvis fanned herself with both hands. "I'd forgotten how many things there are to do on a wedding day. It seems like I've been running my legs off since the crack of dawn. So exciting, the way all this has turned out." She hurried to a cupboard, took out paper, pen, and ink, and sat down at the table.

Seth blinked. "What are you doing?"

Mrs. Purvis dipped the pen in the inkwell and scribbled rapidly. "I'm making a list."

A chuckle rose in his throat. "Isn't it a little late for that?"

Mrs. Purvis made no reply. She scratched a few more words on the paper and held it up so he could read it. "A list of my successes. Look: Annie Trenton and Nick Rutherford; Dinah Mayhew and Seth Howell. I feel it's important to recognize my newfound gift." Her eyes took on a dreamy look, and she stared into the distance. "I wonder who else I may bring together before the fair is over."

She hopped up and scurried over to tuck the writing materials back in the cupboard. "Well, no time to waste. I'll start the music now."

Dinah stood still so as not to wrinkle the dress of her dreams.

Millie finished weaving the last of the summer flowers into Dinah's hair. She stepped back to survey the results and gave a satisfied nod; then her expression clouded. "What a shame your aunt couldn't be here today."

Dinah only nodded, not trusting herself to speak. It would have been wonderful to have Aunt Dora stand in for her mother and to have Uncle Everett walk with her up the aisle. But that wasn't to be. Aunt Dora's time was now occupied with tending to Gladys. The physical effects of the drugging had worn off quickly enough, but it would take far longer for her emotions to heal. Some wounds went much deeper than the physical. Dinah knew that only too well.

As if sensing her thoughts, Millie added, "I'm sorry your

father won't be giving you away."

"He already did that years ago." Dinah blinked rapidly, then shook off her gloom. This was not a day for sadness. The only tears for now would be tears of joy. Today she would forget the past and set her sights on what God had in store.

Millie handed her the bouquet of white daisies, and together they walked down the hallway and waited until the musical strains from the phonograph came floating up the stairs. Dinah gripped her friend's hand and squeezed it tight. "It's time."

Millie nodded and started down the stairs. Dinah took a moment to offer up a prayer of gratitude before following. *Thank You, Lord, for this day. For Seth. For being my Father.*

She paused outside the parlor and peered through the crack in the open door at the faces of people who had become dear to her during her time in Chicago. Mrs. Johnson sat near the front, handkerchief at the ready. Even Mr. Thorndyke had come to witness this special day.

Behind them sat her girls and their families, every one of them dressed in their best. Dinah took a deep breath and stepped forward to meet her future.

The little girls' mouths formed perfect O's when they caught sight of Dinah in the white satin gown. If she needed any further assurance of how she looked, she found it the moment her eyes met Seth's. Smiling, she made her way toward him.

Seth's friend, Mac, stood beside him, and directly in front of them was Reverend Hall. Dinah knew the man would always be connected in her mind with the turning points in her life. The first time she saw him was the night she embarked on a deeper relationship with God. Today he would start her and Seth off on their journey into matrimony.

She joined hands with Seth, gripping tightly as though she held a lifeline.

Reverend Hall cleared his throat. "Dearly beloved," he began.

Dinah heard the words continue to flow, but all she could think about was Seth, standing there beside her, about to become her husband. She responded automatically to the minister's questions and heard Seth do the same.

"I now pronounce you man and wife."

Dinah felt her chest constrict so she could hardly breathe. The moment had come. She and Seth were joined together in the eyes of God and man.

The minister raised his hands in benediction. "Seth, you may kiss your bride. May you walk together in the joy of the Lord from this day forward."

Dinah's heart seemed to stop, then leaped as Seth tilted his head toward hers. His eyes darkened, and she heard him whisper, "From this day forward."

She nodded solemnly, the truth of the words echoing in her soul. She stood on the threshold of a new beginning, a future that held the assurance of God's love and acceptance and a life ahead with Seth.

"From this day forward," she repeated. Lifting her face to his, she melted into her husband's embrace.

About the Author

Author of ten novels and eleven novellas, Carol Cox's love of history, mystery, and romance is evident in the books she writes. A pastor's wife, Carol has a passion for fiction and is a firm believer in the power of story to convey spiritual truths. She makes her home with her husband and young daughter in northern Arizona, where the deer and the antelope really do play—often within view of the family's front porch. To learn more about Carol and her books, visit her Web site at www.CarolCoxBooks.com. She'd love to hear from you!

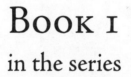